THE HOLY GRAIL

The holy Grail

Its Origins, Secrets, & Meaning Revealed

Malcolm Godwin

VIKING
STUDIO
BOOKS

A LABYRINTH BOOK

VIKING STUDIO BOOKS

Published by the Penguin Group
Viking Penguin, a division of Penguin Books USA Inc.
375 Hudson Street, New York, NY 10014, U.S.A.
Penguin Books Ltd. 27 Wrights Lane, London W8 5TZ, England
Penguin Books Australia Ltd. Ringwood, Victoria, Australia
Penguin Books Canada Ltd.,10 Alcorn Avenue, Suite 30, Toronto, Ontario, Canada M4 3B2
Penguin Books (N.Z.) Ltd. 182-190, Wairau Road, Auckland 10, New Zealand

Penguin Books Ltd. Registered Offices: Harmondsworth, Middlesex, England.

First American Edition
Published in 1994 by Viking Penguin,
a division of Penguin Books USA Inc.

1 3 5 7 9 10 8 6 4 2
Copyright © 1994 LABYRINTH
Text copyright © 1994 Malcolm Godwin
Original illustrations copyright © 1994 Malcolm Godwin
All rights reserved

Produced by Labyrinth Publishing (UK) Ltd.
Design & Typesetting by MoonRunner Design Partnership

Printed by Singapore National Printers, Singapore.

Library of Congress Catalogue in Publication Data
Available upon request

ISBN 0-670-85128-0

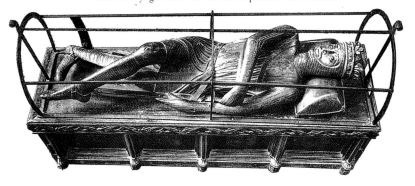

CONTENTS

	PAGE
INTRODUCTION	6

PART I
The Three-fold Tree 14

THE FIRST BRANCH, *The Celtic* 16

THE SECOND BRANCH, *The Christian* 80

THE THIRD BRANCH, *The Chymical* 136

PART II
A Myth for our Time 182

CHAPTER I
A Living Legend 184

CHAPTER II.
The Loss of the Female 196

CHAPTER III
The Wasteland 214

CHAPTER IV
The Wounded King 228

CHAPTER V
The Healing 241

INTRODUCTION

T HE LEGEND OF THE GRAIL, more than any other western myth, has retained the vital magic which marks it as a living legend capable of touching both imagination and spirit. No other myth is so rich in symbolism, so diverse and often contradictory in meaning. And at its core there exists a secret which has sustained the mystical appeal of the Grail for the last nine hundred years, while other myths and legends have slipped into oblivion and been forgotten.

Something seems to grip the Western imagination when we talk of the Holy Grail. Some alchemical process appears to be triggered in our collective unconscious, transforming this often muddled and confused story into an archetypical dream image of the Ultimate Quest for All and Everything.

Few have even read any of the dozen or so original Grail romances. Even fewer are acquainted with all the various pagan and apocryphal models upon which the legend grew, and yet the concept of the Grail Quest is instantly recognized by most westerners as the greatest of all spiritual endeavors. All the more strange is that our attraction to the myth, or the shape behind the myth, appears to be out of all proportion to its baffling story.

Is there any historical evidence to suppose there really was a Grail to be achieved? Or is the legend only a delightful literary device created by troubadours and conteurs to entertain the courts of Europe as they gently dozed off after the stuffed aurochs and roasted boar? In searching for the answers to such mysteries we must step into an enchanted and mythical world which appears to endlessly expand in complexity and beauty wherever we look. Somewhere within the interwoven strands of this medieval tapestry there is a radical and compelling message which is as fresh and alive today as it was in the twelfth century.

The Legend of the Grail first appeared at the end of the twelfth century. It sprung as if fully armed from the head of a gifted poet called Chrétien de Troyes. We know virtually nothing of Chrétien's life except through his work. Many scholars maintain he was the greatest French writer of medieval romances. Certainly his writings were largely responsible for the subsequent popularity of the Arthurian legends of the period. Without him the Grail myth might never have surfaced at all.

In Chrétien's time the written romance was a completely new phenomenon, drawing upon an oral tradition that had been firmly established in the Celtic lands for centuries.

For the Celts, the bard had long been a tribe's most precious repository of their history. He was the authority of their lineage, he sang of their noble deeds, of their father's deeds and of their remembrance of claims to kingship and order. The bard was the maker and holder of the collective memory and the collective myth. Without a bard the tribe would lose its significance and identity.

The new conteurs who peddled their wares across the continent no longer sang to such close-knit tribal families, but rather penned the traditional tales of many tribes, creating legends with which a king, a court or

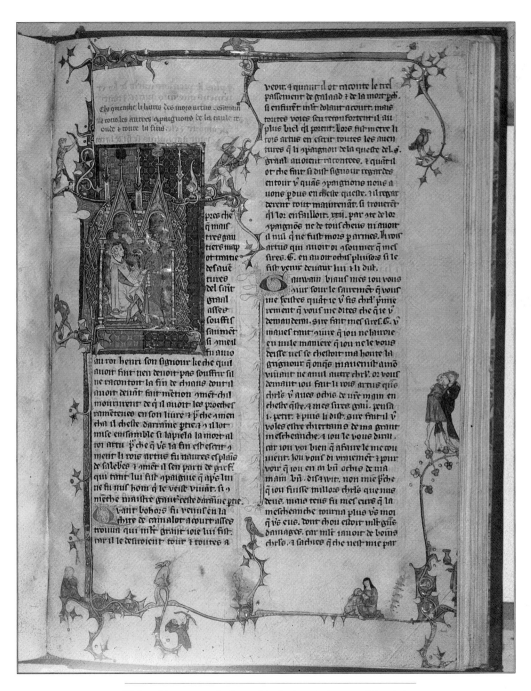

Walter Map *writing the Quest of the Grail at the dictation of King Arthur.*

a cloister could identify, irrespective of tribal background. They became the new literary bards who expressed a collective dream which embraced the whole family of Europe, from the lavish courts of Aquitaine, Anjou and Lorraine to that of Henry II of England.

It is said that an individual who does not dream, who cannot transform his or her fears, tensions and aspirations into significant and meaningful images, becomes sick. A society which has lost its ability to respond to the collective dream, or myth, is likewise unable to heal itself or to fulfill its need for the spiritual or the religious. And Europe in the twelfth century was sick. The male-dominated Church of Rome had subsumed all local myths into its own grand scheme. But its rigid orthodoxy and weird hatred of Eve had resulted in a one-sided, stagnant and corrupt vision.

So the timing of the emergence of the Grail legends is significant and hardly a coincidence. A strange wave of hysteria had swept the Christian world at the turn of the tenth century, alternately swinging between prophecies of doom and ecstasy. The world was supposed to end by the year 1000, bringing a long-awaited New Kingdom of Heaven. But instead of the promised paradise on earth, the people found themselves surrounded by a barren and hopeless wasteland. The Holy City of Jerusalem had been won but then had been promptly lost. The Christian armies were proving no match for the "Infidels" who appeared to have a far more civilized and wondrous culture than their own, while everyone could see that the representatives of the Christian God in Rome were divided and blatantly corrupt. Even the

Pope described his priests as "pigs in a sty."

Most of Europe had entered a great crisis and was passing through its dark night of the soul. Nonetheless it was also the most spiritually charged, crusade-ridden epoch since the vibrant years after the death of Christ. It was a tremendous age of turmoil, full of both experiment and oppression, faith and heresy. The romances of the Grail fulfilled the thirst for a myth with which a changing Europe could identify. Europe was poised to take a radical leap of the spirit, and an exhilarating scent of change was in the air.

Quest for Paradise

The clash of the two religious cultures during the early Crusades, represented on the one hand by the West European Christian princes and on the other by the Eastern Islamic caliphs, created a cross-fertilization of creative ideas and spiritual awareness unparalleled until this present century. And it was often the very Crusaders who had stormed the Saracen strongholds who began to respect and emulate a way of life which was patently far more cultured than their own. These knights returned to Europe infected with the Infidel's ways, and through these carriers dangerously new and revolutionary ideas spread like a virus throughout the various realms. The returning knights not only brought with them miraculous tales of treasure and sacred relics from the Holy Land — as far as the Church was concerned, they also brought heresy.

The exotic atmosphere of the desert and the

Brass of Knight *from Stoke d'Abernum, England 13th c.*

descriptions of the rich and civilized paradises of the Holy Lands caught the imagination of the whole of Europe while the capture of the Holiest of Cities, in 1099, fired the religious fervor of peasant and prince alike. But it was also a time when political power in Europe was fragmented, and armed bands roamed the countryside oppressing the peasants and turning their farms into wastelands. In the last decade of the eleventh century even the weather turned against the poor, with ruined crops, a crippling famine and terrible diseases. Many of the knightly landowners were forced to mortgage their property to the Church in order to be able join the Crusade at all. The price of land fell disastrously. Peasants left their pitiful holdings for the promise of Eastern treasures, both of the spirit and the flesh. Princes faced with the choice of living on their impoverished wastelands, repeated crop failures and a disenchanted peasantry, or going on a crusade to rich and booty-laden paradises, did not hesitate for long. The Church, in dispensing its indulgences so freely, added the incentive that any Crusader would automatically atone for and be absolved of all past sins.

However mercenary the motives of some of the Crusaders might have been, the sincerity, religious fervor and piety of many of the knights and pilgrims was undeniable. And the priests of Rome, who found every advantage in the situation, encouraged the sense of a truly spiritual quest. Sacred, supernatural and miraculous relics flooded the marketplace.

Every abbey or ecclesiastical center advertised its authentic saint, its holy remains, the numbers of its pilgrims and the frequency or power of its miracles. It was into this highly charged, hysterical religious atmosphere that the legend of the Grail was born. But while most eyes were turned greedily to the Holy Lands, a balancing element was arising from Merlin's Isle in the far northwest.

Here Begin the Marvels

The Arthurian stories that Chrétien and his contemporaries recorded so entertainingly, and of which the Grail romance is but one, belong to what was known as the "Matière de Bretagne" ("the Matter of Britain"). Circulated by Breton, Welsh and Anglo-Norman storytellers throughout the courts of France, England and Germany, this essentially oral tradition gave birth to a literature which enjoyed a sudden crazy fashion. There were three principal adventure stories popular at the time which could be grouped as the "Matter of Britain," the "Matter of Rome" and the "Matter of France." The Matter of Rome was devoted to the classical Latin adventures, while the Matière de France was principally concerned with tales of Charlemagne and Roland. But while these were more or less modeled, if glamorized, on historical happenings, what caught the popular fancy in the legends of the Matter of Britain were the weird supernatural encounters, the fantastical sense of wonderment, and an overwhelming variety of magical and mysterious powers.

Contact with the sophisticated Islamic culture had been brought about through the Crusades. New mystical images of the East and of the great Sufi mystics found a ready affinity with the magical, twilight world of the Celtic legends. Together they created an irresistible fantasy genre which fired the imagination of the whole of Europe.

Added to that already potent brew was one of the most radical phenomena of the age — the concept of the Service of Woman. This was in large part born of the Crusaders' exposure to the exquisite Islamic and Arabic love poetry. These quasi-mystical outpourings, in which the woman acquired an exhalted status of literally being worshipped by her lover or admirer, found fertile soil in a Europe barren of any goddess at all. Highly ambitious and independent-minded women like Eleanor of Aquitaine, wife of Henry II of England, or her daughter, Marie de Champagne, quickly seized the initiative and instituted Courts of Love. These outlined a code of behavior in the affairs of love much as Arthur's Round Table gave expression to the code of knightly honor. We do know that Chrétien de Troyes wrote one of his early romances under the strict guidance of Marie de Champagne herself, and much of his later work showed that his lessons at the lady's hands had been well absorbed.

One of the earliest contemporary Christian references to the Grail appears in a passage from the Chronicle of Helinandus, who was a monk of Froidmont at the turn of the twelfth century. Helinandus tells of a hermit living in eighth century Britain who had an extraordinary vision of Joseph of Arimathea, keeper of the bowl used by Christ at the Last Supper. This theme is taken up in the introduction to a work known as the Lancelot Grail which gives the precise date as 717 A.D. on the eve of Good Friday. Christ appears to the hermit and says *"This is the book of thy descent, Here begins the Book of the Holy Grail, Here begin the terrors, Here begin the marvels."* The book was supposedly famous in the time of Ina, King of the West Saxons who was busy extending his kingdom to include Glastonbury, the ancient site of the first Christian church in Europe, said to have been erected by Joseph. Ina attempted to bring peace and unity to the Saxons and Britons and it is possible that the Grail legend could have had an influence during this time.

The legends of the Grail which are familar to most readers are probably those of the Christian hue. Early accounts which show Perceval as the Grail winner have the hero embark upon a quest to become worthy enough to commune with Christ through the agency of the mysterious Grail. He also must heal the King, who is Guardian of the Grail, of a mysterious wound, and restore a land which has become barren and waste. By not asking the right question when he sees the sacred vessel, he not only fails to heal the king, but in many versions he also does not restore the wasteland to its original paradisal state. Only after long and arduous adventures does the knight succeed in his quest, and both king and realm are healed.

The Christianized legend thus reveals itself as a salvic, or salvational myth. It is a story of redemption, recalling the loss of paradise by Adam and Eve which is then regained by Christ. In some versions the savior-hero, the Perfect Knight, is a thinly disguised stereotype of Christ himself.

While ostensibly writing a Christian work, Chrétien does not actually mention any connection with Christ at all in his final romance, *Le Conte del Graal.* That might of course be because the narrative remains unfinished, abruptly interrupted before we learn of the ultimate secrets. However this is doubtful, for to Chrétien the Grail only appears as a costly and magical dish whose function is never quite revealed. All the same, the mystery of this remarkable Grail, along with a bleeding lance, a disappearing castle, and a king grievously wounded between the thighs, piqued the curiousity of both court and cloister.

Whether Chrétien died before its completion or just put the work aside is not known, but the intriguing possibilities of how the story might have ended gave rise to a spate of continuations and imitations which appeared within the following 25 years. And it is these extraordinarily creative variations on an enigma, written in just over a quarter of a century between 1190 and 1225, that we will explore in the following chapters.

Left: **Mappa Mundi,** *13th c. map drawn by Matthew Paris for Hereford Cathedral, England. This map, which has been realigned, as the east was originally at the top, shows Jerusalem at the center of what was believed to have been a flat world. We perhaps tend to forget that this was the view of the writers of the Grail legends, many of whom believed that Paradise itself lay just beyond the Holy lands.*

Below is a map showing the major sources of the Grail legend. It is tempting to look for one single original story but it appears that during the twelfth and thirteenth centuries there was an extraordinary confluence of ideas which somehow reached the talented Chrétien de Troyes who transformed them into one integrated whole. However the myth of the Grail can really be seen as the secular child of the aristocrats of the great courts of Europe and of those bards and conteurs who had to sing for their supper. And although the cloisters continued the legend it never truly had a religious source.

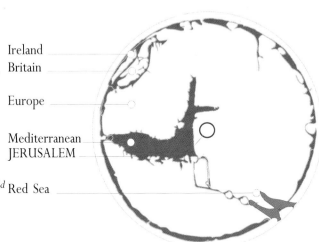

Ireland
Britain

Europe

Mediterranean
JERUSALEM

Red Sea

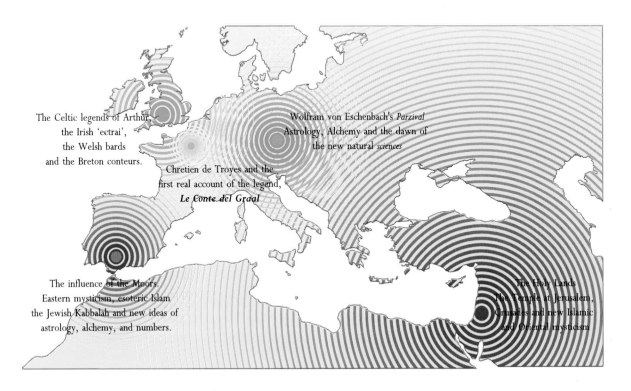

The Celtic legends of Arthur, the Irish 'ectrai', the Welsh bards and the Breton conteurs.

Chretien de Troyes and the first real account of the legend, *Le Conte del Graal*

Wolfram von Eschenbach's *Parzival* Astrology, Alchemy and the dawn of the new natural *sciences*

The influence of the Moors. Eastern mysticism, esoteric Islam the Jewish Kabbalah and new ideas of astrology, alchemy, and numbers.

The Holy Lands The Temple at Jerusalem, Crusades and new Islamic and Oriental mysticism

The Lost Manuscript

One question which has occupied the passions of Grail scholars more than any other is just where Chrétien found the original material for his inspiration. For while most of the later authors owed obvious debts to the French poet, many of the variations suggest that there was a common original narrative shared by them all, which for some unknown reason has been lost. The authors who followed Chrétien were often at pains to reassure the reader of the lofty credentials of their sources, usually by alluding to mysterious and secret documents which were variously claimed to be direct transcriptions from Christ himself, from an angel, from some mysterious alchemical treatise or from an original manuscript from Britain, Spain or the Far East.

As far as Chrétien is concerned, the original imagery for most of the motifs found in his text have obvious and easily traceable precedents in Irish and Welsh traditions. But these do not account for the remarkable variations of later Christian and alchemical writers who appear to be more conversant with the Jewish Kabbala, the Knights Templar and the Cathar heretics than any Celtic twilight of the Gods.

In Parzival, the German version of the romance, the author Wolfram von Eschenbach sees the Quest as one of the individual struggling towards a sense of wholeness. The source of that wholeness is expressed by the Grail. Its very presence nourishes the seeker. In Parzival we read of the split between spontaneous Nature and the rigid Christian belief in God or Super-Nature, separate and superior to Nature. In Wolfram's text the hero's quest is a radical reconciliation, a reunion of the two seemingly irreconcilable opposites – Earth and Heaven, Nature and Super-Nature.

Wolfram's prologue is particularly insightful in the light of what is to follow. He says that "Every act has Good and Evil results." For him the quest for the Grail occurs exactly between the two extremes of black and white. The secret map of the quest is to be found in the natural and spontaneous, and therefore compassionate, impulse. Parzival, or Perceval, can be translated as "Perce à Val" or "piercing the valley" between the two extremes. What is especially precious in Wolfram's story is that he attempts to formulate a spirituality which is firmly based within nature. The natural and spontaneous man will always choose the good, says Wolfram. That is the nature of Nature. He would have celebrated a man like the Chinese master of Tao, Lao Tzu. This is the very first time a voice had been heard in the West which echoes the Eastern Way of Tao, the path of allowing the natural flow of life to guide one's actions.

To speak of the Grail as a single legend is misleading. It is more a central mystery, interwoven with multi-colored strands belonging to different authors, written at different times, and arising from widely differing backgrounds.

The essential story appears to be set in an unspecified Age of Chivalry associated with the Court of King

Arthur. Historically speaking this would have been the sixth century, although most of the accounts show no more than a cursory regard for chronological accuracy, often setting the action five centuries later during the Crusades. The field of the action is likewise found in regions set as far apart as Britain and the Holy Lands, ranging over Wales, Scotland, Brittany, Southern France, Germany, Spain, Egypt, India and the Near East.

Yet, while historical sites and locations are often given with a wealth of accurate detail, the reader must never lose sight of the fact that the real action takes place mostly within the dreamscape of the Otherworld, and far removed from historical time. Into this bardic and mythical place a hero is born who is destined to achieve his quest for a mysterious otherworldly object known as the Grail. That hero is variously known as Arthur, Gawain, Peredur, Perlesvaus, Parzival, Perceval, Galahad or Bors. His conception is usually the result of a mysterious conjunction of parents possessing an admixture of the highest valor and virginal purity, or the most potent magical and spiritual powers. As a child he is reared alone without companions or siblings, either by his mother, or by magically endowed warrior women. Thus, while he often lacks any worldly ways he has an innocence which in some cases earns him the name, the Great Fool.

When he eventually leaves this female domain his first desire is to become the greatest knight of his age. This entails an initiation through the Court of King Arthur and joining the Fellowship of the Round Table. At this point, although the hero distinguishes himself mightily, revealing the telltale mark of destiny, he is always seen as a bit of a gawky yet handsome misfit in the chivalrous company of his fellow knights. His renown through prodigious feats of arms, his impeccable family pedigree, or such fated acts as taking his place at the Round Table on the Seat Perilous, mark him clearly as the Chosen One.

Then, either he rides off to discover the mysterious Holy Grail by himself, or it appears at Arthur's table, giving off such a miraculous and nourishing aura that when it vanishes all the assembled knights vow a fellowship and quest to discover its secrets. The stories then follow the moralizing preferences of the individual author, describing both those perfect knights who will eventually achieve the mystery and those who for some reason are flawed, and fail.

The unfolding story is one of a dream-like journey into the unknown, through the agency of the sacred and mysterious vessel. But the search is individual and the seeker has to face the void alone in order to earn the right to a direct communion with the Ultimate Mystery. The initiate-hero must variously ask a question correctly, avenge a wrong, win the Grail, remain steadfast and loyal, or capture a castle to prove worthy.

By doing so he is transformed, and through his actions manages to heal the wounded guardian of the sacred vessel and restore the surrounding wasteland to a paradise.

PART I

THE THREE-FOLD TREE

UT WHAT IS THE GRAIL exactly, and what is it supposed to do? Not all the authors are as vague as Wolfram when he says, "There was a Thing that was called the Grail, the crown of all earthly wishes, fair fullness that ne'er shall fail." But his is certainly no exception to the wreaths of mists which engulf the object. And just as there is no single account of the quest, there is no single description of the mysterious Grail itself. It variously appears as a dish, a cauldron, a chalice, the cup of the Last Supper, the emerald which fell from Lucifer's crown as he plummeted to Hell, a philosopher's stone and a beatific vision.

The quest is as varied as the vessel sought. It is seen as a search for the Ultimate Source, a search for the Cauldron of Rebirth, the Fountain of Everlasting Youth, Direct Communion with God through the Body of Christ, Enlightenment, Individuality, God, or simply the avenging of a blood feud. The Grail cannot really be separated from the undertaking of the quest for it. Both Grail and quest, the goal and the process towards that goal, embody the ultimate human fulfillment, whatever form the author wishes it to take.

The legend endlessly weaves and counter-weaves brightly colored threads of intrigue and mystery which entice and enfold both scholar and lay reader alike. However, it is imperative not to lose sight of the fact that this myth, the most mystical and alive of any left in the West, must be understood not as a singular story but as a nest of narratives; many versions circling a central theme yet with no one master blueprint.

In order to bring some clarity and shape to what can appear at first glance to be so confusing and contradictory it will be helpful to use, throughout the book,

a time-honored strategem – the Triad. Before there was any written tradition the Cyfarwyddiaid (professional Welsh storytellers) employed a number of devices as aids to memorizing the truly impressive collection of tales and legends which they were expected to know. One of the most successful of these mnemonic devices was the Triad. Triads are persons, places, objects or events which are linked in a way that jogs the memory. There are, for instance, the Three Concealments of Britain (Bran's head buried beneath the White Tower, the dragons of Dinas Emris, and the bones of Blessed Vortimer). Likewise there are the Three Unfortunate Disclosures (the disclosure by Vortigern of the bones, the unearthing of the dragons beneath the castle and the exhumation of Bran's head by an impetuous and arrogant Arthur).

So it seems useful, in wading through the labyrinth of diverse Grail material, to utilize a similar approach. At the same time we can borrow a favorite mythical image, that of the Tree of Wisdom that grows beside the Fountain of Eternal Youth at the center of the world – the Axis Mundi. We might imagine that three separate branches grow from it.

The first can be called the Celtic branch. It could be said to represent the ancient and essentially magical myths of Regeneration and Renewal. The Celts were primarily concerned with the vital relationship between rightful kingship and the sovereignty of the land. Sovereignty is fundamental to the Celtic belief system, and is seen as the Goddess of the Land, or more precisely the Land herself. In order for there to exist a fertile realm there must likewise be a vital and fecund relationship between the Land and the King. In all the legends based upon a Celtic model we find the natural

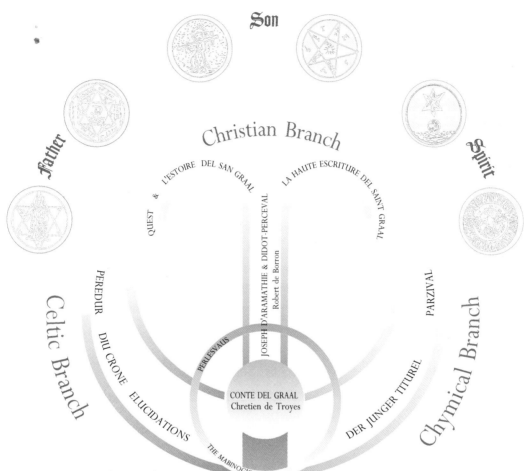

Son

Father

Christian Branch

Spirit

QUEST & L'ESTOIRE DEL SAN GRAAL

LA HAUTE ESCRITURE DEL SAINT GRAAL

PEREDUR

JOSEPH D'ARAMATHIE & DIDOT-PERCEVAL
Robert de Borron

PARZIVAL

Celtic Branch

DIU CRONE

PERLESVAUS

ELUCIDATIONS

CONTE DEL GRAAL
Chretien de Troyes

DER JUNGER TITUREL

Chymical Branch

THE MABINOGION

CELTIC MYTHOLOGY
Pseudo-Apocrypha &
Middle Eastern Sources

harmonies, or more precisely the relationship between mortal Man and the immortal Goddess, have been disrupted for some reason. It is the hero's task to restore them.

The second sacred branch symbolizes the esoteric Christian legends of Redemption and Salvation. In these, the hero seeks his Maker, and through becoming worthy attempts to bring heaven to earth, either reconciling Super-Nature with Nature, or surpassing Nature and entering the Beyond.

The third branch signifies alchemical ideas of Rebirth and the Transformation of the Individual. In this view, Nature is of itself seen as spiritual, spontaneously capable of giving rise to Love and Compassion.

This whole tree can also be seen as symbolizing the three ages of mankind, an idea which engrossed many of the best of medieval minds. The Pagan, or Celtic Age of the Father was represented by the Old Law of the Synagogue; the Age of the Son was symbolized in the New Testament, while the Age of the Holy Spirit looked towards the dawn of a New Awakening.

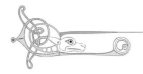

THE FIRST BRANCH

F ALL THE DIVERSE LEGENDS OF THE GRAIL, those which make up the Celtic branch are probably the least widely known. Of course Chrétien was not a Celt but a Frenchman. But from what he tells us there were earlier accounts of the story, both written and oral, which were most likely to have been Celtic in origin. So far none of the works have surfaced which he and his contemporary authors claimed to have used as a basis for their own romances. It is generally accepted that the original sources of all the stories are to be found within the Irish *echtrai*. Themes and motifs may have been obscured, mistranslated or simply muddled by both time and by cultural transference, but evidence of the debt to pagan imagery is clearly discernible.

The *echtrai,* or adventures from which the Grail romances were originally drawn, tell of fantastic visitations of heroes to the island realms and palaces of gods and immortals. Here valorous warriors are sumptuously entertained with food and drink, magically served by golden Vessels of Abundance. In these Celtic otherworldly elysiums neither the inhabitants nor the visitors appear to age. Mystical talismans, magical chessboards, enchanted swords and supernatural spears all bestow their various powers and plenitude. We will shortly be introduced to such artifacts as a Drinking Horn of

Plenty, or a Cauldron of Rebirth and Knowledge, which find their counterparts within the later Grail legends.

These Irish sagas, in both oral and written form, had a profound effect upon their Welsh neighbors, who enthusiastically embraced and adapted them to local traditions. The Welsh had a written and oral tradition unsurpassed by all but their Breton cousins. The Irish had not been conquered by the Romans, so the older traditions had survived in their most virile and untainted form. But as the invading English of the seventh century drove the Britons into Wales and the West Country, so many of these British Celts left greater Britain for the more hospitable lands of Brittany in Northern France, where King Alain warmly welcomed the new arrivals.

And so it was that the Welsh and Britons became Bretons. But they kept the legends of their old land alive through their storytellers, their singers and bards. Breton *conteurs* were considered the best of the wandering storytellers and were reknown throughout the European continent. They gradually elaborated and enriched the Arthurian themes wherever they went. Then the newly formed Cistercian monks took up these essentially pagan stories, and embellished them with Christian ideals and more than a little monkish bias.

The most persistent and remarkable Celtic image found within the Arthurian legends is that of a quest for Sovereignty. Originally the Goddess of Sovranty was an

Irish symbol of the land. True kingship was to be found only in the potent relationship of the hero and the Goddess who represented the land itself. Thus at the very heart of the Arthurian cycle there exists a direct causal relationship between the well-being and health of the king/hero and the fertility of his realm. And nowhere is this more in evidence than in the Grail romances. One character who appears in virtually all the many versions of the story is the maimed Fisher-King whose realm has become mysteriously barren and waste. To the Celts a maimed king was not fit to rule. His infirmity, or in the case of the Grail King, his impotence, would immediately desolate the land.

Chrétien's great unfinished work was a splendid medieval folly built from the ruins of this great tradition. He imparted his own genius to the material and imbued the story with a fresh sense of mystery, which teased the minds of the new Europeans. Although it is clear that his story was in no way original, his poetic and mysterious imagery was the major source and inspiration for nearly all the narratives which followed.

It is quite clear that the *graal* of Chrétien's story, and of those which used his legendary source, had no particular religious significance. If anything, the magical ambience which surrounded both the vessel and the lance was unashamedly pagan. But when the story passed through the sanctified and celibate cloisters of Christian orders it gradually took on an entirely new

significance and power.

As we shall discover later, most modern scholars are of the opinion that the change of both Grail and Spear from pagan, semi-magical objects into miraculously imbued Holy Christian relics, was actually based upon the trivial mistranslation of one simple word – *cors*, which in old French can signify, amongst many other things, both a horn and a body. Through a series of misunderstandings a Celtic Blessed Horn of Plenty,(*cors benoiz*), became the Blessed Body of Christ (*cors benoit*). And thus it came about that a pagan Graal of Plenty was transformed into a vessel intimately associated with the sacrament, in which Christ's Last Supper is commemorated by the consecration of the bread (host) and the wine (his blood). The amazing outcome of the error was a creative and mystical leap of imagination that inspired the medieval spirit and that still reverberates today.

But before we can make out the message written upon the rich and wide tapestry of the myth we must first explore the countless original threads which make up its weave.

Medieval Minstrels and Troubadours *from the* Contigas Sta Maria *14th c. French manuscript.*

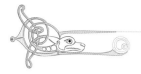

RETURNING TO THE SOURCES

Irish 'Scots' invade the North

Pictish raids

Vikings

IRELAND

Snowdonia (Perceval's birthplace)
○ *Dinas Bran (Grail Castle)*

Bran's Enchanted Isle

WALES
Caerleon,

BRITAIN

The Isle of Avalon ○
Camelot

Anglo-Saxon
expansion

Merlin's Isles at the time of the Grail Legend

I N ORDER TO UNRAVEL THE EXTRAORDINARY Celtic knots which make up the background to the earliest of the Grail legends it is necessary to examine the mysterious world of Merlin's Isles. Merlin was the great British magician who, variously, has been accredited with the building of Stone-henge, being the architect of and the power behind Arthur's throne and arranging the whole Quest for the Grail. There does appear to have been a historical figure who lived during the turn of the 6th century and he epitomizes the air of otherworldly magic which seems to permeate these misty isles and which captured the fancy of the great courts of Europe. For on the one hand he is a druidic figure of great power

wielding a shamanistic magic of the land, while on the other he is a civilized Christian Romano-Briton. This uneasy mingling of a pagan wildman and a sage of great wisdom, within the figure of Merlin, seems to sum up the British predicament after the Romans left. They had been subject to all the civilizing influences of four centuries of occupation, and had acquired a new religion and a radical new perspective, yet had a rich tradition of magic and the otherworld which was never quite resolved within the Christian framework. Soon the villas, the temples and the fine Roman roads were overgrown and forgotten by a people who were hard pressed to repel invaders from all sides. The major threat to the Arthurian world were the pagan Anglo-Saxons, or English, who pushed the Christian British towards the West Country and Wales forcing many families to seek refuge across the channel in Little Britain (Brittany of modern France). They took with them the heroic legends of otherworldly quests and these formed the foundation for the Arthurian legends which grew with the telling. By the time Chrétien de Troyes wrote *Le Conte del Graal* he could have had access to a wide range of both written and oral material from which he could create his masterpiece. The Irish *echtrai* or adventures, which have so many Grail themes and images within them, appear to be the earliest he could have known. The Four Hallows of the Grail have obvious counterparts in the Four Treasures of Ireland and the elaborate material from the Welsh *Mabinogion* finds its way into many of the motifs surrounding the Rich Fisher King and the hero of the story, Perceval.

The map on the opposite page shows the main routes taken by the Grail legend from its original Celtic sources and demonstrates how the original Irish and Welsh material could have influenced the rest of Europe. Of course this was not a one-way traffic of ideas and we shall see later how the other two branches also had their influences upon the emerging myth.

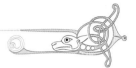

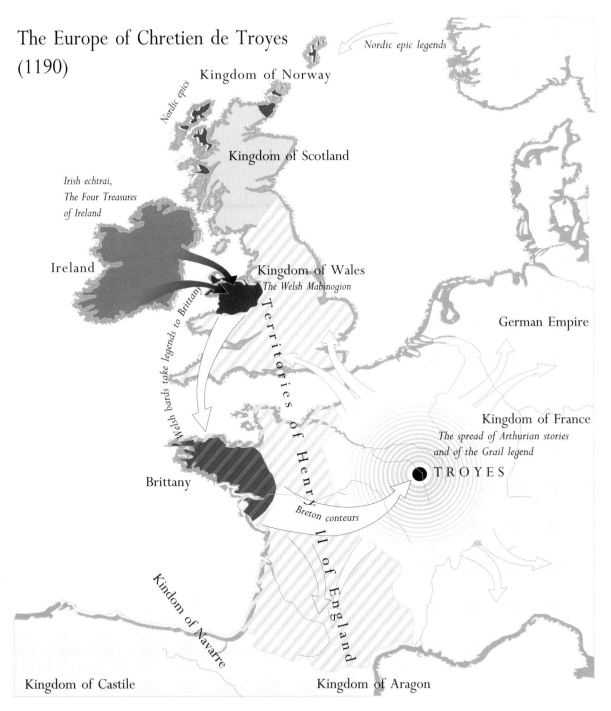

The Europe of Chretien de Troyes
(1190)

Nordic epic legends

Kingdom of Norway

Nordic epics

Kingdom of Scotland

Irish echtrai,
The Four Treasures
of Ireland

Ireland

Kingdom of Wales
The Welsh Mabinogion

Welsh bards take legends to Brittany

T e r r i t o r i e s   o f   H e n r y   I I   o f   E n g l a n d

German Empire

Kingdom of France
The spread of Arthurian stories
and of the Grail legend

TROYES

Brittany

Breton conteurs

Kindom of Navarre

Kingdom of Castile

Kingdom of Aragon

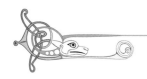

THE PARADISE LAND

HE ELUCIDATIONS, the prologue to *Le Conte del Graal*, opens by inform-ing us how the realm of Logres was once a paradise on earth. The original Celtic Logres was one of two parallel aspects of the land, which the Celts believed had both an outer and an inner nature. Logres was seen as the inner soul of the earthly Britain. So within the first lines of the introduction we are clearly meant to understand we are in another world, an enchanted and otherworldly state. There was, however, no confusion for the Celt to find that the action simultaneously takes place at real locations in his-torical time, supposedly around the end of the fifth cen-tury after the Romans had abandoned Britannia.

Throughout this mythic and poetical land, maidens lived by sacred grottoes, wells and springs. To the Celtic mind the everyday world and the Otherworld were twin universes running parallel to each other. It was at such sacred places as wells and springs that the two worlds were believed to come so close to one another that one might bridge the gap and cross over to the other side.

The Maidens of the Sacred Wells would feed wan-derers and travelers from golden bowls and cups. His-torically we know that Britain was specially favored with hundreds of sacred wells. The Romans reverently main-tained the ancient traditions of occupied Britain and often built shrines around such waters, as the extensive building over the healing springs at Bath shows so clearly.

The twentieth century mind, educated in the ways of Freud and Jung, will note the psychological signifi-cance of drawing from the deep wells of the uncon-scious. But the Celts responded readily to the image of springs bursting up from the land as evidence of the nourishing fecundity of Mother Earth. And it was near the presence of flowing water that the most frequent access across worlds would be obtained.

To return to the story, the maidens served all way-farers and the realm was at peace and fertile until one day an evil King Amangons ravished one of the maid-ens, held her in captivity and stole her sacred bowl.

Amangons' male retainers enthusiastically followed their king's example with disastrous consequences and soon there were no maidens serving at the wells. From that time onwards the Realm of Logres changed into a barren wasteland "worth not even a couple of hazel-nuts." The wells and the waters dried up, animals became infertile, trees no longer bore fruit or leaf, flowers withered and the people left. "And since that time the court of the Rich Fisher, which made the land to shine with gold and silver, with furs and precious stuffs, with abundant foods of all kinds, with falcons, hawks and sparrow-hawks, could no longer be found. In those previous days, when the court could still be found, there were riches and abundance everywhere. But now all these are lost to the Land of Logres."

We are told that the land of Logres "lost the Voices of the Wells." The barren wasteland which was the result bespeaks a loss of contact with the Otherworld. It would appear that the Grail hero, the one who is eventually to "free the waters" has to discover the meet-ing place between worlds where he can re-establish the precious links between the female sovereignty and the kingship of the realm.

"The Golden Age," *by Lucas Cranach, 16th century.*
This painting expresses the paradisal mood of a realm where the sacred springs flowed abundantly. The harmony and joy is about to disappear.

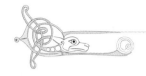

THE LADY OF THE FOUNTAIN

HE ELUCIDATIONS establishes the primary concern of Celtic mythology – the loss of communion between the divine female, queen of the Innerland and the rightful kingship of the outer realm. The king rules the land by right of his true union with her and by his championship of her freedom.

Superficially, it would seem that anyone reading the Celtic legends of the Grail would conclude that they are excessively concerned with a male-dominated quest, with aggressively competitive knights who delight in nothing more than braining the opposition as frequently as possible. But the more one enters into the depths of the myth the more one becomes aware that, instead, the story is actually about the women of the land. And all these women eventually turn out to be the ancient Earth Goddess in her many disguises, variously appearing throughout the narratives as a maiden, a nymph or a crone. We find the most typically Celtic expression of the multi-faceted deity in Eriu, the Irish *Sovranty of the Land*, who first appeared throughout Old Europe over 8,000 years ago.

Springs and wells were thought to be the most powerful outward expression of the life-giving abundance of the Goddess. Thus it is no surprise that the Lady of the Fountain is one of her primary images. In the Welsh *Mabinogion*, the knight Owein encounters the Countess of the Fountain. This is Sovereignty herself, who has a champion to guard her spring. Whosoever overcomes that champion becomes the new consort of the Goddess.

Owein is directed to a great tree beneath which is a fountain, a stone and a silver bowl. He is told to fill the bowl and throw water over the stone. There is a clap of thunder and a shower of huge hailstones falls upon him, stripping the leaves off the tree. A flock of the most beautiful singing birds then alights upon the tree. A black knight appears and accuses Owein of destroying many beasts and men through the storm, and of laying the land to waste. This knight is of course the lady's champion. Owein slays the rider and promptly falls in love with the Countess of the Fountain. Eventually he marries her, and takes his turn as champion for three years after which King Arthur and Gwalchmei appear. Owein is granted leave by the Countess to join Arthur but then forgets all about her. When her messenger, Luned, confronts him with his heartless treachery, he suddenly remembers his time in the Land of the Fountain. Grief-stricken, he wanders the lands in search of this lost paradise. After many misadventures the lovers are at last reunited.

This story illustrates the importance of the fountain-spring in British culture. And the British Isles do have a remarkable and ancient tradition of sacred, miraculous, wishing wells. Even today they are sought for the healing or fertile properties of their waters. Historically, territorial goddesses were associated with the sacred wells which also served as boundary markers for the various Celtic tribes of Britain.

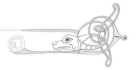

Left: *One curious tradition associates wells with severed heads. The Celts believed that the head possessed magical, healing, prophetic and even fertile powers. Often on the place where a severed head had fallen a spring would gush forth. If a head was thrown into a well its enchanted influence enhanced the power of the healing and fertile waters. When the well at Carrawborough, Northumberland, dedicated to the Celtic Goddess, Coventina, was recently excavated, a human head and*

more than 14,000 coins were discovered at its base.

Opposite: *At* **Mari**, *in Iran, a Goddess of the Flowing Vase stands in the center of the throne room of King ZimriLim. This deity, who shares a common ancestry with the Celtic Well Maidens, dates from the 18th century B.C. She holds a vessel out of which flows water from a hidden pipe. Throughout the world, myths and legends hold the female as the holy vessel, or the sacred water basin embodying life-giving waters.*

Above: *Illustration from the* **Livre du Cueur d'Amours**. *France, 15th C. In this French romance the knight Cueur unsuspectingly drinks from a spring and then pours water from the cup over a stone. Immediately a terrible storm breaks out. The fountain in the story of Owein was later associated with the famous fountain of Barenton in Brittany. This fountain is still reputed to be able to bring on rain if water from it is poured over a stone.*

MAIDENS OF THE WELLS

EFORE AMANGONS AND HIS FOLLOWERS had raped the Maidens of the Wells and had stolen their sacred vessels, communion with the Sovranty of the land had been possible. By drinking from the cups offered by the maidens, seekers might find union with the otherworldly paradise. We will find that the Grail Castle, or Court of Joy, is deep within that paradise, and it is there that the Fisher King guards the Hallows of the Goddess. But with the rape of the damsels the essential harmony between worlds was disrupted.

So at the outset of the legend we are told of the Fall and the loss of paradise. This is one of the most foundational of all human myths, not only occurring in Europe and the Near East but throughout the globe. A Hopi Indian Elder of North America describes the state: "We were created equal, of oneness, living in a spiritual way, where life is everlasting. We were happy and at peace with our fellow men. All things were plentiful, provided by our Mother Earth upon which we were placed." Two thousand five hundred years ago the Chinese sage, Chuang Tzu, talks of a paradisal Age of Virtue when men and women "were upright and correct, without knowing that to be so was righteousness: they loved one another, without knowing that to do so was benevolence; they were honest and generous without ever knowing that it was good faith and trust; in their simple movements they employed the services of one another without thinking that they were conferring or receiving any gift. Therefore their actions left no trace and there was no record of their affairs."

There is now enough substantial evidence to confirm that an Earthly Paradise could have been a historical reality and that many of the myths are actually collective memory traces of that vanished Golden Age. Archaeologists have recently unearthed remains of communities in Anatolia, Yugoslavia, Romania and the western Ukraine, sometimes numbering in the hundreds of thousands. They were gathered in agricultural paradises and apparently coexisted in peaceful harmony for almost four thousand years. Within a time span comparable to that between ancient Egypt and the present moment, these Neolithic peoples evolved virtually all the major domestic technologies we know of today under the benevolent religion of a Great Mother/Land Goddess. Among the over 30,000 artifacts unearthed in the area, now known as Old Europe, no weapons of war were found. The very absence of such objects tells us that here we have discovered a culture which is unlike any previously known. For while these mysterious peoples had all the technologies to fashion swords and shields they chose to make comic masks and fish hooks instead. It would appear that these communities lived in a way that was arguably the most joyous, peaceful and life-affirmative the world has ever known. Seeing the tiny altars and vessels used, we can easily imagine that the nurturing and life-giving spirit of the Goddess must have permeated every aspect of everyday existence. The evidence available suggests it was an age of partnership, cooperation, equality and an overriding sense of shared community. But what was happening in Old Europe, and later in parts of the Mediterranean such as Crete or Malta, can now be understood as a particular stage through which humankind had passed, regardless of geography.

Then disaster seemed to strike. The archeologists tell

us that the paradise communities which stretched over an area equivalent to that of modern North America appear to have all disappeared, as if overnight.

The Grail myth echoes this catastrophe. In the collective unconscious it appears to have been remembered as one of the most fundamental of human tragedies. In the Christian version of the story Adam and Eve were expelled from the Garden of Eden because they were disobedient to the Creator, and they entered the wasteland. That original sin was redeemed by Christ and through his intercession paradise could be regained. In the Celtic myths we are about to examine, that original paradise can only be restored and renewed by the Grail hero.

Opposite: **Bronze Head of Minerva***, dating from the Roman occupation of Britain at Bath.* **Above:** *The most sophisticated of all the Roman shrines in Britain was at Bath, deep in the Celtic heartland. These unique hot springs were venerated by both Briton and conqueror alike for their healing and curative properties.* **Inset:** *The cover to the* **Chalice Well** *beneath Glastonbury Tor. Chalice Well is the most*

celebrated of all the wells and springs associated with the Grail legend. According to some traditions this chalebeate spring is believed to be the hiding place of the Grail vessel. Its uniquely reddish-brown water is said to be caused by the blood of Christ which Joseph of Arimathea caught in the Grail Chalice. The well has never been known to dry up.

THE WASTELAND

I F WE TRACE THE LOSS OF PARADISE in Old Europe we discover that the open rural complexes of the sixth millennium B.C. were replaced by fortifications where none had existed before. The sudden appearance of lethal weapons coincides with an invasion of warlike, pastoral peoples who possessed very different social systems and ideas from those of the peaceful farmers. These invaders murderously swept through the communities and within a few generations the Neolithic paradises had been wiped out and humankind had taken a disastrous new fork in the road.

The new way was based, not upon cooperation and equality of both sex and class, but upon a dominator ideal; a stratified and pyramidal social structure which has continued, essentially unchanged, for the last five-thousand years. As the surviving followers of the Goddess fled their ruined paradise much of humankind became the eternal refugee. Peoples were displaced and found themselves always searching for the safe and peaceful haven in an increasingly divided and violent world. Joy, peace and a sense of harmony with nature and existence could now only be found in the legends of the past.

The essence of the early matrilocal nature cultures of Old Europe can be best expressed as the sacred Chalice of the Womb. The image representing the Nomadic invaders would have to be that of the lethal blade.

So within the opening pages of Elucidations we re-enact what could be described as a dim remembrance of an ancient egalitarian and matrilocal society that was ravished by a people whose way of life was one of slaughter, rape, destruction, and subjugation. The "lost voices of the wells" could well be part of a collective memory when a Wasteland came to Europe 5000 years before the time of Arthur.

Yet, strangely, it is the bloodthirsty heathen Celts, among the fiercest upholders of the lethal blade, who somehow understood the necessity of a balance between a Sky God and an Earth Goddess. And it is out of that intuitive understanding that the Grail legend grew.

Opposite: **The Golden Age**, *by Lucas Cranach 16th C. This shows the change from the idyllic peace and harmony of his earlier painting on page 21.*
Above: **Votive Chariot of the Sun God.** *Celtic, Denmark 2nd-1st C. BC.*

The irony of the Elucidations is that while it was the solar hero of the Sky God who overcame the peaceful maidens of the Earth, only a solar hero can undo the damage and heal the rift between male Heaven and female Earth.

THE LOST CHILDREN OF THE WELLS

HE COMING OF THE WASTELAND coincides with the decline of Arthur's court and the breakup of the Round Table. Just as the Wasteland has been caused by disruption of the balance between the Earth Goddess and the Kingship, so we discover the malaise has spread to Arthur's court and threatens to break up the fellowship of the Round Table. While Arthur was a young man his realm had enjoyed a Golden Age but as the king grew older he had increasingly become a bystander. In the earliest Welsh epics Arthur was always active. In many ways he was the Grail champion but later texts are less than kind to him and by Chrétien's days he has already degenerated into an often foolish old cuckold. When King Arthur and his knights discovered the cause of the Wasteland they swore vengeance upon the descendants of Amangons and went on a quest to rediscover the original sacred wells. They had no success but they did meet certain maidens under the escort of highly skilled knights. One knight who was captured by Gawain was Bliho Bliheris, who turned out to be the greatest storyteller of his age. This knight told Arthur that both maidens and escorts were descended from the original Virgins of the Wells and that they continually searched for the Court of the Rich Fisher and a way to restore the land. This of course presented Arthur with an unsolvable problem, for the very descendants of Amangons were also the

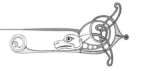

self-same descendants of the ravished maidens.

The appearance of Blihos Bliheris suggests that the author used a literary device to lend authenticity to the tale by enlisting a well known, proven and historical storyteller. For Bliheris was a historical Welsh knight in eleventh century Pembrokeshire, who was famed as the greatest storyteller of his age.

Blihos the Bard appears as much part of the Grail family, forever seeking the lost Grail Castle of Joy, as the legendary heroes themselves. And as one of the great clan of medieval troubadours and bards he is the real, authentic echo of the "voice of the wells."

The second introduction to *Le Conte del Graal* is the *Bliocadron*. Composed as a prologue in the early 13th century by an unknown author, Bliocadron deals with the hero's youth. Bliocadron was the name of Perceval's father, one of twelve brothers who all managed to get themselves killed in battle or tournament. When he also followed his brothers' reckless example, Bliocadron's wife retired to a castle by the sea of Wales. In order to avoid her son becoming a knight, fighting in tournaments and ending up like his father and uncles, the mother raises him in ignorance of knighthood and chivalry. Indeed she goes so far as to say that if he should ever see men *"dressed as though they were covered in iron"* they would surely be devils. He is to cross himself, say his credo and retreat with all speed.

So having established a paradise lost, a wasteland which is caused by an imbalance of kingship and the Sovereignty of the land, and the desperate need of a hero to redress that loss of harmony, we can now proceed to Chrétien's account of the Conte del Graal.

*Left: Stone **"Janus figure"** from Holzgerlingen, Germany, 6th c. BC. This double faced figure stands over seven feet high and once bore a pair of horns.*
*Right: Bronze, copper and silver **Shrine of St. Lachtins' arm**, Donaghmore, Co. Cork , 16ins. high. **Below:** Illustration from the Luttrell Psalter.*

Le Conte del Graal

HIGH IN THE FOOTHILLS of Mount Snowdon the son of a widow is practicing with his javelins when he meets five knights. When he sees their glittering armor for the first time he believes them to be angels. This is in sharp contrast to the prologue we have just seen in which his mother specifically warns him that men in iron are devils. After the boy learns from one of the knights that they come from the court of King Arthur, he confronts his mother. She then admits that his father was a great knight who had been wounded in the thigh and physically maimed. He had died of grief upon hearing of the death of his other two sons and she had vowed that the remaining child would be spared becoming a knight and suffering the same fate.

The young man doesn't pay much attention to what she is saying, he is only interested in going to "the king who makes knights." So his mother sews him an absurd rustic outfit hoping that by looking a fool he will be laughed out of court. She then gives him advice on how to behave honorably towards women. He must only take a kiss or some token like a ring or trinket. She tells him of the Church and of the Son of God. But he is impatient to be off, and soon leaves her in a swoon of grief. He looks back once after crossing the bridge and sees her body lying there but spurs his horse onwards all the same.

The theme of Mother and Son is one common to many cultures and of course finds its most powerful expression in the West as the Virgin and Child. The Celts had many such archetypes, like Modron and Mabon or Rhiannon and Pryderi, who exemplify a very particular veneration of the woman as mother and also confirms the Celts' reverence of the Goddess. This is her first appearance in the legend, in her aspect of the Mother who must give up her child as he outgrows the nest.

Celtic head *from a sacrificial vessel first century A.D. with the gold or silver torque around the neck.*

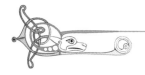

Peredur

THERE IS AN ALMOST IDENTICAL ACCOUNT of the hero's youth in the Welsh romance, *Peredur*. In this story, set in North Wales, the young hero is the seventh son. His father and six brothers all died fighting and the mother had taken him into the wilderness in the hope that he would avoid the same fate. He is raised alone, with no knowledge of his heritage. We are told that *"the son, who had no name, was so fleet of foot that he could outrun two hinds"* and even without training he was an expert with the Welsh

javelin. But his innocence and lack of experience brand him as the Great Fool.

One day he meets the knights Gawain, Urien and Owein, whom his mother had described as angels. Owein explains he is nothing of the sort but just a knight, and Peredur promptly wants to join them. His mother, seeing his determination, tells him to go to King Arthur, for they are kin. She then gives him the advice that he must go to church if he sees one; if meat and drink are not offered courteously then he is to take them; if he hears a cry of distress, especially from a

woman, he must go to it; if he sees a jewel to take it and give it to another and if he sees a fair maiden he should make love to her.

In this account Peredur then comes to a pavilion which he mistakes for a church, which suggests the sacred nature of the place. A beautiful auburn-haired maiden with a golden diadem sits on a golden chair and welcomes him. He asks for food and she gladly gives it, abundantly. He asks for her ring which she also does not begrudge him. He kneels before her, gives her a kiss and leaves. We may assume that this is the hero's first encounter with Sovereignty. But he has much to learn and is not ready to take responsibility for the consequences of his actions. The maidens' own Lord and champion returns, and believing the youth has shamed his wife he determines not to rest, nor let his consort rest, until he has met Peredur and avenged the imagined wrong. In other words he must seek the one he believes to be the challenger.

In Crétien's *Le Conte del Graal* the fool, also mistaking a fine tent for a Church, remembers his mother's advice and enters. He finds a sleeping maiden inside and abruptly wakes her. Just as his mother had told him, he kisses her, very much against her will, and even though she appears frightened he takes her ring as he had been advised. Having rudely eaten his fill at the table he rides off oblivious of the weeping woman and her likely fate at the hands of her jealous husband. When the husband does return he is convinced that she has been unfaithful and vows she will suffer until he is avenged.

As can be seen the poor maiden in this story is very different to the more majestic figure of Sovereignty in the Welsh story of *Peredur*. But in neither case is there any vital and empowering exchange, for the hero has yet much to understand and experience before he can match the gifts of Sovereignty.

Opposite: A Scene from **Le Livre du Cueurs d'Amours**. *Illuminated manuscript, France 15th century.* **Right:** *Celtic bronze god or hero from the river Juine, France., 1st century BC.*

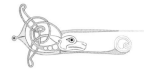

KNIGHT TO KING'S PAWN

ERCEVAL EVENTUALLY ARRIVES AT CARDUEL where King Arthur is holding court but before he can enter he meets a knight in magnificent crimson armor, carrying a golden cup which he has just snatched from the king's table. In the process, he has inadvertently caused the queen's cup to spill over her lap, thus compounding the insult.

In *Peredur* there is no such vague equivalence. The Red Knight forthrightly seizes the goblet from Queen Guenevere, throws the liquor over her face and boxes her ears, challenging anyone to avenge this insult. This is a gross insult and the theft of the cup means a loss of Sovereignty for Arthur, as the Goddess bestows kingship through it.

Both accounts of the episode of this stolen cup have striking similarities with the earlier story of the sacred Maidens of the Wells. Like the queen, as representatives of the Earth Goddess they were shamed and insulted. Now it is the Red Knight who shames Gwenhwyfer, who is also the representative of the Sovereignty of the land.

The Red Knight sends a message with the youth to the king. "Either give me my rightful lands or send a champion to fight for the cup." But our young fool only has eyes for the knight's brilliant red armor and fails to deliver the message. He then meets the distraught king who fears the challenge by the Red Knight. The king's enemy has spilled wine on the queen's dress so both he and his knights are shamed, and yet no one cares to be champion and respond to the challenge. The king himself seems as reluctant as the rest. Chrétien insinuates that the king is in decline.

Although he is said to have just won a great battle, most of the companions of the Round Table have in fact left the court and dispersed, suggesting that all is not well in the kingdom. Arthur increasingly has become a bystander delegating his role to younger champions like Gawain, who does not seem to be present during this episode.

In the earliest Irish epics Arthur was always active, but by now a spiritual and physical lethargy has settled upon the land. The underlying malaise would appear to be Arthur's failure of union with his queen and thus, by implication, with the land.

In the folk ballad of King Arthur and King Cornwall the latter is boasting:

> "I had a daughter by King Arthur's wife,
> That now is called my flower.
> For King Arthur, that kindly cuckold,
> Hath none such in his bower."

This is indeed a far cry from the halcyon days of Arthur's tempestuous youth.

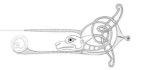

Opposite: **Serpent stone**, *Maryport, Cumberland. This four foot high carving is a fantastic combination of the Celtic Cult of the Head, the Crowned Serpents of Fertility and traces of a Salmon of Wisdom carved on the testes. The head itself is superimposed upon the glans of the phallus.*

Above: The circular amphitheatre at Caerleon, Wales, was thought to be the site of Arthur's court at Carduel. The remains of large buildings hinted that it was an ancient British city but most of the ruins are in fact Roman. The round amphitheater further suggested a link with the legendary Round Table.

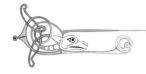

THE RED ARMOR

HE YOUTH IS IMPA-TIENT, WANTING TO be knighted so he can claim the red armor from the knight outside. Kai, Arthur's bluff seneschal, mocks the lad and tells him that certainly the king grants him his wish and gives him those arms. All he has to do now is to go outside and get them. As Arthur rebukes his seneschal for sending the youth out to what must have seemed his certain death, a beautiful maiden suddenly laughs and tells the youth that there will never be a better knight than he. The short-tempered and jealous Kai slaps the maiden and kicks the court fool (in Peredur, instead of the fool it is a male and female dwarf who are beaten) who has predicted that the girl would not laugh until she saw the man who would be supreme among knights. The prophetic laugh is a particularly favored motif among the Celtic story-tellers and only those with the true gift of prophecy would ever use it. Merlin would often laugh as he fore-told even the most doom-laden scenarios. Laughter was considered full of magic, and often heroes laughed as they rode into battle.

The youth glowers at Kai but rides out to arrogantly demand the Red Knight's armor. Losing his temper at the uncouth lad the knight cuffs him with the butt of his lance but is promptly and unexpectedly rewarded by the young man's javelin through his helm into his eye.

The youth is eager to remove the armor from the dead man, but only when helped by a page does he manage to put on the unfa-miliar pieces. Even so, he refuses to take off the homespun clothes his mother had made for him. The page soon discovers that teaching a fool is a very painful business al-though he still manages to explain the rudi-ments of holding a lance, and a shield and the use of stirrups. The would-be knight commands the page to return the golden cup to the queen and vows he will avenge the maiden whose face was slapped by Kai. He then spurs his horse and it carries him off.

At this point in the story the young man's simple desire to become a knight is preempted by the insult to the queen and the king. Fate arrives before the hero can be properly initiated into both manhood and society. Destiny forces him into the premature role of a cham-pion who remains outside of the normal everyday social hierarchy. He does not earn his position, it is thrust upon him. He *is* his destiny.

Opposite: Helmet, Sutton
Hoo Burial Ship, 5th century.
Although the helmet is actually
thought to be Anglo-Saxon in
origin it represents the wide
variety of arms available to the
warriors of the period. These
and the many trophies captured
by all the warring factions of
post-Roman Britain would mean
that any good armor was prized
and worn by whosoever was
tough enough to claim it.

Left: Epona, the Goddess of
the Horse. Epona was worshipped
by the Roman cavalrymen. She is
the counterpart of the Irish
Goddess, Rhiannon, whose son
Pryderi is the early prototype of
Peredur and Perceval.

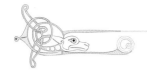

THE CODE

FINALLY OUR HERO, who has yet to claim a name, arrives at a fair castle where he meets Gurnemant of Gohort who undertakes to teach the unskilled lad how to maneuver his horse, and how to use a lance and sword. The youth learns at an astonishing rate and soon the old *vavasour* has taught him all he needs.

He tells the lad that he must now drop his mother's advice and take a new code of behavior more befitting a knight. He is instructed to be merciful to any other knight he vanquishes, to avoid being too talkative, to go to anyone in distress and to attend Church. Gurnemanz offers his daughter's hand but the young man declines. He feels he must earn his bride so he thanks Gurnemanz and leaves to find his mother.

This is the young hero's belated acceptance into male society with its complex chivalric code of behavior. The key to the hero's subsequent failure when tested at the Grail Castle is the instruction that a true knight should avoid being too talkative. The young fool unquestioningly takes these rules at face value so when he is confronted with a situation which requires his true and natural response he falls back on someone else's authority, on a programmed reaction which is totally inappropriate to the situation.

At the next castle he meets an old, lame knight, who is actually his uncle, invites Peredur to join him before a fire where they watch two youths in mock battle. Peredur then fights the best of them and his host predicts he will become the greatest knight in the land but insists that Peredur drop his mother's teachings and learns, instead, the male codes of honor. Peredur leaves and comes to yet another castle where he meets another maternal uncle who this time teaches him how to use a sword. Peredur is told to smite an iron column three times with the sword. He breaks the blade each time but while he manages to mend the broken sword on two occasions, on the third attempt he fails and is told that he has, as yet, only come into two-thirds of his full strength, although already he is the greatest swordsman in the land.

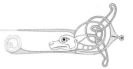

Above: Graffiti, 3rd C. A D.
Above: Graffiti, 3rd C. A D. Roman chain mail, which was copied from earlier Asian sources, protected both horse and rider. During the historical period in which these stories unfold we discover at the end of the Roman occupation of Britain an unusually high concentration of heavily armored cavalry. These included the Sarmatians, horse nomads from the Eastern steppes. These were the first known troops in Western Europe to use body armour of horn or metal scales for both man and horse. They carried long lances and long double-edged swords.

What is fascinating in respect of King Arthur's knights was that these Sarmatian veterans had a battle standard of a windsock-like dragon and their god of war was symbolized as a sword planted upright in the ground, or in a stone-like platform. Even Excalibur derives from Kalybes, a Sarmatian clan of master smiths (Latin Chalybis).
Left: Bronze shield from Witham, Lincolnshire.
Opposite: Shield from the Thames at Battersea in London. Both were probably made in the 3rd century and were votive or ceremonial weapons.

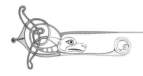

THE FOOL AND THE VIRGIN

HRÉTIEN TELLS OF HOW HIS HERO rides into the forest until he comes to a fortified town which is being besieged. The land around has been laid to waste, and although the townspeople offer him lodgings they are starving and can only hold out for one more day. Blancheflor, the exquisite golden haired young queen of the realm, (in Peredur her skin is 'whiter than flowers of the whitest crystal, hair blacker than jet and two small red spots on her cheeks') comes to the hero during the night and explains that it is an unwelcome suitor, Clamadeu who besieges her castle and that she will kill herself rather than yield to him. The young couple chastely lie in one another's arms all night in the bed and in the morning the young knight offers to fight the queen's enemy on condition that she will be his if he wins. She offers her love without any such condition, but he is determined to fight for her. He first meets Clamadeu's seneschal and defeats him and then remembering that he should be merciful, sends him to King Arthur to be the captive of the maiden who was struck by Kai.

The victor returns to the castle and once again innocently sleeps with Blancheflor as husband and wife. The next day he meets and defeats twenty knights sent against him. The fortunes of the town are changing and that night a ship is driven by gales into the harbor with provisions for all the defenders. On the third day he defeats Clamadeu himself who he likewise sends to Arthur, along with a message for the maiden whom Kai had struck.

Now the land is at peace and the lovers become truly man and wife. But only too soon the young knight wishes to see his mother again to ensure she is well. He promises to return to his love, Blancheflor, and her castle of Beaurepaire, as soon as he can.

Chrétien was well known as a writer of popular romances long before he penned *Le Conte del Graal*. Both the matter and the manner of his earlier poem *Lancelot* was actually dictated by Marie de Champagne. This powerful daughter of Eleanor of Aquitaine created a "Court of Love" at Poitiers imitating the earlier traditions of Languedoc. This court was governed by a great lady, while its laws were drawn up in accord with the outpourings of the poets under the guidance of the Countess Marie herself. Chrétien came under her direct influence during the four years of the Poitiers court. But he appeared to bridle at some of her dictates, one of which was that there could be no courtly love between man and wife. Perhaps she was reflecting on how Henry II had treated her high-spirited and ambitious mother, but Chrétien offers in the scenes between Blancheflor and Perceval an innocence and simplicity which is a far cry from the illicit goings-on between Queen Guenevere and Lancelot. For in these scenes we glimpse Sovereignty in both her Virgin and Nubile aspects, as her champion becomes her lover.

Right: Painted tray, 1400 depicting the rule of love. Venus is adored in much the same way as the Virgin. However in this painting the devotees are the six great historical lovers including Paris, Tristram and Lancelot. The power of the Courts of

Love, of Eleanor of Aquitaine and Marie of Champagne, had already spread throughout the rest of Europe and Chrétien, at one time the court poet of Marie, was well aware of their attraction in his elaboration of the story of Blancheflor.

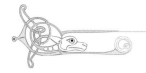

THE CASTLE OF THE FISHER KING

NCE AGAIN PERCEVAL RIDES FOR A DAY until he reaches a wide river with no ford. On seeing two fishermen in a boat he inquires whether there is a lodging nearby. He is directed to a mighty castle with a tall tower which is square and built of dark stone and flanked on either side by two lesser towers. The hall stands in front with an splendid arcade. He is made welcome and later meets his host, who had been in the boat, leaning on one elbow before a great fire. The nobleman apologizes for the fact that he cannot rise, but although the young knight is curious he fails to ask why. We have at last arrived at the Grail Castle. It is invisible to all but those who are worthy. It is tempting to forget that we are deep within the Otherworld, that inner part of Logres which is ailing just as the Fisher King is wounded and impotent. To seek an actual historical location is to miss the point, and yet the two worlds do cross at certain sacred places. The site which fits most descriptions and has an impeccable pedigree is that of Castell Dinas Bran at Llangolan, perched high above the River Dee in North Wales. Tradition has it that it was the home of the god Bran. The legendary King Bran possessed a magical Cauldron of Plenty, which recalls the Rich Fisher, the first Guardian of the Grail who in *Perlesvaus* is named Bron. Chrétien gives no explanation for his Fisher King but we do know that Bran was the Welsh God of the Sea and the River Dee is famous for its fishing. Not only that, both Bran and the Fisher King had wounds that would not heal, and both entertained their guests lavishly.

Above left: Greek vase painting, 5th century B.C. Woman carrying an impressive fish phallus. In ancient Athenian fertility festivals erotica such as these were meant to excite the participants.
This page: Castell Dinas Bran, Llangolan, Wales.
Above right: Carved gravestone, 13th c., Lerida Museum. The identification of Christ with the fish is seen clearly in this image of a huge fish within a vessel. Early Christians, in order to conceal their true beliefs, used the code of 'Iesous CHristos Theou HUios Soter', Jesus Christ, Son of God, the Saviour. This spelled I C H T H U S, which is the Greek word for fish.

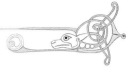

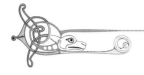

THE GRAIL MAIDEN

The sword and the procession of the Grail, French manuscript, 14th.C.

S THE KING AND THE KNIGHT are talking together a lad enters bearing a sword, which he gives to the host saying that it is from the king's niece. Its blade can never be broken, save in one perilous moment only known to Trebuchet, the man who has forged it. The king gives the sword to the young knight, telling him that he is destined to wear it.

Then a second youth enters the hall holding a white lance, from the tip of which oozes a drop of blood. *"Two more youths appeared carrying candelabras followed by a fair maiden who held a bejewelled, golden grail in both her hands. She was beautiful, gracious and splendidly garbed and as she entered with the grail in her hands, there was such a brilliant light that the candles lost their brightness, just as the stars do when the moon or the sun rises. She was followed by another maiden carrying a silver carving dish."*

The procession and the Grail pass before them once more as the company are all eating, but the young knight does not ask who the Grail served, or what the procession signified. He puts off asking the question until the morning for fear of offending.

The hero has now witnessed the Grail Maiden and, what we later learn are the Four Hallows: the Sword, the Silver Platter, the Lance and the Grail. Sovereignty in her virgin aspect carries the centerpiece of the Grail. The host remains hospitable, but retires to bed being carried out on his couch.

After a sound night's sleep the young hero finds himself alone in what appears to be an empty castle. He puts on his armor, finds his horse, but when he rides across the drawbridge it is raised abruptly and he has to leap clear. Thinking that the rest of the company he had seen the previous night have gone hunting, the young knight follows tracks away from the castle and soon comes upon a maiden grieving over her lover who has just been slain by a knight. She asks where the young man has been staying and he describes the castle. She tells him that it is the home of the Rich Fisher King who was maimed between the thighs. She then asks whether he has seen the Lance and the Grail procession. On hearing that he had remained silent when he saw these things she asks his name.

He intuitively replies that it is Perceval of Wales, although up to this point neither he nor we knew his name. She calls him Perceval the Wretched, for if he had only asked the question which had bothered him, the king would have been healed. He would have been able to rule his lands and great good would have come from it.

She informs the young man that his misfortune is a result of the wrong he did to his mother, who has died of grief on his account and tells him that the sword will fail him in his greatest need.

This is the ever-virgin Sovereignty, accusing her champion yet at the same time offering insights into his predicament.

"Girl Enthroned" by Thomas Gotch, 1894. Private collection.

THE SWORD

HE FOUR HALLOWS, either given to Chretién's Perceval, or carried in the Grail procession, seem to derive from early Celtic sources in Britain and Ireland. Many argue that the Four Treasures of the Tuatha de Danaan – the tribe of the great Irish Goddess, Danu – were the original source of the Hallows. Certainly there is an uncanny resemblance of these fourfold treasures – the Sword of Nuada, the Lia Fail, the Cauldron of Dagda and the Spear of Lugh, to the later sacred Grail emblems.

Blood is the central leitmotif of the whole Grail legend. It is hardly a coincidence that all the Hallows are venerated as much through their connection with blood as for their particular attributes. Later on we will find that Gawain is to win the Hallows Sword, which beheaded John the Baptist. It bleeds at mid-day. We have just observed a lance which drips blood. In the procession which Peredur is about to see, there is a dish with a bleeding head upon it. And in most of the Christian versions the chalice is the vessel in which Christ's last blood was gathered by Joseph of Aramathea. It is this constant image of living blood coursing through the veins of the myth which tends to give the legend some surrealistic immediacy of life. Somehow all the sacred relics are organic and present. Blood only flows where there is life. Even the Fisher King has a wound which, in its refusal to heal, gives us the sense of an ongoing process of life always suspended at its most poignant and immediate moment. This is a myth which truly lives, breathes and bleeds.

In exploring the Hallows at such an early stage of our examination of the legends, we will often step outside the Celtic tradition but it is necessary if we are to understand the extraordinarily condensed richness of the

The Stations of the Four Hallows

The Irish poet, W.B. Yeats appears to have been the first to notice the remarkable parallel betwen the four Treasures of the Tuatha de Danaan and the four aces of the Tarot suites. And when we compare the four isolated aces from the Waite tarot pack with the four hallows of the Grail we do find that they have an uncanny resemblance to each other. Superficially, the spear does not seem to match the ace of wands yet when it is recalled that the spear is the hallow which heals the land, regenerating and restoring fertility and life, then the sprouting wand of the tarot fits snugly into place.

Above: *Arthur's sword, Excalibur, is returned to the Lady of the Lake thus ending the king's claim to the realm and to his marriage with Sovereignty.*

Sword
Air
Spring
Yellow
Arthur
East

Paten
Earth
Winter
Green
Gawain
North

Grail
Water
Autumn
Blue
Parzival
West

Spear
Fire
Summer
Red
Amfortas
South

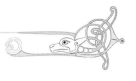

imagery. The Four Hallows can be grouped into the male principle of the Blade – (the Sword and the Lance), and the female principle of the Chalice – (the Platter and the Grail).

The two most likely candidates as prototype of the Hallows Sword are Celtic and Christian. The earliest Celtic example is that of the Sword of Nuadu, one of the Four Treasures of the Tuatha de Danaan in the Christian legend of the *Queste del San Graal*. The earliest Christian weapon is the legendary Sword of David, which Solomon's wife places in the ship of Solomon to be sent down the ages until the Grail knights discover it.

In the Welsh epic poem, *"The Spoils of Annwn,"* a mighty sword is mentioned, wielded by Llwch Lleminawc, alias the God Lugh. This sword appears later in another Welsh epic, *"Culhwch and Olwen",* and is identified as Caledfwlch (Excalibur).

In *"Culhwch and Olwen"* a young hero, Goreu, takes a magical Sword of Light from the giant Gwrnach. This is the legendary Celtic Glaive, the progenitor of all great blades which can only be wielded by a destined hero. Such weapons have unique and extraordinary qualities, often empowering the bearer with superhuman abilities. However, the gift invariably is double-edged, as it exacts a heavy price from whosoever is bold enough to use it. The destiny of the man is bound to the destiny of the weapon.

Often the sword is in two pieces. In *Peredur* the hero breaks a sword twice but is unable to unite the pieces on his third attempt. He will be able to make the sword whole only when he is worthy, after completing specific tasks set along the Grail Road.

In the German *Parzival* the hero is given a magnificent sword but it has a flaw, and at the very moment he needs it in battle it shatters. Fortunately for the hero

this occurs when he is fighting his own half-brother, Fierefiz, who refuses to take the advantage and throws his own sword as well.

In *Le Conte del Graal* it is Gawain who must understand that to trust in the sword alone is perilous, and that the seeker must rather trust his own nature. He, like Parzival, possesses a sword which breaks, is united, and then might break again at a crucial moment.

In the Christian story of *Perlesvaus* it is Gawain who enters a quest for the sword whose blade beheaded John the Baptist. This extraordinary blade, flashes with emerald fire and becomes green when drawn. It bleeds at midday, the time when John the Baptist died. Traditionally, Gawain was supposed to have held Arthur's great sword, Excalibur, in trust until the young king was ready to take its burden.

A sword is, of course, paramount in Arthur's career. His claim to the throne, to kingship and to marriage with Sovereignty and the land rests upon his success in pulling a sword from a stone. Yet his real power is to be found in another sword, Excalibur, which is given to him by the Lady of the Lake, patroness and teacher to both Lancelot and his son Galahad.

The *Queste del San Graal* relates the story of the Sword of David. Solomon's wife placed the weapon in a ship she had built, which sailed out into the ages and was finally discovered by the three Christian Grail knights, Galahad, Perceval and Bors. When they find the wondrous sword, Perceval's sister Dindraine, tells them of its history. In this legend it was the unsheathing by unworthy hands that caused the Wasteland, which the hero must now restore. The last hand which used the sword, before they found it, was that of King Parian who was wounded between the thighs and made impotent by a lance.

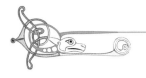

THE DISC

HE DISC OR PLATTER HAS MANY SHAPES and many forms. It appears as a stone, a gaming board, a paten, a table, a dish with a severed head upon it, or even a stone chair. The earliest example of this hallow in the Celtic literature is that of the Stone of Fal, which screamed under every king who took the Sovereignty of Ireland. Also known as *Lias Fail*, it will not tolerate any unworthy Sovereign and appears in the Grail legend as the Siege Perilous. This is the seat at the Round Table upon which only the Grail winner can sit unharmed. Even Perceval, who eventually achieves the Grail, is deemed unworthy when he rashly sits on it at first. It screams and splits beneath him and prophesies that only when the right question is asked, at the right time and by the right knight, will it unite again and the Wasteland be restored to Paradise.

Arthur had to pull the Hallows Sword from the Hallows Stone in order claim his rightful kingship, and Galahad did likewise to prove himself worthy of the Grail. In the Grail procession depicted in the legend of Peredur there is a platter upon which a man's head is placed surrounded by blood. In the story of Bran, King of Britain, Bran was wounded by a spear and his wound could not be healed. He commanded that his head should be cut off, for true to the Celtic tradition he can no longer rule when maimed. As his head is borne to the White Mount in London by seven of his followers they enter a timeless zone for over eighty years where they are lavishly feasted and in which the Head of Bran instructs them in the mysteries.

The Disc is sometimes even represented by the gwyddbwyll board. This chess-like game was obviously a well-known board of the time. It is symbolic of the land and the pieces which move over its surface are the main characters of the Quest. The board, we are told

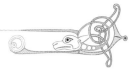

by the Black Maiden, who furiously berates Peredur for throwing it out the window simply because the side he had favored had lost, is the property of the Empress or Goddess of Sovereignty.

Whatever its outward form, the Disc is certainly the most elusive of all the Hallows. The Disc represents the supportive base of human endeavor. It is another symbol of the true nature of the Round Table or the Table of Solomon.

Opposite: **Communion Paten** *Irish C. 700 Patens like this elaborate example from Ireland would have been roughly contemporary with Perceval or Peredur.*

Right: **The Throne** *in Hexham Abbey, Britain, 7th C. This was used as a coronation stone for the kings of Northumbria. Later it became a Seat of Sanctuary. Fugitives seeking sanctuary in a church would have their cases considered by a bishop sitting in the chair.*

Above: **The Seat Perilous** *at the Round Table. Manuscript illustration, French 15th C.*

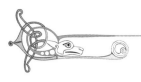

THE SPEAR

HE SPEAR, OR LANCE, SIGNIFIES THE PIERCING, arrow-like perception which aims at and penetrates the essential core of things. It offers insight yet wounds that which is corrupt. At the same time it is the greatest healing influence of the Hallows. This double-edged quality is seen in the appellation of "the Spear which Heals and Wounds."

Excellence with the lance featured in every Celtic stratagem, and the Welsh warriors were especially known for their skill with the weapon. In medieval times the spear had been largely replaced by the jousting lance, a chivalric symbol of challenge.

The Celtic spear, within the essential Grail myth, renders impotent whosoever it strikes, leaving him in a strange state in which he can neither be healed nor actually die. This "Dolorous Blow" lays waste his lands and only a hero of exceptional powers and worthiness is able to lift the burden and heal the sufferer by using the selfsame spear that wounded him.

In the Christian legend the spear becomes the sacred Lance of Longinus, the centurion who pierced the side of Christ at the crucifixion. It was from this wound that Joseph of Arimathea supposedly caught Christ's blood in a vessel and brought it to Glastonbury in southwest Britain.

Above: The **Tombstone of Longinus** at Colchester, Eastern Britain. Christian legend has it that Longinus was a blind Roman centurion who thrust the spear into Christ's side at the crucifixion. Some of Jesus's blood fell upon his eyes and he was healed. Upon this miracle Longinus was converted. The prototype for this story is to be found in the Norse legend of Hod, the blind God who slew the hero Balder. The feast day of the Blessed Longinus falls on the Ides of March, the same day devoted to Hod.

Above right: **Ivory plaque** of the spear wounding Christ. Anglo Saxon 9th century.
Right: **The Fisher King** and the wound, French Illuminated manuscript, 14th C.

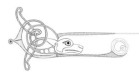

THE GRAIL

HE GRAIL AS DESCRIBED BY CHRÉ-TIEN was a fairly common article of his times. *Scutella lata et aliquantulum profunda* can be translated as a wide and slightly deep dish, about 60 or 70 cms across in which, the Abbot of Froidmont tells us in 1215, *"costly viands are commonly placed for the rich."*

Among the legendary Thirteen Treasures of Britain, which Merlin the Magician is supposed to guard, we find one clear counterpart of Chrétien's Grail. This is the Dysgl of Rhydderch, the sixth century king of Strathclyde. It was described as a wide and deep platter: *"Whatever food are wished for thereon was instantly obtained."* In the Manessier continuation of Chrétien's romance the Grail passes, or moves by itself. *"Then all the tables were provided with delectable delicacies nobly filled that no man could name a food which he did not find there."* This description could as well describe the blessed drinking horn of the British king Bran, in which one received "the drink and food that one desired." Bran's brother had a stepson, Pryderi, who was not only a prototype of Perceval, but also instrumental in bringing about the devastation of South Wales by sitting upon a Perilous Mound just as Perceval, in the *Didot Perceval*, brings on the enchantments of Britain by sitting on the Seat Perilous at Arthur's Court.

There are other images of the Grail in which we can detect the meeting of the twin streams of Celt and Christian. It is discernable in the miraculous and magical cauldrons of Ireland and Wales, or in the cup of the Last Supper into which Christ poured wine, saying "this is my blood," or the chalice which contains Christ's blood from the crucifixion.

The Irish *Cauldron of the Dagda* is a Vessel of Plenty

from which *"no one came unsatisfied,"* while the *Cauldron of Diwrnach* gave the best cut of meat to the most valorous hero, yet would not cook meat for a coward. There are the various "Cauldrons of Cure" into which the hero is plunged only to be tempered and hardened a few moments later by being thrust into a "Cauldron of Venom."

The *Cauldron of Cormac* would break into pieces if three lies were told over it, and was restored if three truths were spoken.

The *Cauldron of Ceridwen* in which the Goddess brewed a potion of knowledge for her misshapen offspring, brings about a transformation in Gwion who, on licking his fingers when accidentally splashed by the liquid, acquires all knowledge. Ceridwen chases him in a fury and he keeps shape-changing to avoid her wrath. She finally manages to catch up with him as he becomes a grain of wheat and she becomes a chicken. But nine months after the encounter she gives birth to a transformed Gwion in the

*The **Ardagh Chalice**, Irish 8th C. This exquisite example of Celtic workmanship, only seven inches in height, was used in the sacrament of the Last Supper. The wine was drunk from it in remembrance of Christ saying "this is my blood."*

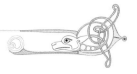

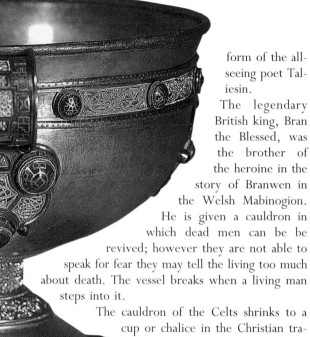

form of the all-seeing poet Taliesin.

The legendary British king, Bran the Blessed, was the brother of the heroine in the story of Branwen in the Welsh Mabinogion. He is given a cauldron in which dead men can be be revived; however they are not able to speak for fear they may tell the living too much about death. The vessel breaks when a living man steps into it.

The cauldron of the Celts shrinks to a cup or chalice in the Christian tradition. The first written versions of the Grail legend coincided with the years in which the Church first introduced the Eucharist for laymen. In this of course, the cup contains the wine which symbolizes the blood of Christ. The cup is that of the Last Supper, the blood is the redemptive symbol of Christ's sacrifice. But it is also the cup which Christ prays might pass from him in the Garden of Gethsemane.

Yet, while the Grail is seen as a healing and nurturing vessel its transforming powers often completely disrupt the established order. For instance when the Grail first appears at King Arthur's table his earthly kingdom appears to be still flourishing; however, there is an unseen stagnancy within. The Fellowship of the Grail, initiated by the King Arthur's Champion, Gawain, destroys the Fellowship of the Round Table. The spiritual energy passes from the worldly and chivalrous court to the Quest for the Grail.

For although the Grail is a healing force, it will scourge as often as it will nourish. Those chosen few who pass its rigorous tests are transformed, but those who attempt to grasp its meaning before they are ready are purged and often destroyed, in much the same way as the servants of that other holy artifact, the Jewish Ark of the Covenant, had been destroyed before. Lancelot, and even Gawain in the later legends, are found to be flawed men and not worthy of facing the Ultimate Source which the Grail embodies.

Of all the Hallows the Grail is the cup of the ultimate transformation. It transforms both the individual and the land.

In certain traditions it was believed that when Lucifer Morning Star fell from Heaven, the emerald stone from his crown fell to earth. As it did so, it changed from Stone to Sword, to Spear and finally to the Grail Chalice. Yet another tradition tells that when Lucifer the Lightbringer rebelled in Heaven, one-third sided with God, one-third descended to Hell with their fallen leader, and one-third remained neutral. It was the latter who brought the Grail to humankind to show them they should follow the middle way between the extremes.

But, however complex the imagery surrounding the Grail might be, essentially this centerpiece of the legend is the ultimate life-giving and life-sustaining vessel. As nurturing as a mother's womb, it is that uterus from which there is spiritual renewal and the rebirth of both individual and the land.

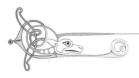

THE HIDDEN HALLOWS

 E NOW REJOIN PEREDUR whose experiences in the Castle of Wonders differ greatly from those of Chrétien's hero. Peredur sees two youths enter the hall carrying a great spear with three drops of blood issuing forth from its tip and running to the floor.

At the sight of the spear there is a great cry of despair from the company, yet the host does not interrupt the flow of his talk. Then two maidens bring a great salver, or dish, upon which is a man's severed head surrounded by blood. There is another great outcry from the company and yet the feasting continues. But Peredur does not ask about these wonders. This account is unique amongst the Grail legends. The Grail here is a gruesome dish which serves as a reminder of some deed which needs avenging. Here the question which is not asked concerns the nature of the head. If Peredur had asked *whose* head, and how it

concerned him, he would have known how to lift the enchantments of the Wasteland. The severed human head is the most typical of all the Celtic religious symbols, as it appears to signify divinity and otherworldly powers such as divination and prophecy. We find striking parallels to this whole scene in the feasting at an otherworldly hall at Grasholm, an island off the Welsh coast, by the wondrous Head of Bran and his followers who did not age for eighty years. Chrétien has been beautifully economical in limiting the Hallows to four. The author of Peredur is less frugal. The hero has already taken a Ring from the Maiden of the Tent, restored the Cup of Sovereignty to Gwenhwyfer, wielded the Sword which was Broken, seen the Dish with the Head and the Spear which drips blood. He is about to be given a Ring of Invisibility, and to win three Cups of Sovereignty, a Chessboard and the horn of a Unicorn.

Opposite: **Head of John the Baptist** *by Odilon Redon. Four Celtic heads, three of which are decorations from pottery. The head was believed to be the seat of the soul and possess powers of fertility,* divinity and prophetic knowledge.
Above: **Drinking Horn,** *8th c. Germany.*
Center: **Gundestrop Cauldron,** *Denmark; gilt-silver Celtic ceremonial bowl, first century B.C.*

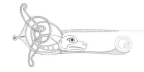

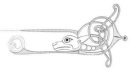

THE NINEFOLD HAGS OF GLOUCESTER

IN LE CONTE DEL GRAAL Perceval leaves his lamenting cousin to bury her lover while he goes in search of the knight who killed him. Instead he meets a wretched woman on a nag. She is the maiden Perceval had so uncouthly kissed in the tent, and whose husband had shamed and ill-used her as a result. He defeats the jealous husband, reunites the couple and sends them to surrender at Arthur's Court. This exploit adds to the increasingly impressive list of vanquished knights sent to Arthur, and the king is so intrigued that he sets out with his great company to find the unknown knight who is responsible.

Peredur, like Perceval, also meets a maiden lamenting her dead husband. She is trying to drag his body onto a horse, and she curses Peredur that he is the cause of his mother's death. As it turns out, she is his foster sister. Peredur eventually defeats the knight who killed her husband and sends him off to Arthur. By now he has sent so many defeated knights to the king that Arthur is determined to find him and let him avenge Kai's churlish behavior.

Peredur comes to a mountain castle which has been

afflicted by a plague of witches. This is the first of the hero's tasks of ridding the land of a host of plagues which have followed in the wake of the Wasteland. Although unarmed and only in his shirt, Peredur manages to overcome the leader of the Nine Sorceresses of Gloucester. She begs mercy as she recognizes a prophecy which tells that she will train him in arms. He agrees to spare her and is trained by the witch and her warrior sisters for three weeks.

The nine sisters of Gloucester represent the hag aspect of the Hallows queen. They are a group of female warriors who in reality guard the Hallows and ensure that the cycle of the waxing and waning power of the goddess can be reenacted. As an aspect of the goddess they must provoke the hero into restoring the rightful kingship which brings about a union with the land. So it is they who train Peredur so that he can fulfill the prophecy that he will eventually overcome them. The hero who seeks the Grail is usually harried, mocked and encouraged in turn by the Grail Messenger in the guise of a hideous hag. For Peredur this is multiplied ninefold. The Triple Goddess is tripled, and the ninefold aspect of Sovereignty encourages the young hero so that eventually he can achieve the quest and once again empower the Hallows of the Goddess.

Any unworthy hero would receive the Dolorous Blow, causing a wound, so the land could not heal. Like the Hallows themselves, the witches have the twofold effect of being both regenerative and destructive.

Opposite: **"La Femme sans Merci"** *by J.W. Waterhouse, 1893.*
Above: *Stone relief of the* **Triple Earth Goddess**, *Cirencester, Britain, 2nd century. The three Mother Goddesses hold trays abundant with bread and fruit. But the self-same goddesses who can nourish can also destroy, often taking a ninefold hag aspect when they do so.*

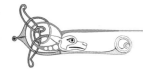

BLOOD ON THE SNOW

E HAD LEFT ARTHUR and his court setting out to find the mysterious knight who had defeated the best warriors of the land. On the first night of their journey they encamp near the forest. In the morning there is a freak snowfall. By chance, Perceval is riding near their pavilions when he sees a flock of geese attacked by a falcon, which knocks one of the birds to the ground. The goose escapes but three drops of blood fall on the snow. Perceval falls into a trance, for the blood and the snow have the appearance of his beloved's face, her red cheeks and lips on a pure white skin.

In *Peredur* the details are more in tune with the Celtic tradition. Celtic taste ran more towards dark damsels so the description is subtly changed. According to the Welsh author a wild she-hawk kills a duck but is disturbed and flies away. A raven alights on the snow near the duck. The three colors remind Peredur of the whiteness of his beloved's skin, the red of cheeks and lips, and the raven-black of her hair, and contemplating these he falls into a deep trance.

Returning to Perceval we find that while he sits in his saddle, totally entranced by the memory of his love Blancheflor, he is challenged by Segremor, one of Arthur's knights. He defeats the knight as if in a dream and calmly returns to his reverie. Kai then challenges him and is promptly unhorsed. In both French and Welsh accounts Kai breaks his shoulder, which confirms a prediction made by the fool that the slap he gave to the maiden would be painfully repaid. Both Peredur and Perceval have avenged the original insult. It is only when the gentle Gawain greets him as the snows are melting that Perceval slowly comes out of his enchantment and the two knights immediately take to one another as if they were twins.

Detail from **Portrait of a Woman** *by Rogier van der Weyden, 15th C.*

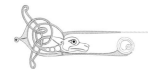

THE WOMAN ON THE MOUND

T THIS POINT IN THE DRAMA Chrétien's French romance and the Welsh narratives diverge. For the Welsh *Peredur* there is now an interval of over fourteen years. Although the tale appears to have little to do with the Grail there are many themes and elements which are crucial to an understanding of the relationship between the hero champion and the goddess. We will follow the complex adventures of the Welshman first.

At Arthur's celebration Peredur meets Angharad Golden-Hand, (Sovereignty as virgin) and he so falls in love with her that he swears never to speak to a Christian until she pledges her love, which at first she steadfastly refuses. From this point onward we enter a Celtic knot of interweaving adventures until he wins her love.

But Peredur is not a man to stay faithful for long. Soon he is off seeking adventure. This time he discovers a hall in which three men are playing gwyddbwyll and three maidens who warn him that their father, the Black Oppressor, will slay him. Peredur defeats this one-eyed black knight, who turns out to be yet another of the terrible scourges of the land. But before dispatching him, Peredur learns that the man's eye had been plucked out by the Black Wyrm of the Dolorous Mound as he attempted to steal an enchanted stone the Wyrm had in its tail.

In his quest for this Wyrm, Peredur first comes to the court of the Sons of the King of Suffering. Peredur sees three sons dead, carried across their horses. Women take the corpses from the saddle and bathe them in a tub and apply precious ointments. The men are instantly revived and tell Peredur that a terrible monster called Addanc slays them every day and every day they are resurrected. Here we can surely recognize

Bran's Cauldron of Rebirth in another guise.

Our hero then meets the fairest woman he has ever seen. This is the first time he has met Sovereignty in her true form, seated on a mound symbolic of the land she represents. Instead of taking the ring from the maiden in the pavilion, this time he is given a magical ring with which to kill the Addanc, on the condition that he will love her most of all women. The enamored Peredur readily agrees. Before disappearing she tells him to seek her in the direction of India.

Journeying into what is obviously the Otherworld, Peredur comes to a river with a flock of white sheep upon one side and a flock of black upon the other. As one sheep bleats, a black exchanges for a white across the stream, the process being reversed the next move, like a game of chess. The image of a tree, one half of which is burning while the other half is full of green leaves, leaves no doubt but that we are crossing the boundaries between two realities.

The reflecting images suggest that at such borders the earthly realm is mirrored by its opposite in the Otherworld. This is a supra-reality superimposed upon the normal landscape. It is analogous to the experiences of heightened states of consciousness in which the meditator or shaman sees the normal world in literally "a different light."

With the help of the ring, which renders him invisible, Peredur kills the Addanc but declines the kingdom he is offered as a reward.

Having met his double, Edlym Red-sword, he sets out for the Dolorous Mound but must now fight 200 of the 300 owners of the pavilions set up around the mound before the rest agree to become Peredur's men. He slays the Wyrm in the mound, gives the stone in its tail to Edlym, and continues on his way.

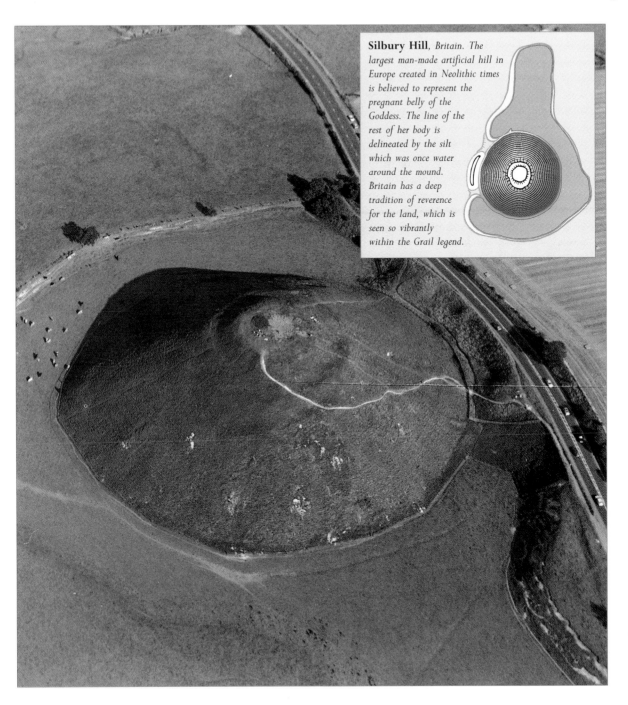

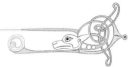

Silbury Hill, *Britain. The largest man-made artificial hill in Europe created in Neolithic times is believed to represent the pregnant belly of the Goddess. The line of the rest of her body is delineated by the silt which was once water around the mound. Britain has a deep tradition of reverence for the land, which is seen so vibrantly within the Grail legend.*

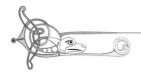

THE EMPRESS FOUND

EREDUR COMES TO WHERE a great tournament is being held and takes lodging with a miller and his wife. The miller lends him money, so he can enter the tourney. The Empress of Constantinople has offered herself as prize to the bravest of all the knights, and Peredur is so entranced by her beauty that he forgets to enter the tournament. Only when the miller gives him a hearty blow on the back as a reminder does he recover from his reverie, smile and then defeat all comers. He sends the knights to the Empress, and their armor and horses to the miller's wife to repay his debts. Finally he defeats three challengers: a black knight with a goblet of gold, another black knight with a goblet shaped as a beast's claw, and a red curly-haired knight with a goblet of crystal stone. He drinks from each vessel. The three cups from which Peredur drinks can also be understood as the three cups of Sovereignty. The beautiful maiden, the queen and the hag are symbolized by the white milk of fostering, the red wine of kingship and the dark potion of forgetfulness.

Thus he wins the love of the Empress who turns out to be none other than the Woman of the Mound who gave him the stone ring by which he defeated the Addanc. They rule together for fourteen years.

It is at this point that the oldest surviving manuscript of *Peredur*, known as the *Peniarth,* ends. In the later sequels this whole fourteen-year episode is compressed into a minor and brief diversion. But on closer inspection this is a vitally important sequence, as it allows some insight into the underlying nature of the quest. So far the hero's quest has been for the female, and that female is Sovereignty in many disguises. She has appeared as an overprotective mother, and as an immature maiden, as in his immature, first encounter with a maiden in the Pavilion. She can be as royal as Gwenhwyfer or as deformed as the silent female dwarf. The female characters who appear so regularly throughout the narrative are as mysterious as the maiden who carries the dish in the Castle of Wonders, or as sharp-tongued as Peredur's foster sister. She can assume the shape of his first besieged and virgin love, or the countess of the mountain castle who is harrassed by the Witches. Her three-fold aspect can become the ninefold warrior hags, or her virgin form that of Angharad Golden-hand. She appears disguised as the Black

Oppressor's daughter, or undisguised as the Woman of the Mound. In the final episodes of the *Peniarth* the goddess appears as the Countess of the Games, the miller's wife, and the Empress of Constantinople whom he eventually marries. Shortly he will meet the ugly Black Maiden who, as the hag of the three-fold goddess of the Hallows, berates him for his tardiness in healing the king and the land.

Peredur is really dogged by a very persistent goddess! But after all, he did inadvertently become her champion by avenging the insult to Gwenhwyfer and killing the challenger, so he only has himself to blame.

In this legend the goddess appears in her essentially healing role as the Grail Maiden, and in her provoking role as the Black Maiden. The old Irish tales tell of the hero being plunged into a life-giving cauldron, and then immediately immersed in a cauldron of venom. This is precisely what happens in the Grail legends. Healing is usually administered through the agency which wounded in the first place.

Opposite: **Celtic Bronze Vessel** *containing a cremation from a warrior's grave at Milavec, Bohemia. Such urns symbolized the rebirth of the warrior.* **Above:** **Tapestry***, French 15th C.*

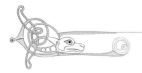

THE CHALLENGE OF THE LOATHY HAG

WE NOW CAN RETURN TO CHRÉTIEN'S NARRATIVE. We had left Perceval at King Arthur's great celebration of the young hero's arrival at court. But the festive atmosphere does not last long, being cut short as a hideous hog-faced maiden approaches the feasting on a mule. She greets everyone except Perceval whom she curses and upbraids for holding his tongue at the castle of the Fisher King. Because of his thoughtless and foolish act the king cannot be healed of his wounds and can no longer rule his lands. Because of Perceval, women will lose their husbands, the land will be waste and maidens will be left as orphans and helpless.

She then tells the company that if they want a joust or chivalrous battle they should go to the Proud Castle Orgulous, where there are 566 knights and their ladies.

The Loathy Hag then proposes that those who would have the supreme glory should raise the siege of the Maiden of Montesclaire and win a mysterious Sword.

Gawain swears he will seek the maiden, while other knights choose the Proud Castle. Perceval, however swears he will not spend two nights in the same lodging until he discovers the answers to the two questions he had failed to ask: Who was served from the Grail? And what was the truth of the bleeding Lance?

As they are all preparing to leave, the knight Guigambresil rides up and accuses Gawain of slaying his Lord. Gawain contests the slander, and they agree to meet to decide the matter before the King of Escavalon within forty days.

Gawain sets out for the appointed meeting and on the way reluctantly but gallantly takes part in a tournament as the champion of a younger daughter, and wins the day. At Escavalon he encounters a stranger who entrusts him to the care of his beautiful sister. They immediately are infatuated with one another but an old seneschal recognizes Gawain. Believing him to be guilty of slaying Guigambresil's Lord, the seneschal incites the townspeople to attack the lovers. The two defend themselves using a chessboard as a shield, huge chess pieces and the sword Escalibord. The King of Escavalon, appears in the middle of the melee and stops the brawl. The forthcoming combat with Guigambresil is postponed for another year on condition that Gawain goes in search of the Lance at the Grail Castle.

The sequel to the first edition of *Peredur* picks up an almost identical tale of the ugly hag arriving at court. In the sequel she mentions the bleeding lance, but avoids mentioning the head on the bloody platter. Peredur, like Perceval, is so goaded by the hag's curses that he leaves in search of the Castle of Wonders in order to heal the king.

Above: **The Wheel of Fortune**, *14th c.* *Opposite:* '**The Entry to the Castle of Maidens**" *by Alan Lee.*

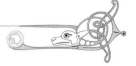

THE THREE SCOURGES OF BRITAIN

FOLLOWING PEREDUR'S PROGRESS we find that on arriving at a castle he is offered lodging and his host's daughter falls in love with him. Fearful that Peredur will take advantage of the maiden, her father imprisons him. However, with the connivance of the girl, Peredur secretly leaves his prison for three days in order to defeat his host's enemies who surround the castle. On discovering the identity of the unknown victor, the host releases him and offers both kingdom and daughter. But Peredur is resolute and only wants to find the Castle of Wonders.

He is directed to a castle in the middle of a lake. Upon entering the hall Peredur finds a gwyddbwyll board with the two sets of pieces playing each other. He grows angry when the side he supports loses the game, so he throws the board and pieces into the lake.

The Loathy Hag appears in the hall and bemoans the fact that Peredur more often does harm than good. The chessboard belongs to the Empress, and the only way to recover it is to go to the Castle of Ysbidongyl. If Peredur can kill the scourge who is laying waste the kingdom he will recover the board. Peredur manages to defeat this first scourge of the land, but the Loathy Hag then tells him that he must then rid the realm of a second plague: a stag with a single horn.

He beheads the stag, but then a lady arrives who grieves at the death of the beast, the greatest jewel in her domain. Peredur asks if he can do her some service as recompense. She directs him to fight a knight who appears from beneath a huge stone. Peredur fights him until he disappears. Peredur learns from a cousin that his kinsman had been killed by the third scourge of Britain, the Nine Sorceresses of Gloucester who also maimed Peredur's uncle. The cousin predicts that Peredur will avenge his kinsman and undo the effects of that Dolorous Blow.

The spear which wounds the land is revealed as the horn of the unicorn, "as long as a spear shaft and as sharp as the sharpest thing." It had dried up the ponds and killed the fishes, it devastated all living and growing things and killed the other beasts of the forests.

And the black maiden who has encouraged Peredur to kill the stag with one horn is the selfsame horsewoman who berates Peredur for doing so. Both are none other than Sovereignty whose land is being scourged because of the stag. By killing the beast Peredur restores the land and "frees the waters."

Out of this complex imagery two types of female, with entirely separate aims, can be distinguished in the

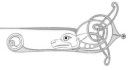

Perceval/Peredur/Grail romances. One is the Grail Bearer, whose prototype was probably Eriu, the Sovranty of Ireland, who served visitors to the Otherworld from her enchanted vessel. The other is the kinswoman concerned with avenging a blood feud.

The theme is really quite simple. There was a *maimed* king and a *dead* king, one to cure and one to avenge. The maimed king's realm was a Wasteland yet, paradoxically, he was guardian to a vessel of inexhaustible abundance and everlasting life which surely could have helped his infirmity. But it does not. The dead king was the rightful champion who had been killed by an unworthy contender and who must be avenged in order that a proper champion restores the union with Sovranty.

Throughout *Peredur* the figure of the Celtic goddess variously appears as mother, warrior, hag, virgin, a symbol of fertility and benefactrix of the land. She is known in the Irish epics to possess a very healthy, if on occasion overwhelming, sexual appetite. More archaic by far than the male gods it is she who is both responsible for the land while at the same time she *is* the land.

Opposite: **French illumin- ated manuscript**, *14th C.*
Center: **Chesspieces,** *9th C. from the Orkney Islands, Scotland.*
Above left: **Gaming Board,** *Viking 9th C.*

Above: **Glass Gaming Pieces** *from the burial of a Belgic Chieftain, South West Britain.*

Below: **Unicorn** *from the Westminster Bestiary, 13th C. England. In the Middle Ages it was believed that the mythical unicorn could only be captured by a naked virgin who was seated alone beneath a tree.*

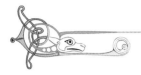

Gawain and the Woman of the Fountain

MEANWHILE AS WE RETURN TO Chrétien's *Perceval* we discover that he has totally forgotten God. For five years he has wandered, seeking the Grail, without entering a church. On Good Friday he is chastised for wearing armor and by coincidence meets a hermit and begs his council. The hermit tells him that his suffering is caused by his mother's death. "Sin stopped your tongue to ask of the Lance but it was only foolishness that stopped you asking about the Grail." The hermit turns out to be his uncle, the brother of the Fisher King and of Perceval's mother. Perceval stays with the hermit in order to do penance, and from this worthy man Perceval learns that his failure to ask about the procession and the Fisher King's infirmity is a social, worldly flaw. He is attempting to live by someone else's set of rules and is not true to his own promptings. The second reason is far more serious, for the death of his mother from his thoughtless and egocentric behavior shows him his own lack of love and compassion. This is a spiritual or even religious shortcoming. It will be this illumination at the Pascal season which is to assure his later success.

Chrétien now switches to Perceval's alter-ego, Gawain. He too is seeking Sovereignty. Gawain encounters a beautiful but haughty woman under a tree by a fountain. She responds arrogantly to his advances but agrees to ride with him if he gets her horse from a nearby garden. Those he meets within the garden warn Gawain against the woman but he ignores the warnings. He sets out with her and they are followed by what appears to be a hideous and rude dwarf. In one of their subsequent adventures Gawain's horse is stolen and he has to ride the broken-down nag of the dwarf. He is continually mocked and maliciously reviled by the beautiful woman of the fountain but somehow Gawain remains true to his chivalrous code. He also appears to really love the woman. Eventually Gawain encounters a knight riding the horse which had been stolen from him, defeats the knight, and reclaims the horse. When the party must cross a river, the ferryman demands the horse, Gringolet, as a toll. Gawain persuades him to accept the defeated knight instead, and the description of the ferryman who takes him across the waters reveals him to be an otherworldly guide who warns Gawain that this Castle of Marvels is enchanted.

Gawain boldly enters the castle and encounters the Perilous Bed on which he is assailed by seven hundred bolts and arrows, and on top of that he must kill a ravenous lion. He manages to survive all these trials, and by doing so the enchantments of the castle are ended. He meets the three queens who have been held prisoner there. They are Gawain's grandmother (who is also Arthur's mother) his own mother, and his sister.

Above: Lion of St. Mark,
7th c.
Right: **Shield of Parade**
15th c.
Opposite: **Sir Gawain,**
Illuminated Manuscript 14th c.
*"Gawain rides into a deep
forest, wondrous and wilde."*

Gawain has thus won through the trials and becomes the Lord of the Castle of Marvels. He has freed the goddess in her triple aspect of maiden, nymph and crone, and finally wins the love of the haughty Woman of the Fountain as he fulfills all of her demands. At this point Chrétien's narrative abruptly ends with Gawain awaiting King Arthur's arrival at a tournament he has arranged.

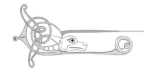

THE FIRST CONTINUATION 1180 ~ 1200

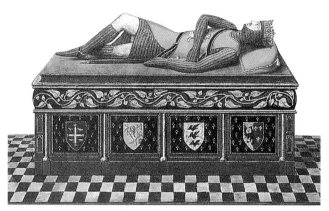

THERE ARE FOUR DIS- TINCT continuations to Chrétien's unfinished romance and each of these have many vari- ations. The shortest of the four begins as a knight passes by without saluting Queen Guenevere. She sends Gawain to bring him back. The stranger, whose name is Silimac, agrees to return only on condition that Gawain will help him on a secret errand. But just as they reach the queen's Pavilion Silimac is felled by a javelin thrown by an unknown and invisible assailant. Before he dies he entreats Gawain to put on his armor, mount his horse and give it free rein in order that his mission can be completed. Gawain, having given his promise, obeys and rides away, allowing the horse to guide him. This simply signifies to the audience that one can only discover the hidden realm in a natural state of let-go.

He is overtaken by a thunderstorm and seeks refuge in a chapel. There, a black and hideous hand extinguishes a candle with a wild lamenting cry. This is one of the few references to real evil in the Grail legends. One of the most distinctive attributes of the entire body of legends is the remarkable lack of the usual medieval preoccupations with Good versus Evil. In this particular case the Devil is behind the hand, and the Perilous Chapel signifies Hell itself.

Fearfully, Gawain departs and rides through the night. He is totally exhausted by the time he reaches a strange hall set on a causeway far out into the sea. In the hall there is a huge company awaiting him with great joy, saying that they have waited long for this moment. But when Gawain is stripped of Silimac's armor the assembled company discovers their error and knowing *"It is not he,"* they vanish. Gawain is left alone in the huge hall save for a bier in the center with a corpse lying on a scarlet cloth.

On the corpse's chest lies one half of a broken sword.

A procession of mourners enters, only to vanish once again. Another large crowd appears and sets up tables, and then a kingly figure enters and invites Gawain to eat. A rich Grail serves everyone with a magnificent feast. In the earlier Chrétien romance there is no mention of the Grail serving anyone but the Fisher King's old father.

In this continuation however, the Grail actually dispenses a sumptuous and abundant feast. In this sequel it resembles not Chrétien's *Graal* but the enchanted *dysgl* of Rhydderch — *"Whatever food one wished thereon was instantly obtained."*

In this continuation, and in the Manessier which follows it, we are told, *"Then all the tables were provided with delectable delicacies, nobly filled that no man could name a food which he did not find there."*

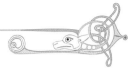

Gawain often appears to lead a split life. On the one hand he proves worthy to be the Grail hero, and on the other hand too flawed. In this account we will discover both aspects are in action.

This twin aspect appears in some earlier traditions of two brothers. Gwalchmai, who was earthly, and Gwalcheved, who was more heavenly. Both names signify the hawk, one of May and one of Summer.

Gawain's devotion to women is often cited as his major flaw, and yet as a knight he is especially associated with the Virgin Mary. He is known to bear her symbol, for he is the Knight of the Goddess. The symbol is a pentangle, the most human of all geometries. In "Gawain and the Green Knight," this motif signifies that he is faultless in the five senses, the five fingers and the five pure virtues of faithfulness, (cleanliness, courtesy, compassion, frankness and fellowship). The pentangle is the Solomon's knot of love which is endless and joined at no point. The pentangle is the symbol of balance. We recall Gawain's link with the East when it is discovered that Sophia, the gnostic female principle of wisdom, would only allow entrance to the realm of light if an initiate wore a pentangle.

Left: **Effigy** *of the Duke of Normandy from Gloucester Cathedral, Britain.*
Above: **St. Michael's Mount**, *Cornwall, South West Britain. Tradition tells of this island, being the only part left from the legendary Lyonesse, the land which disappeared beneath the sea.*

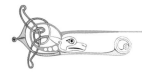

A Man for All Seasons

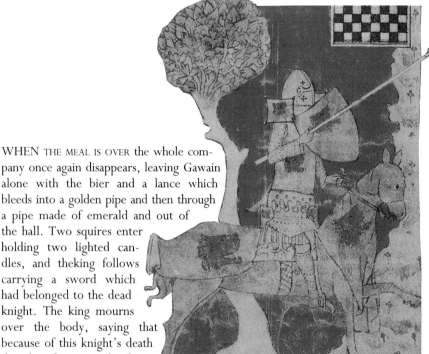

WHEN THE MEAL IS OVER the whole company once again disappears, leaving Gawain alone with the bier and a lance which bleeds into a golden pipe and then through a pipe made of emerald and out of the hall. Two squires enter holding two lighted candles, and theking follows carrying a sword which had belonged to the dead knight. The king mourns over the body, saying that because of this knight's death the kingdom is desolate. Only when the death is avenged will the people and the land be restored. He then draws the sword which has been broken and asks Gawain if he can bring the two pieces together. Gawain tries but is unsuccessful – here we see his flawed aspect. But immediately the worthy side surfaces, and although he is completely exhausted he forces himself awake to ask about the lance and the sword he has seen. No one has ever dared to ask before, and the king tells him it is the lance with which the Son of God was smitten at the crucifixion. The sword destroyed the entire kingdom of Logres. But as he continues the story Gawain can remain awake no longer and he falls asleep, so knows no more. However, the readers of the story are told how Joseph of Arimathea went to Mount Calvary where the Son of God was crucified and collected the savior's blood at the foot of the cross in a vessel called the Grail. He kept the Grail in safekeeping, was imprisoned but miraculously released by the Lord. Accompanied by Nicodemus and a small retinue, he set sail and landed on the White Isle in Britain. Whenever he was in need Joseph would blow a horn and the Grail would come and serve wine and food in abundance. Since then the Grail has been handed down only to those of Joseph's lineage.

Gawain awakens the next morning in a field of gorse by the sea. He is dismayed to realize he has not heard all the king's words, but nonetheless resolves to become mightier in arms and wisdom in order to be able to unite the sword. As he rides through the country he marvels at the surrounding land. No realm is more beautiful or so fertile as this, and yet the night before it had been a barren wasteland. In the night the streams have been restored and all the woods turned green. The people bless him as he passes for having asked about the lance. Yet they are sad that he has not asked whom the Grail served, which would have brought great joy to the realm.

Left: **Gawain** *(Walewein) from a 14th c. Dutch illustrated manuscript, Leiden.*
Above: **Green Man,** *Roof boss from Norwich Cathedral, Britain.*

This mysterious seasonal figure challenges Gawain in a 14th century poem, "Gawain and the Green Knight," to a lethal beheading game to choose the new yearly champion of the Goddess.

C E L T I C   B R A N C H   73

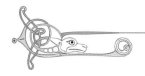

PARADISE REGAINED

RIGINALLY GAWAIN WAS the Grail winner in the earliest traditions of the legend. Nowhere is this more evident than in the *Diu Crone*. This "Bejewelled Crown," written in 1224 by the great Arthurian scholar of the age, Heinrich von den Turlin, makes Gawain the actual Grail winner and draws upon what must be the earliest Celtic tradition.

We join this particular account after Gawain, who has been searching for the Grail, comes to a land so beautiful that it might well be taken for an earthly paradise since "twas full of all delights that heart of man might desire." At the entrance to this wonderland was a building of glass, but the way was guarded by a flaming sword. This scene, reminiscent of the gates of Eden guarded by the Seraphim with the fiery sword, marks the boundaries of the Otherworld. After wandering for twelve days Gawain discovers his fellow knights, Lancelot and Calogreant. The three meet a squire who invites them to his Lord's castle. The floor is strewn with roses. The host is a hospitable old man dressed in white and gold who reclines on a couch. As they sit to eat, a youth enters and lays a sword before the host. Wine is served, but when Gawain notices that the host neither eats nor drinks he likewise refuses. Lancelot and the other knight do eat and drink however, and immediately fall into a deep and drugged sleep.

Two maidens then enter bearing candlesticks. Behind them walk two youths carrying a lance between them. Next come two more maidens bearing a silver salver filled with precious stones, followed by "the fairest being whom, since the world began, God had wrought in woman's wise, perfect she was in form and feature,

and richly clad withal." She bears a jewel of red gold in the form of a base on which another, rich with gold and gems, sits like a reliquary on an altar.

The spear suddenly sheds three drops of blood into the salver, which the host takes immediately. The maiden then places the fair reliquary upon the table and Gawain sees within it bread of which the old host partook. This is surely the clearest image of the Christian Eucharist in the entire Grail corpus. This sacrament of the Host embodies the Corpus Christi, both the blood and the body of Christ. Gawain can no longer keep silent and asks what the meaning is of so great a company and the mysterious ritual he has seen. At this question the whole company rises with a joyful shout.

Gawain is then told that he has achieved the Grail, and many have been released from a great sorrow by his question. They had trusted that Perceval would learn the secrets of the Grail but he had failed to ask the question by which they might be freed. For the company had to abide in the semblance of life when they were actually dead. This was a punishment for kinsmen slaying kinsmen over possession of the land. The question had to come from one of their own kin. And Gawain was one of their lineage who had to demand the truth of the marvels in the hall. The blood from the spear and the one-third of bread is all that is needed to nourish the king once a year. But the penance is now over and the maidens who are not dead are released. It was by their purity that God had laid upon them the service of the Grail, but that obligation was now withdrawn. With this explanation the king gave the sword which lay before him to Gawain and at dawn the entire company, save the maidens, faded from sight.

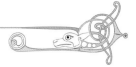

The Troubadour, Werner von Teufen, *Manesse Codex.*
In one of the many stories of Gawain we are told how he once agreed to marry a Loathy Hag to save Arthur. He transformed his wife, by a kiss, into a woman of surpassing beauty who tells him she can only be beautiful half the time. He can choose whether she is beautiful by day or by night. His act of compassion in giving her the freedom to choose for herself breaks the enchantment and she remains beautiful all the time.

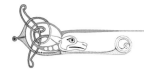

END OF A CYCLE

MANESSIER'S SEQUEL TO THE CONTE DEL GRAAL was written for the Countess Jeanne of Flanders. She was the grandniece of Phillipe, Count of Flanders for whom Chrétien had originally composed the Conte – which brings the legend the full cycle of three generations.

Manessier continues with Perceval at an abundant feast. He sees two maidens bearing the Grail and the serving dish. The first is the Fisher King's daughter while the other is the daughter of his brother Gron (Bron), the King of the Wasteland. This brother-king had been killed by the Lord of the Red Tower with the sword which broke.

In this sequel the Fisher King had managed to maim himself with the fragments of the sword and could not be healed until Gron's death was avenged. Perceval has the sword fully reforged and kills the Lord of the Red Tower. As he returns to the Grail Castle the Fisher King is immediately cured of his wound.

Now we can also round off the Welsh epic of *Peredur*. The hero has summoned the war-band of Arthur to attack the nine witches of Caer Loyw. These were the sorceresses who had taught Peredur about arms, so he gives the chief witch three chances of stopping the fighting. She refuses, so he is forced to kill her. As she dies she shrieks that it was prophesied that Peredur was destined to slay all her sisters, which comes about. And

Below: **The Book of Durrow**, *9th* C. *Illuminated Gospel of St. Matthew* **Right**: *Rustic Scene by Samuel Palmer, 1825. Inscribed are Virgil's lines "When Libra makes the Hours of Day and Night equal (Autumn Equinox) and divides the Globe in the middle between Light and Shade."*

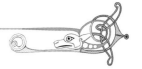

thus all is told of the Castle of Wonders.

As this legend comes to an end we are aware that throughout its pages Peredur lives on the two levels of World and Otherworld. In his empowerment through the Hallows and his relationship with the multi-faceted Sovereignty he is able to act as a channel between the two realms. But the cycle must change, just as the natural seasons occur and as life is followed by death. Of all the Grail legends, Peredur clearly accepts the repeating cycle of barrenness and fertility. The Wasteland will return. Sovereignty, like nature in death and winter, will assume the guise of a hag and scour the land for a new champion. The Hallows will be lost once again. Paradise will be lost and the power of kings like Arthur will wane and disappear. Golden ages will be replaced by dark eras awaiting the destined knight and Sovereignty in her queenly aspect. This is the message of the legend for our own times. The Sacred Land has been raped and misused, we have not been conscious of the excessive male dominated attitudes to the earth. We hopefully enter an era in which Sovereignty's consort can once again heal and restore paradise.

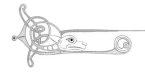

THE ROOTS OF THE MYTH

ALTHOUGH WE WILL NOW FOLLOW the intricacies of the two other branches of the legend considering the imagery we have just explored it appears to grow out of the oldest and deepest roots of all. We have seen that originally these images arose from an almost inexhaustible spring of Irish *echtrai* or adventures. These were heroic sagas of fantastic voyages, through twilight Wastelands to the crystal halls of the otherworldly and timeless realms of the pagan gods. As the legends passed across the Irish sea into Wales the immortal gods and goddesses gradually took on mortal flesh and blood, along with a curious new veneer of Celtic Christianity.

It has also been seen that one abiding mythic theme is that of the Sun God and the Earth Goddess, once represented by Lug and Eriu the Sovranty of Ireland. The concept of Sovranty was an ever shifting motif of the Goddess as both separate and yet inseparable from the land itself. The Sun Hero's task was to unite the Sun King with the Sovereign Queen in order to restore a harmony to the Wasteland. This had been brought about by a Dolorous Blow, which castrated the ruling kingship. In order to accomplish this quest the hero must heal the king or assume the responsibility for the realm himself.

A second favorite motif is

that of avenging the rightful kingship of the land which had, through killing or treachery, fallen into the wrong hands. The knights of the Round Table exemplify this theme by seeking vengeance upon the descendants of King Amangons.

Such complex material was transmitted through the Welsh bards and Breton *conteurs* to an essentially sophisticated French culture throughout a Europe which was fascinated by the mysterious, outlandish imagery from far-off lands still glowing from the embers of an abundant Celtic mythology. It hardly mattered that the tradition was in ruins. In fact, it was an advantage for the French authors could create whatever fantastical folly they liked from the fallen masonry.

We shall now discover how a magical Platter of Abundance, a Horn of Plenty, and a Cauldron of Rebirth and Knowledge were transformed by continental poets and clerics into a eucharistic artifact of the flesh and blood of the Holy Body of Christ. We will examine the reasons why the bloody spear of the Sun God became the lance which pierced the side of the crucified Messiah. And we will find how the great Irish sea god Bran became transformed, first into a British chieftain, then a miraculous, feasting head, to finally the maimed Fisher King, grandson to Joseph of Arimathea and guardian of the Holy Grail.

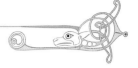

Pagan images which symbolize the abundant vulva of the Earth Goddess transform into the entrance of the Mother Church.
Opposite top: **Sheela-na-gig**, *Kilpeck, Britain.* **Bottom:** **Pagan God** *with drinking horn, Roman Britain.* **This page, top:** **Neolithic Barrows**, *Britain.* **Below right:** **Tarxien**, *Malta 4,500 B.C.* **and** **New Grange**, *Ireland, entrance to Celtic Tomb.* **Below left:** **St Brendan's Cathedral**, *Galway, 12th c.*

THE CHRISTIAN BRANCH

Dominican   *Franciscan*   *Benedictine*   *Cistercian*

ANY READERS who felt they were already familiar with the legend of the Holy Grail might have been surprised by the versions we have just explored in the pages of *Le Conte del Graal, Diu Crone* or *Peredur.* In these, while the Grail is certainly a remarkable and even magical vessel of plenty, it hardly deserves the mystic appellation of "Holy." Undoubtedly the Irish, Welsh and Breton Grail stories were closer to the original source of the myth than the second branch which we are about to explore, and yet these Christian legends have a mystery, a richness and complexity all of their own.

The beauty of each of the Christian threads of the Grail tapestry is best appreciated in the light of the sheer ingenuity and creativity of the monkish writers. They managed to cloud a work of the deepest heresy in such pious mystery that both legend and authors survived the fiery zeal of the Church fathers. The orthodox minds of papal Rome, while never actually acknowledging the existence of the Grail, were surprisingly faint-hearted about denouncing it either. Perhaps the whole "Matter of Britain" was such a popular and complex weave that it bewildered even those most single-minded and fanatical theologians who determined what was acceptable to God and what definitely was not.

Even more curiously the legend remained untainted by the fall of the heretical Cathars, the Albigensians and even the Knights' Templar who feature implicitly within the various texts.

Deep under the surface of the popular romances lurked something far more seriously heretical than any of their implicit links with the Church's claimed enemies. This makes it all the more puzzling why there was no violent orthodox reaction to the various texts. The strange hybrid strain of Christianity found within the pages of the whole Vulgate Cycle, the *Roman du Graal* of Perlesvaus, bears little or no resemblance to that espoused by the priests of Rome.

In this second branch of Grail legends we discover an apocryphal tradition based, not upon the teachings of the Apostles, but rather on the mysteries surrounding a little known and very minor character within the gospels called Joseph of Arimathea. In the legend it is he and his family line who carry the true message given to the disciples at the Last Supper by Christ. And if that wasn't heresy to the fanatic Dominicans who were founded during the peak of the Grail's popularity, what on earth could be?

So how did a spirited, essentially Celtic adventure based on myths of kingship and the healing renewal of the land, take on the salvic, religious significance of Redemption? And why should the tale of a hero seeking the Goddess of Sovereignty become the inspiring quest of an individual to encounter his God face to face?

In attempting to answer these questions we are presented with an intricate tangle of threads. First, visions of spirituality held within Celtic Christianity and those of Rome were profoundly different. The British church had long claimed to be the first church of Europe. And they fundamentally differed with Rome in their concepts of an otherworldly realm just beneath the surface of the everyday, tangible world — as opposed to that essentially Middle Eastern concept of a separate Kingdom of Heaven somewhere outside of nature. The great British sorcerer, Merlin, epitomizes the rift between the pagan and Middle Eastern roots. Originally created by infernal powers to be the anti-Christ, Merlin even had a demon father and was born covered in hairs. However his diabolic nature was unexpectedly altered by being baptized. Thus he was split between the pagan, otherworldly realms and the Christian kingdom of Heaven. But while he could wield great power there is a sense of unease and a lack of harmony to his life. He was after all a man of nature with a deep shamanistic connection with the Earth and her powers. The Church's message, on the other hand, was of a supernatural agency which was directly opposed to nature. And by the time the Christian Grail legends appear, a seeming hatred of all things of nature was part of the Church's creed.

In these legends the already unorthodox views of the Celtic "Pagan-Christianity" are mixed with ingredients imported from the apocryphal world of the Middle East and its mysterious "hidden scriptures." From these arise strange tales set within the traditions surrounding the sacrament commemorating the Last Supper — the Eucharist. And it is the remarkable combination of Christ's secret teachings given at the Last Supper, the blood of the crucifixion, and the Celtic "pagan religion", that form the heretical foundation of most of the Christian Grail mysteries.

Shaman *This image of a sorcerer was painted 15,000 years ago on a cave wall at Les Trois Frères, in the French Pyrenees. Representing the pagan Otherworld, the British magician, Merlin, continued the mystical, shamanic tradition whilst simultaneously, having one foot in the Christian world.*

THE BACKGROUND HISTORIES

THE MAJOR ROMANCES of the Christian branch appeared in the remarkably short span of twenty-five years at the turn of the thirteenth century.

The first of these romances, which had such a profound effect upon what was to follow, is thought to have been *Le Roman du Graal*. This is a prose trilogy attributed to Robert de Borron, comprising Joseph d'Aramathie, Merlin, and what is now known as the Didot-Perceval. This early Christian work describes the history of the Grail vessel and its arrival in Britain. It traces the coming of Arthur and the Round Table, the quest for the Grail, and the final decline of Arthur's Golden Age. The author was a Burgundian poet in the service of the Lord of Montfaucon, who died on the Fourth Crusade in 1212. The work is generally thought to have been written sometime between 1191 and 1202.

The second and most well known romance is found within the massive collection of The Vulgate Cycle, also called the Lancelot-Grail cycle. This was compiled from 1215 to 1235 and greatly expands the earlier Borron trilogy into five narratives – the *Estoire del Saint Graal*, the *Estoire de Merlin*, the *Prose Lancelot*, the *Queste del San Graal* and the *Mort Artu*.

Most scholars agree that the Vulgate is the product of multiple authors under the guidance of a main "architect." If these authors were not actually monks they were most probably lay clerics engaged in writ-

ing for the Cistercian order. The Christianity they espoused was a curious blend of monastic ideals and an imitation of apocryphal scriptures. For while there is seldom any direct reference to the apocrypha, the ambient atmosphere of the stories seems identical.

The third, Perlesvaus, is a romance in Old French prose dating from the beginning of the thirteenth century, and is associated with Glastonbury Abbey. The author is obviously acquainted with Chrétien's Perceval and the work of Robert de Borron, although his writing predates the Vulgate Cycle. Perlesvaus is a wild mixture of religion, magic and violence, which stamps this author as the anarchic rogue amidst the more sedate and sanctified company of his Christian brethren. The Post–Vulgate cycle attempts to remodel the earlier cycle by centering upon the Grail rather than upon Lancelot and the Queen. Also named by the author as *La Haute Escriture del Saint Graal,* it tells of *Logres* before and after the Dolorous Stroke, and ends with the coming of the good knight, the adventures of the quest, and Arthur's death.

But the work we will be examining in detail is the *Queste del San Graal,* which falls within our time frame of 1190 to 1230 and was probably written by a clerk whose work took him to both court and cloister. At this time there were great armies of scholars and clerks who worked for both lay and ecclesiastical houses. A powerful Cistercian influence is clearly discernible within the pages and it is likely that the author had found employment in one of the great Cistercian monasteries which had been founded in 1098 as part of a great monastic reform. The

Post Vulgate Cycle
Known as La Haute Escriture del Saint Graal
Author Unknown

The Vulgate Cycle
Estoire del Saint Graal, Estoire de Merlin, Prose Lancelot, Queste del San Graal, Mort Artu
Compiled by Cistercian Monks from 1215 to 1235

Perlesvaus
Romance in Old French prose written about 1205
Author unknown

Le Roman du Graal
(Joseph d'Arimathie, Merlin, Didot-Perceval)
Written by Robert de Borron from 1191 to 1202

Cistercians were exemplified by Bernard of Clairvaux who also supported the establishment of the Knights Templar. Indeed the white-robed monks were closely linked with that military order of the knights of Christ who gained respect in a society where all supremacy was to be measured and expressed on the back of a horse. The Cistercians had reached their peak of influence in the years in which the bulk of Christian Grail legends first appeared. Their own theology was a blend of Charity, Chastity and Grace. It was to their hierarchy of monastic virtues that the author of the *Queste* turned. As chastity was the prime virtue, and lust topped their list of deadly sins, it is hardly surprising that the author infuses the *Queste* with more than a little monkish celibacy. This is in sharp contrast to the texts we have already explored. While such virgin prudery often looks absurd to our modern understanding, throughout the rest of text there is an enlightened call for charity and mercy towards sinners, and above all a sense of real Love of one's fellow humans. And whereas the Celtic tradition is full of blood and the severed heads of challenged adversaries, the *Queste* is thankfully almost empty of corpses, save those slaughtered by knights who have failed to embrace God's grace. Even those wounded always seem to be within easy distance of the white-robed monks who restore them to health, vigor, and God's ways.

The perfect knight in the *Queste* had to enter a rigorous spiritual cleansing involving confession, communion, fasting, prayer, and above all, abstinence. While the author is at considerable pains to recite scriptures for his readers he also particularly, and somewhat surprisingly, chooses to draw upon the rich symbolism of the most mystical and sexual book in the orthodox scriptures – the Song of Songs, which had also proved an inspiration for many a troubadour.

Left: **Moralia in Job** *An illustration of monks cutting trees from a French manuscript of the 14th century.*

The Luminous Experience

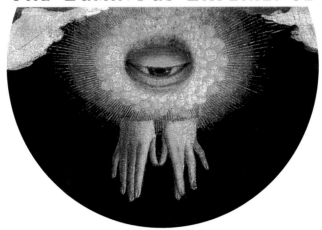

 HRÉTIEN'S GREAT UNFINISHED WORK was a splendid medieval folly built from the ruins of an ancient Celtic mythology. He imparted his own genius, imbuing the story with a fresh sense of mystery which teased the minds of the European courts. Although his story was in no way original, his poetic and mysterious imagery was the major source and inspiration for virtually all the narratives that followed.

It is quite clear that the *Graal* of his story, or of those which used his legendary source, had no particular religious significance. If anything it was unashamedly pagan in the magical ambience that surrounded both vessel and lance. Yet once the story passed through the sanctified and celibate cloisters of the Cistercians it gradually took on an entirely new significance and power.

Most modern scholars are of the opinion that the change of both Graal and Spear from pagan, semi-magical objects to miraculous Christian relics was actually based upon a curious misunderstanding and mistranslation. Whatever the truth is in such a theory, and we will be examining this in some detail, the outcome was a creative and mystical leap of imagination which still reverberates today.

It has already been shown that while the Holy Grail is essentially a Christian sacred image, it has never been accepted into the orthodox church. It would seem, in retrospect, that there were simply too many disturbingly heretical threads woven into the texture of the legend. One such thread is a lineage which carries the transmission of Christ's inner teaching outside that of the accepted Apostles. We know from the Church itself that the deepest communion of Christ's teaching occurred at the table of the Last Supper. The Grail tradition sees this as the first of three great tables, the others being the Round Table and the Table of the Grail. It was here the true seeker could be in direct contact with God. So even though Joseph of Arimathea was not actually present at the Last Supper he was still chosen by Christ to be the first Guardian of the Grail. By this point the Grail has been transformed into a vessel intimately identified with the eucharistic sacrament commemorating Christ's Last Supper.

Sacred Allegory *by J. Provost. The Eye of God stares out at us from above Christ who wields the double-edged sword of the Word. On the right Christ's bride holds the Lily of Mercy and frees the dove of the Holy Spirit. The soul, with its thumbs, shapes a vulva while gazing upwards.*

THE NEW TRANSMISSION

 T IS IN ONE OF THE NEW TESTAMENT APOCRYPHA, the *Evangelium Nicodemi*, written around the fourth century, that we find the legend that changed the whole nature and message of the Grail.

Joseph of Arimathea is mentioned in all four Gospels as being a rich disciple who begged Pilate for Christ's body after the crucifixion. He took the body, wrapped it in fine linen and placed it in the tomb. Nicodemus is known to have brought spices for the embalming. In the apocryphal texts the story is much elaborated. In these accounts Nicodemus, an influential ruler of the Jews, testifies on Christ's behalf which infuriates the Jewish elders. They manage to take their revenge, not upon Nicodemus himself but upon Joseph, and imprison him immediately after he has laid Christ's body in the tomb. But on Easter Day they find him gone. Eventually discovered at his own home in Arimathea, Joseph testifies that on the Sabbath the risen Christ appeared to him, freed him from prison and returned him to his own home.

This story appears to have been the foundation of

Opposite: Joseph and his company receives the blessings from the Holy Grail. French 14th c.

Left: **Dream of the Virgin** *by Simone dei Crociffissi. The Tree perpetually renews itself.*

one of the versions of the first Continuation of *Le Conte del Graal* which we have already briefly examined. In it Joseph has a golden vessel called the Grail and in it he takes the blood from the crucified Christ. He then begs Pilate for the body and is allowed to remove it to the sepulcher.

In his home he has a small altar with two candles burning continuously at which he prays each day before the blood within the Grail. But he is observed doing this and imprisoned. As in the first apocryphal account, the walls of the prison rise to release him but even in the face of this miracle he is banished along with Nicodemus, his sister, and his friends. Joseph then sails to the White Isle, which is part of England, and the little community settles there. It significant to note at this point, for we will be examining the role of the horn, that in times of famine Joseph blows a horn and the Grail serves them all abundantly. Joseph is therefore the first of the lineage of Grail guardians which would pass on through the Fisher King to Perceval.

Joseph d'Arimathie

HILE THE FIRST CONTINUATION gives a broad outline to the story, it is really Robert de Borron's poem, *Joseph d'Arimathie,* that was largely responsible for the real incorporation of a leitmotif which radically changed the Christian legend. Robert's account differs considerably in detail from the Nicodemus' version. He maintains that it is Pilate who gives Joseph the vessel that Christ had used at the Last Supper. Joseph collects the blood in the vessel but is imprisoned when the Jews find the Tomb opened on the third day. Christ appears to Joseph in prison with the vessel and tells him that he will have the guardianship of it. In token of the Trinity, there will only be three successors. He is also told that the vessel is to be called *"calice."*

Joseph is joined by a small company including his sister and her husband Bron. This little band settles down for a while but begins to go through hard times. It is believed that some of them have sinned and are responsible for the famine. A voice issuing from the vessel announces that some of Joseph's company are guilty of lust. It instructs him to find a table to commemorate the Last Supper, and for Bron to catch a fish. Joseph takes Christ's place at the table, which has one empty seat which will be filled by Bron's child.

Only some of the company can take their places at the table. They are nourished to their hearts' desire by the fish, but the lustful remainder feel nothing and depart. In this episode the discriminating power of the vessel suggests parallels to the legendary Celtic dish endowed with miraculous properties of nourishing, and the cauldron which knows the worthy and the unworthy.

However, one who has failed to pass the test insists on sitting in an empty seat, at the place of Judas, and is promptly swallowed up. We then learn that only a grandson of Bron will be able to take that perilous seat.

The Last Supper. *A miniature from a 12th century Syriac Codex.*

CHRIST, ANTI-CHRIST AND THE CORPUS CHRISTI

JOSEPH'S SISTER, ENYGEUS, bears Bron twelve sons of which one, Alein, is to be the forthcoming guardian of the Grail. Joseph delivers up the Grail to the safe-keeping of Bron, now known as the Rich Fisher, and teaches him the secret word that Christ taught him in the prison. A certain Petrus is told to depart to the west to the vales of Avaron where he will be joined by Bron and Alein, thus fulfilling the prophecy of the Trinity.

Within this story we have the bridge between the Celtic and Christian worlds, but also the source of a far-reaching error. Scholars are now of the opinion that the Cistercian monks and clerics mistook or misread the original Celtic stories and, finding a reference to the *cors benoit,* or the Blessed Horn which had the miraculous properties of providing whatsoever food was desired, transferred this magical Irish imagery into a Christian framework. For *cors* is a word with multiple meanings. It can signify a court, a corner, a course, a horn or a body. The monks were completely unfamiliar with a nature myth which included a Horn of Plenty, whereas they were only too familiar with the Host, or Holy Body. Every day of their cloistered lives they celebrated the Eucharist and knew the Sacrament of the Last Supper, the Corpus Christi, the wine and the consecrated bread, as quite literally the blood and body of Christ. Any cleric translating Welsh or Breton texts would assume that *cors* meant the Corpus Christi. Once the error was made all the curious passages which could only fit the earlier "horn" were subtly altered to fit the new image. Even the Land of the Grail and its castle is called Corbenit or Cor-

lenot, echoing the original Cors Benôit, the Castle of the Blessed Horn.

This is, of course, not the only difference between the two branches. In the earlier Celtic versions we find a leitmotif of rebirth and renewal. The major theme is one of healing both king and realm, while a sub-plot of avenging a murdered kin weaves into some accounts. In contrast the Christianized texts show this transformation is through redemption and not renewal. The salvic message is that such a change can only come about through faith, compassion and a chaste and pure love. The theme of chastity must have been a central obsession with the cloistered and apparently celibate scholars for when any emotion is repressed it becomes the abiding preoccupation. Thus chastity and a concern with both male and female purity took on a significance completely lacking in the earlier sexually explicit goings-on of randy and debauched Welsh knights.

The sequel to Joseph in Robert's account is Merlin. At the beginning of Joseph, Robert clearly states that the coming of Christ was God's scheme to thwart the devil. But in his second poem the plot radically changes to that of the devil attempting to thwart the sacrifice of the Son. Merlin was created as an anti-Christ with this in diabolic mind, but Merlin's baptism was unforseen and he was transformed. It was also Merlin who created Stonehenge and constructed the Round Table, modeled upon the tables of the Last Supper and the Grail.

Opposite: **The Mass of St. Gregory**, *Flemish 15th century. This painting depicts the moment when Christ miraculously appears as a Real Presence during the Eucharist while Gregory, the first monk to become Pope, is officiating.*

Didot-Perceval

HE TWO SURVIVING VERSIONS of the final part of the romance known as the Didot-Perceval differ considerably from the previous accounts. They were almost certainly flawed copies of a lost original.

In one version the Holy Spirit tells Alein of his father Bron who lives in Ireland. It has been foretold that Alein's son Perceval will heal the old man of a long standing infirmity, but only after he has become a knight at Arthur's court. In the second manuscript Alein dies and Perceval goes to the court, jousts brilliantly, and wins the favor of Gawain's sister. Against all advice however he rashly takes his seat at the Siege Perilous which promptly splits beneath him and breaks with such an agonizing sound that it seems that the world might sink into the abyss. A voice tells the company that because of this act a great wrong has been perpetrated which will affect the entire Round Table. But the knight Perceval has been especially rash and he will suffer mightily because of it. Had he not been of the Grail lineage he would have joined Moyses in the pit. The Fisher King will not be healed of his infirmity, the stone will not be joined together, or the enchantments of Britain be lifted, until a knight who surpasses all other knights asks what the Grail is and whom one serves by it.

Perceval then swears he will not sleep two nights under one roof until he has found the castle of Bron, the Rich Fisher. The narrative then roughly follows the many versions already encountered.

Left: **St. Mary's Chapel** *at Glastonbury. The original wattle church was traditionally believed to have been the first church in Europe and was founded by Joseph of Aramathea.* **Right***: Throne of St. Mark, Venice. The Tree of Life is shown with the four rivers of Paradise flowing from its roots.*

THE BIRDS

ERCEVAL COMES TO A CASTLE where he plays a wonderful chessboard but is checkmated thrice. In his pique he is about to throw the pieces when the lady of the castle beseeches him not to. She entertains him and asks a favor: he is to bring her the head of a white stag. She lends him a small hound to flush out the stag. He procures the head but a loathy witch steals the hound. She tells him she will give it back if he goes to a tomb and calls out, *"False is he that hath painted you here."* Perceval follows the witch's order and a black knight emerges from the tomb and they battle fiercely. Just then another knight rides up and takes both hound and head. The black knight withdraws into his tomb and Perceval is forced to follow the robber knight. As he is searching for the thief he meets his sister and his uncle, who inform him that he is destined to find Bron and receive from him the Grail.

There are then a number of adventures and misadventures with all the motifs most usual to the Grail themes. The Loathy Hag appears with her champion, the Handsome Coward, who Perceval defeats but sends

to Arthur. Then occurs a hauntingly strange story that does not appear on the surface to have any theme in common with the rest of the Grail legends.

Perceval is challenged and does battle with a knight at a ford and defeats him. The knight, Urbain, tells that he has fallen in love with the enchantress of the nearby castle and has pledged to guard the ford on her behalf. He has been there almost a year but in defeating him Perceval has broken the enchantment, and the castle shatters for love of the knight. Now, even in the Christian text we unexpectedly enter the wondrous Otherworld of Sovereignty. A flock of birds attacks Perceval, who appears to kill one. It instantly shape-changes into the sister of the enchantress and is borne away by the rest of the flock. Even though the defeated knight has also attacked Perceval in this interval, he is allowed to rejoin his beloved.

Above: **The Tomb of Archbishop Theodore,** *6th century Italian, at St. Apollinare in Classe, Ravenna. The Dove of Heaven descends into what appears to be one of the earliest images of the Grail.*

Above: **Glastonbury Tor**. *Considered by many as the most sacred site in Britain it is traditionally associated with Joseph and the Grail.*

A NEW MEANING

L ATER IN HIS ADVEN- TURES Perceval sees a vision of two children in a wondrous tree, and a mysterious "shadow" of Merlin. Both direct him to the Fisher King's castle. He meets the Rich Fisher in a boat and is offered lodging in the castle.

As they feast together in the evening Perceval witnesses a richly dressed maiden enter with two little silver platters. After her comes a youth bearing a lance, from which issue three drops of blood. He is followed by a second youth who bears the vessel Joseph had been given in prison. But Perceval does not ask what they signify for fear of appearing rude and offending his host. He does not know that Christ had told Bron that he would never be cured until the best knight in the world would ask who was served by the Grail.

The next morning Perceval awakes to find the castle deserted, so he rides out. He then meets a maiden who reproaches him bitterly for having failed to ask the question which would have healed his grandfather Bron, would have given him the guardianship of Christ's blood and would have undone the enchantments of the land. Perceval once again swears he will seek his grandfather's house until he can finally achieve his quest.

He unexpectedly then finds the head of the white stag and the hound which had been stolen. He defeats the robber knight, discovers that the Black Knight of the tomb had been enchanted, returns the head and hound to the Lady of the Chessboard Castle, and adroitly avoids that lady's very tempting offers. He then wan- ders in desperation for seven more years, forgetting God in the meanwhile. Finally he discovers his hermit uncle and confesses and does penance.

Setting off once again to find his grandfather he enters a tournament at the White Castle and in doing so breaks his vow not to stay in the same place twice. Merlin appears again to upbraid him for this lapse but then directs him towards his goal. When Perceval finally manages to reach the Grail Castle the enchantments are immediately broken. The Fisher King is instantly healed and at the bidding of the Holy Ghost he relates the secrets of the Grail to Perceval, entrusting the vessel to him just before he dies. At this a paradisal melody and scent arise from the vessel and simultaneously the split in the Siege Perilous is reunited. Merlin appears at court to announce that the Quest is ended, and the enchantments fall and disappear throughout the realm.

Robert de Borron gives a new meaning to the Grail by giving it the miraculous properties of the Eucharist. The Grail thus becomes the agent of the Corpus Christi – for the *SangRaal*, or Holy Blood, was more important than the *San Graal* itself.

By transferring the holy vessel to Britain, and creating an entirely different Holy lineage than that of the Church of Rome, he has raised the sacramental and religious tone of the whole legend. Before we can enter the major legend of the Christian branch, the *Queste del San Graal*, we must detour to explore the surrealist landscape of the wild card of the Christian Grail pack, *Perlesvaus*.

Perlesvaus

THE NEXT ACCOUNT of the Christianized Grail that we explore is that of the French prose romance, *Perlesvaus*. The author, probably a pious chaplain in some aristocratic household in Northern France or Belgium, must have had access to a rare library indeed for he seems familiar with most of the Arthurian literature of the period. His unique contribution to the Grail corpus is in the wealth of archaic Welsh material which imbue his text with an often macabre and surreal atmosphere, combining the Celtic twilight world with remarkably bloody Christian zeal. His work remains the linch-pin between the pagan hub and the later Christian spokes. Written some time between 1192 and 1225, *Perlesvaus* reflects the contemporary crusading passions of the "New Law," most happily expressed at the point of a sword. The hero is conspicuous in his enthusiasm for cheerfully slaughtering any pagan who is not prompt to embrace the New Order.

The author claims he obtained his story from a Latin book found in a holy house on the Isle of Avalon in the Adventurous Marshes. This is clearly Glastonbury Abbey in Southwest Britain. While this certainly suggests that the author knew of the place it is unlikely that he was party to the whole Abbey propaganda surrounding the sanctity of the spot. Glastonbury was claimed as the original site of Joseph's first church in Britain and the bodies which were unearthed in 1190 in the Abbey grounds were said to be those of Arthur and Guenevere.

Left: **Glastonbury Abbey.** *Joseph was supposed to have planted his staff on the Isle of Avalon where it sprouted into a Holy Thorn. It still blossoms at Christmas time. Arthur's grave was claimed to have been discovered in 1190 and the lead cross (**above**) with his name was found with the bodies of the King and his queen.* **Inset:** **Joseph.** *Stained glass, Langport, Glastonbury, 15th C.*

No Family is Perfect

ALTHOUGH AT FIRST THE AUTHOR OF THE STORY OF *PERLESVAUS* keeps pretty much to Robert de Borron's tale, his story quickly shows some curious discrepancies. It claims that a priest called Josephus took the story from an angel, and tells us that the hero of the tale, the Good Knight, was descended from Joseph of Arimathea. Later on we discover that the hero's maternal uncles are the Fisher King, King Pelles and the evil King of *Castel Mortel*.

This King of Castle Mortal is warring with his brother, the Fisher King, who has the Lance and Grail. In this version the Grail appears in the form of a dish. The hero has a sister, Dandrane. On the father's side the grandfather is Nicodemus, while the father, Alain li Gros, was the youngest of twelve brothers, eleven of whom died in battle attempting to bring the New Law to the realm. The family is said to come from Kamelot in Wales and Perlesvaus is called "le Gallois."

We learn later in the story that the boy hero had lived in the wild and was an expert with the Welsh javelin. One day he meets two knights fighting, one white and one red. When he sees the latter overcoming his opponent he throws a javelot at the Red Knight and to both his and the White Knight's surprise, slays him. This almost accidental act creates a complex web of vengeance and death which threads throughout the narrative. It appears that the Red Knight is, anyway, the hereditary foe of Perceval's house. Perceval then goes to the court of King Arthur who knights him before he departs to seek adventure as the best knight in the world.

Above left: **Crusader** *14th century bronze horse and rider from Italy.* *Above:* **Vice and Virtue.** *Twelfth century knights from a capital in Clermont-Ferrand. The reality, as opposed to the romance, of feudal knights was that they were for the most part an arrogant, brutish, squabbling and essentially violent lot, feared by both kings and peasant alike and by the time the Grail legends were written, chivalry was a thing long past.* **Right:** **Illustration** *from a 13.C. manual on fencing from South Germany showing the use of arms which would have been familiar with the contemporary writers of the Grail legends.*

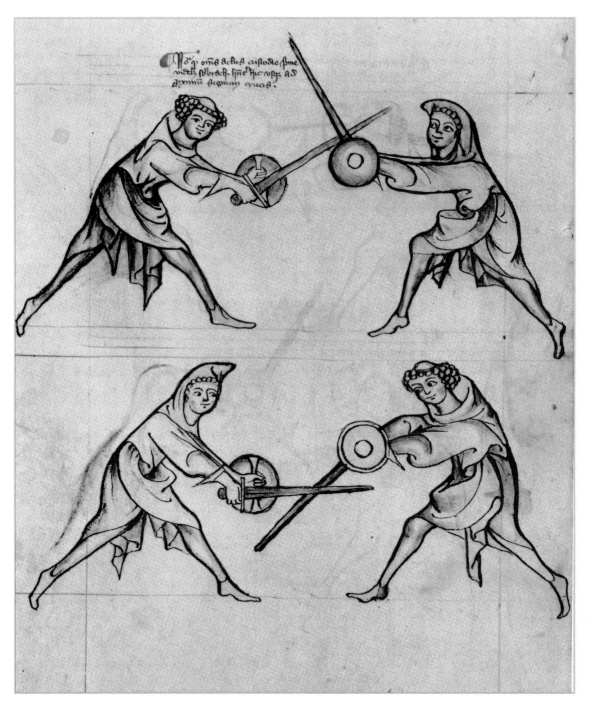

THE PERILOUS CHAPEL

 HRONOLOGI-
CALLY, *PERLESVAUS*
BEGINS WITH AN
episode about
King Arthur. The
king's fame has sadly diminished and his court has so
declined that it is almost deserted. He has fallen back
into pagan ways and no longer observes Christmas,
Easter or Pentecost. His knights have dwindled from
365 in the golden age of the Round Table to only 25.

His queen, Guenevere, reproaches him bitterly for
his apathy, lethargy and lack of spirit. Finally shamed,
he agrees to go on an adventure to the Perilous Chapel.
He decides to take the squire, Cahus, with him. But,
on the night before they set out, Cahus dreams that he
is attacked by a black man at the chapel for trying to
bring a candlestick to the king. On awakening Cahus
finds he has actually been mortally wounded and the
candlestick of his dream lies at his side. This appears to
be the remnants of an ancient story in which an initiate fails a crucial Druidic test.

However, Arthur ventures on alone and learns at the
chapel that misfortune has come to the land because a
knight has failed to ask the right question concerning the

Grail and Lance at the castle of
the Fisher King.

Arthur regains some of his lost
energies, defeats a black knight
and presents the head to a
maiden who is seeking the Best Knight.

This prelude sets the context of the plot, the twilight
and dreamlike atmosphere and the essentially pagan
ingredients bound within a Christian framework. From
this brief account we see that Arthur, as the earthly representative of the realm, has fallen into lethargy along
with his kingdom and his knights. Because Perlesvaus has
not asked the fated question the Fisher King has fallen
into a dolorous languor, his kingdom has split apart and,
evil stalks the land. We learn that the knight who failed
the question test, apparently because of this failure, has
also been mysteriously wounded and is grievously sick.

The twin aspects of outer and inner Britain, symbolized outwardly by the Round Table and inwardly by
Logres and the Table of the Grail, are both ailing.

St. Catherine's Chapel, *Abbotsbury, Dorset, Britain, 13th c. This
lonely chapel, overlooking the sea, fits the description of the Perilous Chapel.*

THE THREE DAMSELS OF THE CART

 HEN ARTHUR RETURNS TO COURT, three damsels arrive with a cart drawn by three white harts. Inside the rich cart there are the gruesome heads of 150 knights, some sealed in caskets of gold, some in silver and some in lead. The Damsel of the Cart who leads the party is described as plain and bald. The author appears to baulk at describing this Grail Messenger as the hideous Loathy Hag she usually appears to be in other versions, so he coyly tones down the ugliness to just being bald. In one hand she carries the head of a king sealed with silver and crowned with gold, while her right arm is in a sling of gold resting on a rich cushion. She explains she cannot alight from the horse until the Grail quest is achieved, and only when a knight asks the right question or wins the vessel will her hair grow back. A second damsel brings a brachet (hound) and a shield with a red cross. This is to be left with Arthur until the knight who will win through to the Grail arrives. Within the boss of the shield, which we later learn belonged to Joseph of Arimathea, is a fragment of the true cross and the blood of Christ. This damsel also carries the head of a queen sealed in lead and crowned with copper. This queen has betrayed a king, whose head her companion carries.

Much later we learn that the heads of the king and queen are those of Adam and Eve, which reveals the author's ideas about women. This macabre imagery suggests that the sources of Perlesvaus share elements of the fascination and reverence found within the Celtic cult of the head. The Christian veneer which appears to explain that imagery is patchy to say the least. The heads in the cart which are sealed in gold are supposed to belong to the New Law of Christ, while those in silver represent the Jews and the Old Law of the Synagogue. Those sealed in lead represent the False Law of the pagans and Saracens.

The author treads tricky ground when he claims that the bald Damsel of the Cart signifies Fortune. According to one Christian tradition she was said to have been bald before the crucifixion and only regained her hair when Christ had redeemed his people. The cart itself can

---

Above: Reverse side of the Wilton Diptych, 14th C. English The white hart is often associated with the Grail bearers. Perceval's original shield is, itself, one of a white stag on a red background. In the Wauchier Continuation of Le Conte del Graal, Perceval has to bring the head of a white stag to a maiden who lends her brachet to flush out the animal. In one manuscript the knights of the Round Table encounter a white stag in the forest with a red cross on its forehead, and a lighted taper between its horns, carrying a precious Grail-like vessel on its back and followed by a white brachet.

be seen to represent the Wheel of Fortune.

The three maidens leave the court and encounter Gawain on the road, who agrees to escort them past the Castle of the Black Hermit. Even so, he cannot prevent the 152 knights issuing from the Castle of the Black Hermit from carrying off all the heads in the cart. Later we find this event signifies Lucifer and his minions imprisoning the souls in Hell. Gawain defeats a knight who yields up the shield of the Jewish hero, Judas Maccabeus. Gawain gives his own shield to the bald Grail Messenger and sets off towards the Fisher King.

THE SWORD AT NOON

OW APPEARS THE FIRST INDICATION of the Grail's youth-bestowing powers, which only appear elsewhere in Wolfram's *Parzival*. Gawain meets a hermit who serves in the chapel of the Holy Grail and who appears young even though he is over 75 years old.

Gawain learns that a knight of the lineage of Joseph of Arimathea lies grievously sick in a hermitage, but being unable to learn more he rides on to the entrance to the Fisher King's lands. Before he can enter he is told he must gain the sword with which St. John the Baptist was beheaded. The sword is found to be in the possession of a pagan king called Gurgaran who promises to relinquish it on condition that Gawain rescue the king's son who has been abducted by a giant. In the ensuing battle Gawain kills the giant but not before the son is strangled. The pagan king (whose name can mean werewolf) has his son's body cut up and distributed to his people to eat. But he is then baptized and gives Gawain the sword, which has the unique property of being covered with blood if it is unsheathed at noon. (Likewise Gawain himself gains his greatest strength at noon, which then wanes from that point as he weakens throughout the rest of the day.)

After some mischance Gawain finally crosses three perilous bridges to arrive at the Castle of the Fisher King. In the hall he meets the king who reclines before a pillar of copper which supports an angel holding a piece of the True Cross. The king receives the sword and gives it to his niece, thus reversing the sequence of events as told in Chrétien's version.

We have firsthand evidence of the rejuvenating powers of the Grail when *"Gawain was led into the hall and found twelve ancient knights, all grey-haired though they seemed to be not so old as they were, for each was a hundred years of age or more, and yet none of them seemed as if he were more than forty."*

Bamburgh Castle, *Northumberland, Britain. Traditionally the site of Lancelot's castle of "Joyous Garde." This perfectly matches the description and atmosphere of Gawain's perilous entrance to the Grail Castle. It is also reminiscent of the site of the great feast of Bran's head which was said to have lasted over eighty years, in which the followers of this great king of Britain "did not perceive that his fellows did not age."*

THE KNIGHTS WHO FAILED

DURING THE FEASTING two maidens come from a chapel, one holding the most Holy Grail into which blood drops from a lance which the second damsel is holding. Into the vessel of eternal redemption flows the blood of the lance, the eternal sacrifice. They walk into the hall where Gawain and the knights are eating, but so sweet and holy is the odor of the relics that all forget to eat. Gawain gazes enraptured at the Grail, and it seems as if there is a chalice within it. He sees the point of the lance from which the red blood flows, and two angels who bear two candelabra of gold with lighted candles. The maidens pass before Gawain into another chapel while he is lost in thought, and such great rapture fills his mind that he thinks of nothing but God. The knights are all downcast and doleful and look at him.

Then the maidens pass once more and this time Gawain seems to behold three angels and in the midst of the Grail the form of a child. The Master of the Knights calls upon Gawain but he only gazes before him in a silent trance as he sees three drops of blood fall upon the table. The three drops of blood on the snow are now recalled in the other versions. Gawain is actually in the midst of a great mystical experience and although he fails to ask the fateful question concerning what he is witnessing there is no blame attached to him.

He is not the fated knight. The maidens withdraw and the knights are filled with fear as they look at each other. Gawain is entranced by the three drops and tries to pick them up but they elude his hands.

"Once again the two maidens come before the table and Gawain seems to see three, and it also appears that the Grail is wholly in the air. And there appears to be a man nailed to a cross, and the spear was fixed in his side. Gawain sees him and has great pity and can think of nothing but the pain the king suffers. The Master of the knights once again calls on him to speak, saying that if he delays longer the opportunity will be for ever lost. But Gawain is silent, not hearing the plea."

It will be noticed, unlike virtually all other versions, in *Perlesvaus* the king is not present at the meal. The Grail itself has youth-restoring and preserving powers and the Grail appears to change from a dish to a chalice. This is the only Grail romance in which the vessel shifts its shape. Later, when Arthur assists at mass at the Grail Castle he sees the Grail undergo five changes, the last being that of a chalice. The entire sequence within the realm of the Fisher King rests upon a repetition of the number three and a preoccupation with the Trinity. Gawain has failed to ask the question three times and the hall empties and he is left alone. It is then that he notices a chessboard and as he begins to play with

Opposite: **Sparrow beak**
helmet 1462. **Below:**
Brasses *of 14th c. knights.*

the ivory pieces he is checkmated three times by the gold. Impatiently he sweeps the pieces from the board but a maiden appears and orders a page to remove the game before he does more damage.

He sleeps until dawn and finds himself locked in. A damsel tells him that a service is held in the chapel in veneration of the sword he has given the king, but he cannot be admitted because he had failed to speak the words which would have brought joy to the castle. A voice warns him to leave and he does so.

After two minor incidents we come to the end of Gawain's failed quest and turn briefly to the other peerless knight, Lancelot, who takes up the story. They meet at the castle of the Poor Knight and dispose of some robbers. Gawain leaves for Arthur's court while Lancelot travels onwards to the Grail Castle. On the way he has a macabre adventure in the Castle of Beards where he is served by terribly mutilated knights, in yet another version of the beheading game, and is warned that such an amorous knight as he will never be allowed to witness the Grail. Although he manages to pass through the perilous cemetery to the Waste City, gains entry to the castle and is warmly entertained, the Grail does not appear.

THE CHALICE

AVING WITNESSED TWO WORTHY BUT FAILED ATTEMPTS to win the Grail we turn to the real hero of the romance. Perlesvaus is now recovered from his mysterious illness having been cared for by his uncle, King Pelles.

As soon as Perlesvaus has recovered he by mistake fights with Lancelot, neither recognizing the other. Both sustain terrible injuries but Lancelot fares worst as befits the theme of Perlesvaus being the greatest knight.

From now on the plot weaves and counterweaves plots of carnage and vengeance in which the hero proves his valor and a particularly bloodthirsty Christian zeal, bringing the New Law to the pagans. Perlesvaus kills the fierce Cahot the Red and retakes the castle called Key of Wales, which was originally his mother's. We are then introduced to Perlesvaus's sister, Dandrane, who is the first to learn that the Fisher King has died. His castle has been seized by his evil brother, the King of Castle Mortal and now the Grail no longer appears.

A Holy Circlet of Gold which encases the Holy Crown of Thorns is won, lost, and then won again and

Perlesvaus finally reaches the Grail Castle. He overthrows 27 knights who guard the nine bridges leading to the Grail Castle. The evil king finally throws himself off the battlements and Perlesvaus becomes the Grail Guardian. The castle is encircled by a river which runs from the earthly Paradise. It is known as Edein, The Castle of Souls and the Castle of Joy. Arthur visits the Castle and during mass sees the Grail appear in five forms, the last of which is a chalice. It is made known that this was the first time such a vessel had been used for the consecration of the Host in Britain.

Perlesvaus's sister is abducted but her persecutor, who was also responsible for the death of Pelles, is slain by Perlesvaus and there is a reunion with their mother. They both take up residence in the Grail Castle.

*Above: **The Nanteos Cup.** As Glastonbury Abbey was destroyed seven monks fled to Wales with an olive wood bowl, said to be the cup of the Last Supper. Water poured from the bowl is claimed to have miraculous healing powers. **Right**: **Manese** Anthology. Images from a 14th c. German manuscript.*

AXIS MUNDI

FTER MORE GRIM MISSIONS of vengeance, Perlesvaus sets sail with only a steersman for company and visits the Isle of the Ageless Elders. It is here that at last we leave the violence of establishing the New Law and enter the miraculous Celtic Otherworld which acts as a subterranean vein beneath all the outwardly professed imagery of the Church. This under-current of the Old Law is constantly surfacing, however earnestly the author tries to mask it with Christian ritual. There is actually very little spiritual-ity to be found anywhere within this text and the thin veneer of mis-sionary zeal never quite manages to entirely cover the miraculous wonder of Otherworld scenes or the macabre fascination with sev-ered heads which is one of the unique facets of the earlier Celtic society.

But in the closing pages of the romance we arrive at the penultimate par-adise, and here the full splendor of a Celtic Elysium appears. The description of the castle which rises from an island in the sea could come directly from Irish and Welsh legends of the Blessed Isles in the Voyages of St. Brendan, or the feast of the followers of Bran on the Blissful Isles of Grassholm from the *Mabinogion*, the *Caer Siddi* (Faery Fortress) of Taliesin, or the otherworldly realm found in the *Spoils of Annwn*.

Four trumpets sound sweetly at the four corners of the walls, and as they walk to the castle they see the fairest halls and mansions that have ever been built. *"Per-lesvaus looks beneath a very fair tree, which was tall and* broad, and sees the fairest fountain that anyone might describe. It was set with rich golden pillars and the very ground seemed to be of precious stones."* This is the Fountain of Youth which appears in many legends throughout the world. Often this fountain is found beneath the Tree of Life and Knowledge at the center of the world, the Axis Mundi.

"Above this fountain two men were sitting. Whiter than new fallen snow was their hair and beards yet they seemed young. As soon as they saw Perlesvaus they rose to meet him and bowed to worship the shield he bore at his neck. They kissed the cross and the boss in which the relics were enclosed."

The Axis Mundi is a predomi-nant feature of most world cos-mologies. It is usually seen as the center point of the earth and that place where the earth is joined to the sky, the heavens, or the Other-world. It is the threshold between worlds and is usually a source of fertility, abundance and life. The Grail itself is partially a manifestation of the Axis Mundi. It is the point from which all directions are established. This also applies to time, for as all directions flow from this point so at the center all times occur simultaneously. Thus it could be said to possess youth-restoring properties.

We now learn that Joseph of Arimathea bore the shield, which was once pure white. After the crucifix-ion he added the red cross and the holy fragments within the boss. Then, *"Perlesvaus looked beyond the foun-tain and saw in a beautiful spot a tower-like casket of what appeared to be glass. It was so big that inside there was a fully armed knight. He peers into it and sees that the knight is*

alive. He tries to speak to him but the knight gives no answer."

Perlesvaus is led into a great hall with an image of the Savior of the World in majesty with his apostles about him. Here is a gathering of holy men and with them a number who wear an emblazoned red cross. While they all feast, a golden chain with a crown of gold descends and a hideous pit opens beneath it and from its maw come piteous cries. The chain and crown then ascend and the pit is covered over once again. Perlesvaus learns that he must return to this place, for he is to be king of a nearby isle. The present king has proved to be so worthy that he has been chosen to reign in an even greater realm. Perlesvaus is warned that if he does not rule well he will be placed on the Isle of Suffering from which he heard the cries from the pit. He leaves his own shield and is given a pure white one in exchange, and is told to go back to his home and be prepared to return when a ship arrives here to fetch him.

Opposite: **Zodiac** *by L.V. Ringbom. The Grail Castle is at the center of the world. The Moon is in Cancer where the Divine meets the World. The Sun is in Libra showing the equilibrium between earthly and heavenly planes*
Above: **Fountain of Life** *by an imitator of Hieronymous Bosch, 16th C.*

THE BLESSED ISLES

PERLESVAUS, ON HIS RETURN to the Grail Castle severs any remaining threads within the narrative He slays the Black Hermit, meets the Damsel of the Cart (whose hair has grown back because he has regained the Grail), and finally settles down in the Grail Castle with his mother and sister. Eventually he disposes of all the holy relics of the castle to the hermits of the area. A voice announces the *"Holy Grail shall appear here no longer"* and shortly afterwards a ship arrives with a white sail upon which is a red cross. Perlesvaus embarks with the coffins of Nicodemus, Joseph of Arimathea, the Fisher King and his mother and sister – the entire lineage of the Holy Grail – and sails back to the Isles of the Fountain of Youth where we suspect the Grail will now reappear.

The Grail Castle itself begins to crumble into ruins once its last guardian has died. Eventually only two Welsh knights dared to enter the place as it had the rep-

utation that none ever returned from exploring its ruins. They were right fair youths and gay. They entered light of heart and remained a long time and when they emerged again they led the simple life of hermits. When asked why they were so happy they replied *"Go where we have been and you will know why."* As we have already seen, the traditional site of the ruined Grail Castle is Dinas Bran, the abode of Bran, one original source for the Fisher King.

Another beautiful dreamlike romance which appeared after Perlesvaus seems to share a common source. *"Sone de Nansai"* is a thirteenth century French narrative written by a poet of Brabant, and although the two stories are completely independent, some of the details are remarkable in their similarity. In the later legend we learn that the hero, Sone, has killed the Irish king in battle and has undertaken single combat with the champion of the king of Scotland. In order to win favor from heaven for this enterprise, he sails with Alain, king

Labels on the illustration: *Is: S. Brandano.* · *Cabo Finis terræ:* · *Hispania.* · *Gades.* · *Babaria.* · *M. Canaria.* · *Insula Fortunata.* · *Cabo de No:* · *M. Attlas.* · *Africa.*

of Norway, to an island monastery. The fortress abbey is a circular hall with four towers around it. A fireplace is in the center with four pillars. Around the walls are paintings of the Annunciation, the Life of Christ and the Descent into Hell. The abbott meets the two voyagers and together they feast in a meadow overlooking the sea with marble walls around them. On the walls are ten leopards which turn and make harmonious sounds when the wind blows. The castle is set in woodlands of almond and olive and beautiful birds and exotic animals roam the forests. Three streams meet at the castle where there is an abundance of fish. The feast is sumptuous. The abbot tells them that Joseph of Arimathea had founded the castle. As custodian of the Lance and the Grail, Joseph sailed to Norway where he conquered the king and desired and married the heathen daughter. But she would not embrace the new religion. Testing his faith, God struck him between the thighs, so that he was unable to walk. His only relief and amusement was to fish. Eventually he was healed by a knight and

founded the abbey and bequeathed it to twelve monks and an abbot. But during the time he was maimed, the realm of *Logres* lay waste and infertile.

The abbot opens a vessel of ivory and takes out the Holy Grail which illuminates the entire land. The abbot then takes the Lance, at the point of which hangs one drop of blood. He shows the visitors the coffins of Joseph and his son. The abbot gives the very sword with which Joseph had guarded the land to Sone, who then defeats his gigantic Scottish foe.

Left: **The Great Cross,** *Mosaic from San Giovanni, Laterano. This is the center of the world with the Four Rivers issuing past the roots of the Tree of Life.* ***Above:*** **Voyage of St. Brendan***. Detail from a 17th c. map which shows the saint disembarking on what appeared to be an island but turns out to be a friendly whale..This Irish saint would have been a contemporary of Perceval and his fabulous adventures which tell of a wondrous elysium to the west of Ireland called the Fortunate Isles which can be seen at the top of the illustration. His legend could well have inspired the later writers of both Perlesvaus and Sone de Nansai.*

THE VULGATE CYCLE

Queste Del San Graal

THE STORY OPENS AT THE SEASON OF PENTECOST. Three nuns present a young man to be knighted by the greatest knight of the Round Table, Lancelot. He knights the lad with the help of Bors and Lionel. Lancelot does not know, however, that the young man, Galahad, is his own son. He had been tricked one night into lying with the daughter of the Fisher King when he thought it was his beloved Guinevere. The nuns do not allow Galahad to join the knights at King Arthur's court until the moment is right.

In the morning when Lancelot and his friends reach Camelot they discover on the Perilous Seat at the Round Table a freshly traced inscription. This tells that 450 years have passed since the Passion, and on the day of Pentecost the seat will find its true master. Before they can sit to eat there comes news of a great wonder: a stone of red marble has appeared and is seen floating by the river's edge. Held fast within the stone is a sword with the inscription *"None shall take me hence but he at whose side I am to hang. And he shall be the Best Knight in the World."* Not even the great knights Gawain or Perceval can remove it. We already can sense that the heroes of the earlier romances, Gawain and Perceval, are to be eclipsed by a new, worthier and supremely Christian knight. They return to dine at the Round Table. Suddenly the windows and doors close by themselves and a great light enters the hall. An old man is seen leading a knight in red armor. This red motif appears hard to lose in any of the versions, but in this now Christian setting, red and white are the colors of Christ. The company is told that this is the desired knight, who stems from the House of David and the lineage of Joseph of Arimathea. Through him the enchantments of the land are to be lifted. Galahad takes the Perilous Seat with impunity and the old man departs with messages to Galahad's uncle, King Pelles, and his grandfather, the Rich Fisher King at the Blessed Castle.

Opposite: **The Round Table of Pentecost**, *12th c. French. Galahad is being introduced by the white robed monk.* **Above: Arthur draws the Sword** *from the Stone. Galahad will join Arthur as the rightful champion and king of the realm by enacting precisely the same scene.*

THE FELLOWSHIP

AVING ESTABLISHED THE HERO'S UNDENIABLE PEDIGREE the author proceeds to demonstrate that he is indeed the Best Knight. For not only does he draw the sword from the stone, he also unseats all but Lancelot and Perceval at the jousts.

A maiden on a white palfrey then arrives to tell Arthur that the Holy Grail will appear in his court and feed the companions of the Round Table in honor of Galahad.

As they feast there is a loud clap of thunder and the hall is lit as if by a sunbeam. All are struck dumb as the Holy Grail appears, filling the palace with a fragrance of spice and providing all the company with whatever food was most desired. But then it disappears.

Gawain is the first to swear to go on a quest for the Grail in order to look upon its mystery. The other knights all join him, swearing Fellowship of the Grail. This spontaneous gesture of his nephew and heir saddens Arthur for he knows that the Fellowship of the Round Table has been superceded by the new Companions of the Grail. The hermit Nasciens sends a message that if any knight takes a woman with him he will fall into mortal sin. The Cistercian author would see no oddity in imposing such strict monastic vows upon the secular Round Table. They had the example of the celibate Order of the Knights Templar to inspire them. Even their founder, Bernard of Clairvaux, was instrumental in forming these warriors of Christ.

Each knight must be pure and cleansed and must seek the Grail alone. So as the Companions finally depart Arthur's court, each go his separate way.

Opposite: *Galahad sits in the siege Perilous, 15th c French.*
Left: *Boyhood Knights from Romans de Chevalerie c.1280*
Below: *Arthur's knights swear a Quest for the Grail which inadvertently destroys the Fellowship of the Round Table.*

THE SHIELD AND THE SEVEN DEADLY SINS

 ALAHAD THEN RECEIVES A SHIELD that only he is worthy of bearing. Its history is worth recounting. Joseph of Arimathea was sent to Sarras forty two years after the crucifixion. There, his son Josephus fashioned a shield for King Mordrain of Sarras to help him overcome a powerful rival. The shield had an image of a cross with the bleeding Christ upon it. It perfomed a miracle whereupon the cross vanished. Josephus and his father traveled to Britain where they were promptly imprisoned. Mordrain, with his brother-in-law Nascien, sailed from the Holy Lands, released them, and brought Christianity to Britain. Josephus left the shield in Britain for the time when the perfect knight would come.

After one of many moralizing episodes Galahad eventually rides to the Castle of Maidens. This is situated by the River Severn in the West Country of Britain, where he defeats seven knights who hold the castle in thrall, and releases the maidens within it. It turns out that the seven knights are really the Seven Deadly Sins and the castle is Hell. This is a symbolic reenactment of Christ's descent into Hell in order to release the souls of the just, represented in this case by the maidens. We will discover, as the story unfolds, that Galahad is not only the Perfect Knight but that he is also a thinly disguised shadow of the Christ reborn.

The next adventures concern two Grail seekers who, although brave and valiant, have some fatal flaw which

the authors are at pains to show in relation to the Perfect Knight. The first is our original Celtic hero,
Gawain. By now his earlier behavior of womanizing and
willingness to do battle is frowned upon by the peace
loving and celibate monks. So when he is admonished
for being a bad and faithless servant of God he ingen-
uously and honestly replies *You know me well!* admitting that the hardship of Christian penance is more than
he can bear.

Meanwhile the second knight, Lancelot, along with
Perceval has been challenged and defeated by an
unknown adversary. Neither man recognizes the other.
Lancelot rides on alone to discover who his adversary
might be and while he sleeps in a chapel he seems to
see the Grail healing a knight, who subsequently takes
Lancelot's armor while he lies asleep. When he awakes
a voice rebukes Lancelot for wasting the great talents
God had given him. He stays with a hermit and swears
he will change his sinful ways, become celibate, and
never lie with his lover the queen again.

So far both of these great knights have proved too
worldly for the quest. Gawain proves the more stub-
born Celt in his earthly ways, while Lancelot chooses
the path of penitence.

The Fellowship of the Grail *sets out from the Court of King Arthur
leaving their women behind, as each must seek alone. 13th c. French ms.*

THE THREE FELLOWSHIPS

THE STORY NOW SHIFTS TO PERLESVAUS who meets his aunt at a chapel. She had once been the Queen of the Waste Land and from her he learns of the death of his mother. He also learns of the three great Fellowships. The first was the Fellowship of the Last Supper at the table of Christ, where the bread of Heaven sustained the twelve. And there was found the perilous Seat of Judas.

Then there was the Table of the Holy Grail at which Joseph fed 4000 with only twelve loaves through the agency of the Holy Grail. At this table there was also a perilous Seat of Dread upon which only the true leader or guardian could sit.

Lastly there was the Table Round devised by Merlin, symbolizing the earth, the planets, the stars and the spheres, a true epitome of the universe. Merlin had forecast that although the Grail was withdrawn in his age, there would come a later time when three knights would triumph. He prophesied that two would be virgins while the other, although knowing a woman, would be chaste. And Merlin then created the Seat Perilous which Galahad had sat upon. Perlesvaus is further told that just as the Holy Spirit came down among the Apostles in a pillar of fire at Pentecost, so both the Chosen Knight and the Shepherd wear red armor. The author thus reinforces the implicit hint that Galahad is the new Christ.

Perlesvaus' aunt insists that he keep his virginity and remain celibate without the stain of lechery and Perlesvaus gives his promise to do so.

Visiting a church he meets an ancient man, King Mordrain who, 400 years before, had ventured too near the Grail and had been maimed for his imprudence. We see how, like the Ark of the Covenant before it, the Grail can wound if the seeker is deemed unworthy. Mordrain had begged to live until he could clasp the Good Knight to his breast. Nine generations of his line have passed and in this time he has been nourished, like Titurel, the Rich Fisher, by only a wafer of the Host.

King Arthur's Round Table, *Winchester Castle, Great Hall, Southern England. This 13th century table has twenty four places with the names of the knights reading clockwise from King Arthur: Sir Galahallt, Sir Launcelot Sir Gauen, Sir Percyvale, Sir Lyonell, Sir Trystram , Sir Garethe, Sir Bedwere, Sir Blubrys, Sir Lacotemale, Sir Lucane, Sir Plomyd, Sir Lamorak, Sir Born, Sir Safer, Sir Pelleus, Sir Kay, Sir Ectorde , Sir Dagonet, Sir Degore, Sir Brumear, Sir Lybyus, Sir Alynore, and Sir Mordrede.*

The Maiden, the Lion,
the Crone
& the Serpent

FTER A FURTHER SERIES of adventures and misadventures Perlesvaus now has to face a number of crucial tests. At one point he is offered a horse by a beautiful maiden in recompense for being obedient to her service. He agrees, little knowing the horse is actually the Enemy. As he rides into the night he is only saved at the last moment by crossing himself, which is too great a burden for the Demon to bear. Perlesvaus then awakens the next morning to find himself on an island which he is sharing with a lion and a serpent. He kills the serpent, who had the lion's little cub in its jaws, and through this act manages to befriend the lion. The next night he dreams of a young woman mounted on a lion and an old crone upon a serpent. The young maiden warns him that he will be facing a great test against the Enemy but the ancient crone rebukes him for killing her serpent. We learn later that the young woman on the lion symbolizes the New Law and the New Trinity. The lion signifies the Christ while the woman symbolizes Faith, Hope, Belief and Baptism. She is as fresh and new as the resurrection. However the ancient crone, old through countless generations, is in reality the Synagogue, the Old Law and the False Scripture.

As Perlesvaus plays with the lion another ship arrives all covered in black. In it is a beautiful and sensual maiden who offers food and wine and then herself. Perlesvaus is on the point of succumbing to her advances and about to forget all his vows of celibacy when he sees a red cross on his sword and manages to cross himself in time. The maiden vanishes in a puff of foul stench revealing that she was in fact the Enemy all the while. A voice tells us that Perlesvaus has passed the test and is deemed worthy. He then sets sail, eventually meeting Galahad and Bors.

Perceval and the Two Riders. *14th C. French manuscript. Perceval rests upon the lion and sees in a vision a crone, signifying the Old Law of the Synagogue, riding on the Dragon Beast of the Apocalypse. The other rider is the beautiful virgin, Ecclesia, who symbolizes the New Law of the Christian Church. She is mounted upon a lion and warns Perceval of a time of testing which lies before him.*

THE SLOW ASCENT

E NEXT TURN TO LANCELOT who is about to undergo his particular test of worthiness. In the company of a hermit he finds a dead man dressed in a white linen shirt beside the remains of a fire. Beside him lies a hair shirt. The hermit is unsure of whether the man has sinned, for he was wearing a linen shirt and not the one of hair befitting a holy man or a penitent. So he summons the Devil to determine what is the true case, so that he will know how to bury the man. The devil reveals that the victim has indeed been a holy man. Two knights had tried to burn him alive but he had told them that even his linen shirt would not burn. Although he had died, it was because of God and not because of the fire, for his body had been untouched by the flames. The point of the story is, of course, to demonstrate the powers of faith.

The hermit accuses Lancelot of having wasted his great talents and purity _ which are significantly rank-ordered as *virginity, humility, long-suffering, rectitude* and *charity.* The Enemy found lust in Lancelot, being seduced by the womanly wiles of Guenevere, who, the author notes primly, had never made confession since she was married. These author-monks had a programmed distrust of women, especially whenever they got a whiff of the powerful lusty odor of a pagan goddess like Guenevere. So instead of virginity and chastity the Enemy finds lust and instead of humility he finds pride. But Lancelot gladly agrees to wear the hair shirt of the corpse and swears once again to penance and celibacy.

He learns from the hermit the meaning of a dream in which he has seen a man all set about with stars, two knights and seven kings. He learns that the seven kings are the founders of his lineage, the last being King Ban (Bran). The man set about with stars is the first king to bring Christianity to Britain and the two knights are himself and his son Galahad. Galahad is represented in the dream as a lion with wings soaring over the rest of humanity.

Lancelot joins a tournament between white and black knights. He joins the dark knights and is defeated. On visiting an anchoress he learns that he has fought on the side of the Earthly Knights of Sin against the Heavenly Knights of Virtue.

Lancelot falls into the dark night of his soul as he fights a black knight on a black steed who kills his horse. Lancelot is left alone with an un-fordable river before him and dark forests and cliffs behind him.

Meanwhile the other representatives of the worldly warriors, Gawain and Hector, have both been dreaming. Gawain dreams he stands in a green meadow watching 150 bulls feeding at a hayrack. They are all proud, and all but three are dappled. Of these three one bears traces of spots while the other two are pure white. All the bulls exclaim in a body, *"Let us go farther afield to seek better pastures,"* and they move off into the waste moorlands, ignoring the meadow. Of the three without spots one returns but the other two stay in the meadow. The rest fall to fighting until their fodder is destroyed and they disperse. Later this dream is explained to Gawain. The hayrack is the Round Table and the bulls are its knight companions. All except the three undappled bulls are proud, lecherous and sinful. They ignore the meadow, which symbolizes the original humility and patience upon which the Fellowship was founded, while the moorland is the Wasteland and the path of Hell.

Hector, on the other hand, dreams that he and Lancelot stepped down off a throne, mounting two powerful horses, saying *"Let us seek what we shall never find."* After wandering for many days Lancelot is struck from his horse and his assailant strips him and then arrays him in a robe spiked with holly and puts him on an ass. Thus mounted he arrives at a clear spring but when he stoops to drink from it the spring vanishes. Seeing that he might not drink from it Lancelot goes back the way he had come. Hector, however, wanders aimlessly until he chances on a great wedding feast. He stands outside the gate of the castle shouting, *"Open up!"* But he is not allowed in, as none can enter so proudly mounted. Crestfallen, Hector goes back to the empty throne he had left. This dream is interpreted by Nasciens the hermit, that same holy man who originally warned the Fellowship that they must go separately and without a woman. He tells Hector that

the throne was a sign of power and sovereignty and that he had vacated honor and prestige at the Round Table. Both he and Lancelot mounted the Enemy's steeds of pride and arrogance. Seeking what they would not find was of course the Grail, which they are not worthy to receive. But Lancelot falls from his pride, discovers he is naked of any Christian virtues and pleads forgiveness. His assailant is Christ who arrays him in patience and humility. He sets him on an ass just as Christ himself had chosen the lowliest of animals to ride into Jerusalem. The clear spring is the grace of the Grail, but Lancelot is blinded and cannot see it. He returns to Camelot to tell of what happened. Hector, however, has spent his life astride the powerful warhorse which signifies mortal sin and pride, so that when he comes to the Castle of the Fisher King, where there is a celebration that the Grail has been won, he is not allowed to enter. So both the worldly knights return to Camelot having gained nothing.

Above: **Lancelot and the Holy Grail**. *Illustrated manuscript 15th c. French. For Lancelot, the Grail will always be beyond reach simply because of his catastrophic liason with King Arthur's wife, Guenevere.*

THE SHIP OF SOLOMON

 OW WE COME TO THE ADVENTURES, the trials and tests of the knight Bors. Unlike his worldly fellows, Hector and Gawain, Bors sets out properly armed in Christ. Both the Mass and the Eucharist are celebrated throughout the narrative, but the body of Christ in the form of a wafer is seen by each knight in different ways. Bors declares that what he looks on *is truly flesh and truly man and truly God,"* a statement that demonstrates Cistercian preferences in the dispute over the reality or the mere symbology of the Eucharist. He observes as a pelican on a leafless tree stabs out its own breast to feed its young. This is later revealed as a symbol of God suffering for our sakes. The leafless tree is the cross and the beak that wounds is the lance.

Bors also undergoes a series of tests, including one in which he must choose between saving his brother Lionel from being beaten by two knights, or going to the aid of a maiden being abducted. He chooses the compassionate path of defending the girl and earns his brother's enmity. A voice tells Bors to meet Perlesvaus by the sea, which he does, and joins him in the white-sailed ship.

So already two of the companions of the quest have succeeded in their trials. It is now the turn of the last member, Galahad. Without at first recognizing each other, Gawain and Galahad fight and Gawain is dealt a terrible blow. What was seen as his arrogance in trying to wrest the sword from the stone, even though he tried on the orders of Arthur, has now been repaid in full.

One morning Galahad is woken by a fair maiden who tells him that he must follow her for the greatest adventure of all. The girl brings him to Perlesvaus and Bors and they all embark on a magnificent ship with an inscription in Chaldean upon its side warning that *"I am Faith and True Belief Itself. So before entering be without sin."* The girl reveals herself to be Perlesvaus' sister. They board and find a marvelous sword which, long before, had wounded King Parlan between the thighs for his presumption in drawing it from its sheath. Henceforth he was known as the Maimed King.

Also on the ship is a bed made of timber which has a long and holy history. When Adam and Eve were banished from the Garden of Eden, Eve still carried a part of the branch of the Tree of Life which she planted and it took root. If argument were ever needed to display the essentially male chauvinist attitude within the Christian Grail texts, then the passages surrounding the narrative of the bed would be considered prime evidence. Eve is known both as the sinful one, and the one who should obey Adam. In every way she is described as his inferior. But the writers lived in a time when the cult of the Virgin Mary was fast gaining popularity so were somewhat caught in a double bind, nowhere more evident than in this story. For this branch was carried out of Eden by the very woman who betrayed Adam.  So we are told that through the female we lost our eternal life yet through a woman, the Virgin Mary, life would be restored. This is a vital theme which runs as a swift currrent through the entire Christian corpus of the Grail. The twig took root and became a tree, but white as snow, signifying the pure soul and the virgin body. For at the time Eve plucked it from the tree in Eden she was still a virgin. Abel was conceived beneath that tree which then turned green. And just as he was conceived on a Friday so he died on a Friday, as did Christ himself. Adam and Eve were also cast out on Friday. God curses Cain and the earth upon which the

blood of Abel had been spilled, except for the tree, which underwent a transformation, becoming red in remembrance of the blood of Abel. The shoots from the tree were each red, white and green and it was from these trees that Solomon's wife had cut the three posts around the bed in the ship. The ship had been made on her instructions so that the Perfect Knight, last of Solomon's line, would receive the sword, would lie on the bed and receive the message that Solomon had foreseen his coming.

The magnificent blade is the Sword of King David, but it has only a poor hessian hanging. Perlesvaus' sister has woven a precious belt of her hair and the sword is thus named the Blade of the Strange Hangings. Any remaining doubt of a direct identification of Galahad with Christ must be dispelled by the fact Christ also took up the *"Sword of David"* as the Messiah, King of the Jews and was crucified on a cross made of the Tree of Life.

Opposite page: **Tree of Life** *in the center of the Holy City. Four rivers issue from its roots. 14th c.* **Above:** **Pelican,** *Stained Glass 14th c. The pelican was thought to peck its own breast to feed its young. Christ was identified with the bird.* **Above:** **Expulsion from Eden,** *Bronze doors, St. Zeno's Basilica, Verona 11th c.*

The Death of Perceval's Sister, *from a 14th century French ms.*

THE VIRGIN AND THE LEPER QUEEN

THE SHIP REACHES LAND and the three knights and the maiden disembark near a castle and are immediately attacked. They defeat their assailants and release the count who had been held captive. From him they learn they must visit the Maimed King. On their way they see a vision of Christ as a white hart, on a throne surrounded by four lions, which passes through the glass windows of a chapel towards heaven. *"In like manner did the son of God enter the Virgin Mary, so that her virginity was left entire and perfect."* This curious explanation in which the Son of Man is disguised as a hart with the four attendant Evangelists carries an earlier Celtic theme of Modron and her Divine Son.

They are then stopped by a band of knights who demand a bowl of blood from Perlesvaus' virgin sister. There is a fight against tremendous odds but the valiant three manage to hold their own. However, on learning that the blood is to heal the queen of the castle who has leprosy, Perlesvaus' sister agrees to the blood letting. Her blood does heal the queen but the maiden dies. She has them place her embalmed body on a ship to sail to Sarras where she wishes to be buried with Galahad and Perlesvaus.

Her brother carefully composes a letter to be laid with the body explaining who she is and where she is bound. But after she has died the three companions see a mighty storm demolish the castle and all within it and discover it is God's vengeance for the blood taken from sixty virgins who all died that the wicked queen might be healed. This recalls an almost identical destruction of Sodom and Gomorrah in Genesis.

The companions split up as Bors follows a wounded knight pursued by another knight and a dwarf, while Perlesvaus and Galahad continue their separate ways towards the Castle of the Grail.

Above: **Knight and Princess** Pisanello 15th c., Verona
Left: **Galahad, Perceval and Bors** meet for the last time at the Table of the Grail, *14th century French illustrated manuscript.*

LANCELOT AT THE CASTLE OF CORBENIC

Lancelot at Corbenic, *the Castle of the Grail. 15th century manuscript, Italy. Here he sees the stag, which symbolizes Christ, leap through the window.*

*Right: **Castle**, Les Trés Riches Heures du Duc de Berry, 15th c. This popular image of a castle is unlike any historical fortress of the 9th century when the Grail legend supposedly occurred.*

E HAD LEFT LANCELOT DESPONDENTLY seated on the bank of a wide river. A voice tells him to board the first ship he sees. He does so and sleeps in bliss. He awakens to find he is on the funeral barge of Perceval's sister. He reads the letter that Perceval had written explaining who she was and how she had come there.

Shortly afterwards Lancelot is reunited with his son Galahad and they live together in great accord on the boat for half a year. After Easter they meet a white knight who leads a white horse for Galahad. Father and son take leave of one another for the last time as Lancelot sails off again. He reaches a castle with a gate guarded by two lions. He comes to a door behind which he hears singing and knows that this is the place of the Holy Grail. The door opens on a room full of brilliant light, but Lancelot is forbidden to enter. He can see the Holy Vessel on a cloth of red samite, surrounded by ministering angels. When an aged priest comes to elevate the Host, Lancelot sees three men above the priest's outstretched hands placing a figure in the hands of the celebrant. But it so appears that the priest is overburdened by the figure and about to fall that Lancelot unthinkingly rushes forward to help. But he is *as if shot through with flames and rooted to the ground like a man paralyzed.* He languishes in this state for 24 days, being the number of years he had been in sin with Guenevere and served the Enemy. He wakes up in the Castle of Corbenic, the home of King Pelles whose daughter was the mother of Galahad. He is completely transformed by his experience of being in the trance. On the fifth day of his sojourn with the king, the Holy Grail serves the entire company. At that point proud Hector rides up demanding entrance, thus reenacting his own dream. He is so mortified upon hearing that his brother Lancelot is amongst the celebrants that he rides off in shame. Lancelot himself rides off to Arthur's court. He finds it sadly depleted of all the knights who were lost on their unsuccessful quest.

THE HOLY GRAIL

ALAHAD NOW VISITS KING MORDRAIN who at last sees the Good Knight after having waited 400 years. At last he can die in peace, but before he yields up the spirit his wounds heal and his sight is restored. Galahad also releases Simeon, who once had wronged Joseph of Arimathea, from the torments of fire which he had endured for 350 years.

Galahad and Perceval join one another again and for the next five years they attempt to resolve all the wrongs of *Logres*. At last they reach the Castle of the Maimed King at Corbenic.

Galahad welds together the broken sword, but then gives it to Bors. A great wind sweeps through the hall of Corbenic as nine knights arrive, which now, in accordance with the Cisterican symbolism, makes up the number of the twelve apostles. Three come from Gaul,

three from Ireland and three from Denmark.

Four maidens bring in a bed with an old king upon it. Josephus, the first Christian bishop consecrated in Sarras, descends as if in a vision and officiates before the Grail. Two angels bear candles, a red cloth and the bleeding lance which drips into the vessel. Josephus takes bread from the holy vessel and a figure descends, becoming a child, and enters the bread, *"which quite clearly took on human form."*

A naked Christ then appears from out of the holy vessel and feeds them with the bread. He tells them that they have won a place at his table, which has not happened since the Last Supper when twelve disciples were there. Now the companions are his new apostles. And although many knights have eaten from the Grail and have been filled with grace, never before have they come face to face with its innermost secrets as they do now. They learn that the Holy Grail is *"the platter from which Jesus Christ partook of the paschal lamb with His disciples,"* but that it must leave Logres for the people of

that realm have lapsed into dissolute and worldly ways and no longer serve the Grail. Britain is no longer worthy to harbor such a glory. Galahad, Bors and Perceval must journey to the Holy City of Sarras, but not before Galahad heals the Maimed King with blood from the lance. The healed king then predictably ends his days in a Cistercian monastery.

The three companions board the ship of Solomon with the Silver Table, the Grail, (now in the form of a chalice veil) and the Lance. Galahad desires only death now, as he feels he has already died in the flesh at the Grail Ceremony. He sleeps in the bed of the Tree of Life (reenacting the crucifixion) and the next morning they arrive at Sarras.

They carry the Grail to the palace and as they do so Galahad performs a miracle on a cripple just as Christ had done. They discover that Perceval's sister has arrived in the boat before them, and they bury her as she had wished. The pagan king Escorant, however, imprisons them all for a year but on his deathbed finally

releases them and asks forgiveness. Against his wishes Galahad is made the new king, but only a year afterwards he experiences the ultimate source of the Grail and in the company of the son of Joseph of Arimathea he ascends to heaven. A hand comes down from heaven and takes both the Grail and the lance, and they have not been seen since.

Perceval entered a hermitage and survived his friend by only a year and three days. Bors returned from Sarras, which is said to have been situated on the borders of Egypt, to Logres and the court of King Arthur. Here Bors relates the tale to the knights of his household. And with that the tale falls silent and has no more to say about the adventures of the Holy Grail.

The Quest for the Holy Grail, *a tapestry designed by Burne-Jones and carried out by William Morris. As Perceval and Bors hold back, the destined and perfect knight, Galahad, finally achieves his long and arduous search for the Grail and dies in ecstasy and bliss.*

THE THIRD BRANCH
THE CHYMICAL

THE THIRD BRANCH of the Grail tree is a single work, written about 1220. This poem of some 25,000 lines, composed in rhymed couplets in Middle German, is created on a huge canvas. The action is no longer limited to the Isles of Celtic Britain or to the narrow confines of Wales, but stretches from the heart of Bavaria to as far away as the lands of the Near and Far East. And, whereas the other branches are set in the vague time frameworks of the Otherworld Parzival has a firm foothold in this world, and a precise date. The hero's mother is said to have lived eleven generations before the author of the poem, Wolfram von Eschenbach, which would be about 870.

Wolfram himself lived in what was probably the old Franconian city of Ober-Eschenbach, now near Ansbach in Bavaria. From what he charmingly tells of himself he was not of the nobility. He may have been a knight, but a poor one, judging from his joking aside that even the mice in his home have difficulty in finding something to eat. He appeared to have been dependent upon such patrons as the generous Heinrich von Thuringen, whose court at that time was famous as a center of learning and literature.

Wolfram's claims to be illiterate seem a tongue-in-cheek jest, although it appears that he did not enjoy a classical upbringing. His work suggests he had little knowledge of authors of the Latin school, but this lack is more than compensated by his wide ranging acquaintance with much of the German and French literature available at the time. Yet it is significant that he seldom quotes from books. He never says "I have read," only "as I have heard tell" or "as the story goes."

The chief source of material for his poem is certainly Chrétien, although Wolfram differs significantly from the romance of the French author as his own vision unfolds. He even scolds Chrétien for not having done full justice to the original story, and claims that at least he has an authentic original given him by one Kyot of Provence. Whether this character is another of Wolfram's many jokes has been a source of countless and rather fruitless speculations. But the history given by Wolfram of his so-called original gives some idea of the radical difference between the old Grail material and his new and essentially cosmopolitan variant.

Supposedly, Wolfram's master, Kyot, found an Arabic script in Toledo which told of the Grail. We are told that this had originally been written by a heathen Jew named Flegetanis, 1200 years before the birth of Christ. Flegetanis is Persian for "familiar with the stars" and if we are to take the account seriously the book would have been astronomical in form. Kyot supposedly augmented this with his own researches into Latin chronicles of various countries, and this composite work was said to be Wolfram's actual source.

"*Flegetanis knew the starry script*
could read in the heavens high
How the stars roll on their courses,
how they circle the silent sky
And the time when the wandering endeth
– and the life and the lot of men
He read in the stars, and strange secrets he saw"

Wolfram claims Kyot's research had revealed a genealogical connection between the account of the Grail and of the coming of Christ foretold by Flegetanis. From a belief in the forces of heredity he was able to reconstruct a family tree of the Grail. "*And the sons of baptized men hold It and Guard It with humble heart and the best of mankind shall those knights be.*" These are the Grail Guardians, whose lineage and destiny stretch as far back as Cain, the son of Adam.

Alchemical Tree *from the Treatises of Raymond Lull. This Spanish theologian, kabbalist and mystic alchemist, was a contemporary of Wolfram and traveled throughout Christian Europe and the Islamic East.*
Opposite page: **Alchemical manuscript,** *Hebrew, 12th century, Spain. Jews, Christians and Moslems collaborated under the tolerant Islamic Caliphates of Spain. The Moorish kingdoms supported the mystical and heretical Sufis and it was these Islamic mystics who furnished many of the female precedents within the Grail legend.*

THE WIDE CANVAS

HERE IS A GENERAL CONSENSUS among Wolfram scholars now that the poet drew upon a wide range of readily available sources and took more than a little impish delight in confounding his critics with the enigmatic figure of Kyot and his ancient astronomer, Flegitanus. But certainly Wolfram does make the most of a remarkably wide spectrum of interests current at the time.

Historically, Europe was passing through a wonderfully rebellious and alive spiritual upheaval, full of doubts and questions. The crisis years surrounding the turn of the thirteenth century marked the horrible crushing of the Albigensian and Cathari heretics, yet at the same time saw the enlightenment of St. Francis, perhaps the greatest spiritual figure in the West since Christ himself. The Moslem world witnessed the flowering of a cluster of Sufi masters including Rabiya, Shams-y-Tabriz, Byazid and Mevlana Rumi, while the Dominicans were rooting out Christian heresy in the infamous Holy Inquisition. Jerusalem had fallen to the Saracens, while the Knights of the Temple were still enjoying the peak of their power within Europe. The Courts of Love were flourishing, and the mystery Cult of the Virgin Mary was gathering strength. This was the greatest period of the troubadours and Europe was poised for a leap in consciousness that was, sadly, never to survive the Inquisition.

This was the tumultuous background to Wolfram's *Parzival* and he drew upon the remarkable cross fertilization that the clash and fury of the Crusades had fermented. From the West had come the Celtic storytellers and from the East the shock of encountering a civilization far in advance of anything that Europe could offer outside the Moorish realms of Spain and the

mystical experiments of Languedoc.

Wolfram manages to include it all in the sweep of his huge canvas. In his poem we can find traces of the new Arabian astrology, Islamic love poems, alchemical symbology and the Jewish esoteric traditions of magic and mysticism.

Parzival deals with essentially two realms: one, the Arthurian world popularly known as the Matter of Britain, and the other, a transcendent realm which owes

— twin aspects of the same individual. Gawain is Parzival's worldly alter-ego, the perfect knight who represents the peak of Arthurian chivalry within the Fellowship of the Round Table. Parzival, in contrast, is Gawain's spiritual self, the perfect knight within the transcendental realm of the Fellowship and family of the Grail.

As the poem opens we are firmly set down in the Arthurian world of courtly virtues. Parzival himself even seeks to become part of that world as his father had done. But for him, even the highest knightly honors are not enough. He possesses an inner integrity which finally prevents him from following the social ideas of others, and forces him to seek the Divine Source within himself.

This is why of all the Grail romances *Parzival* speaks most clearly to the modern reader. His quest is a desperate search for truth and that, as anyone who has embarked upon such a path will agree, is a very lonely road. The ideals of the Near East, however, were essentially centered on the community, with each person taking his or her part within the greater whole. This often fanatical combination of Judaic law, coupled with Rome's administrative zeal, overwhelmed a Europe whose ancient epic traditions show a far greater concern with the individual and far less with the community's behavior. The northwestern hero would challenge the gods themselves, if the idea took his fancy, or if he was spurred on by a pretty woman's goading. The Church of Rome, on the other hand, was founded on obedience to God's laws, so there was a deep distrust of any individual who sought to find that God alone.

Parzival proved to be that remarkably modern man, the man who dared to doubt.

much to esoteric Christianity and newly acquired spiritual ideas from the Orient.

These twin themes of the Worldly and the Beyond are exemplified by Gawain and Parzival. The two greatest warriors of the age are like the hero and his shadow

Jerusalem and the Valley of Jehoshaphat *from the Valley of Evil Council by Thomas Seddon, 1854.*

Parzival

THE BLACK & THE WHITE

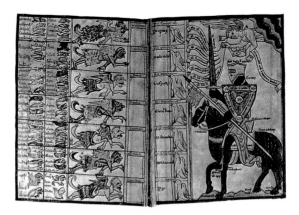

PARZIVAL OPENS WITH A LONG introductory passage in which Wolfram shows that darkness and light, black and white, are to be found within every act. And since every act carries with it both good and bad effects, the best that can be done in such circumstances is to err on the side of the good.

When the human heart begins to stir from its customary unconscious lethargy and pass into the awakening of doubt, the soul feels both dishonor and yet at the same time, grace. The condition is like that enchanted bird, the magpie, which appears to be half dove and half raven. Life holds both hell's darkness and the light of heaven at one and the same moment and it is no use pondering their contrary elements. Rather, one must learn to flow with life, running after the hind one moment and being chased by the boar in the next. According to the poet there are three stages that the hero must pass through. He slowly evolves from a dull, stupor-ridden unconsciousness, passing through the suffering of doubt to finally arrive at a transformed illumination of his or her being.

The image of the black and white magpie is a leitmotif which flits from chapter to chapter throughout the entire work. At the very outset Parzival's adventuring father defends his first love as she is besieged by a white and a black army. He marries this black princess and they have a child who is both black and white and who is Parzival's half brother. This is a natural dialectic, as if Wolfram is warning the reader to take the middle path. Even the hero's name is said to arise from *Perce à val* – to pierce the valley between the two opposite peaks. This is the first real whiff of Eastern Tao ever found within the whole European experiment. Almost two thousand years before the Chinese master, Sosan wrote a verse that would best express what Wolfram seems to have been hinting at. *"The Great Way is not difficult for those who have no preferences. When love and hate are both absent everything becomes clear and undisguised. Make the smallest distinction, however, and heaven and earth are set infinitely apart."*

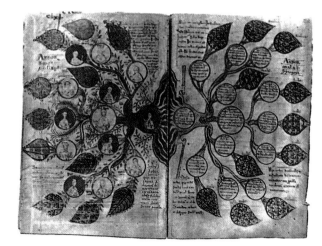

If any more evidence is needed of the author's concern for keeping to the middle path, then all we have to do is turn to the story of the origins of the Grail. This story is told by a mystic hermit, who tells the hero that the Grail was a stone vessel brought from heaven by the neutral angels. When Lucifer fell it was because he stubbornly refused to bow to anyone but God. When ordered to bow to *Adamel*, the original man, he refused. According to the Shiite Muslims this shows that actually Lucifer remains God's greatest worshiper. So, the edges between what is good and what is evil are blurred. When the war came in heaven, one third of the angels sided with the Almighty, and one third with Lucifer, but the last third were neutral. They were neither on God's side nor Satan's. Nature, also, knows nothing of the ethics of good and evil. By insisting that, when in doubt, all that anyone can do is to choose the light, Wolfram is really pointing past all polarities. And in this he touches the traditions of Far Eastern Tao and Near Eastern Gnosticism.

The expressive devices he uses in order to get his message across are alchemy and astrology. Throughout the text we will discover the whole cycle of the astrological zodiac. For to Wolfram the legend of the Grail is an ongoing and unending cycle of events and seasons. While the Celtic concerns were for the Sun Hero to reunite the earth and sky, Wolfram's Sun Hero Parzival must move through the signs of the zodiac in order to enact the order of the stars, enfolding the cosmos within the micro-cosmos, supernature within nature.

Opposite: **Peraldus**, Summa de Vitiis, *1240. A knight armed with the Shield of Faith, accompanied by the white doves of the Holy Spirit, confronts an army of devils and dragons representing the vices he must overcome.* **Above:** **Tree of Good & Evil,** *12th c.*

SARACENS MOURN HIM YET

E LEARN AT FIRST OF PARZIVAL'S FATHER, Gahmuret. He is of the line of Anjou, but on the death of his father leaves for foreign lands. His quest is to serve the mightiest man on earth, but he displays complete indifference to whether this man is Christian or Infidel. As this was written virtually at the same time as Jerusalem fell to the Saracens, it tells much of Wolfram's bold approach, as it does for his audience who appeared to readily accept such a situation.

Gahmuret serves Baruch, the Caliph of Baghdad and then assists the black Moorish queen Belakane, who is besieged by both white and dark armies. Her name, meaning Pelican, was also the alchemical symbol for Christ in the Middle Ages. The bird was believed to wound its own breast in order to feed its young. Belakane has a son by Gahmuret, called Feirefiz. He is spotted black and white like a piebald. But Gahmuret is not steadfast in his loves; the lure for adventure proves too strong for him. He leaves the black queen, much to her sorrow.

In marrying Belakane Gahmuret had become King of Zazamanc. He journeys to Northern Europe, where he jousts at a tournament and wins the hand of the fair Herzeloyde. By marrying the little queen he is not only Lord of Zazamanc but becomes King of both South and North Wales, and, on the death of his brother, the whole realm of Anjou. We learn that his brother had been killed by a knight called Orilis, whom we shall meet shortly. But adventure calls and once again Gahmuret is off to help Baruch. This time he dies from a treacherous wound in battle. The great diamond within his helm which protected him is made soft through sorcery. Gahumet dies what might be termed a true alchemist's death. On his tomb the Caliph inscribes *"Baptized was he as a Christian tho' Saracens mourn him yet."* This is an extraordinary start to the poem considering that as *Parzival* was being written the Christian knights of the Second Crusade were being pulverized by the troops of the Saracens. Which said a lot for Wolfram's contemporary audience that the distinction between the good and the bad guys was not exclusively partisan.

While Gahmuret was certainly an exemplary and fearless knight, fit for King Arthur's court, Wolfram shows he lacks the two most essential qualities of any seeker of the Grail: steadfastness and loyalty. And these are just the characteristics that both his sons, the white Parzival and the piebald Feirefiz, will have in abundance.

Above: **Richard I defeats Saladin**. *Inlaid tiles from Chertsey Abbey, 13th c. England. In actuality the Saracen, Saladin, was a far more chivalrous and civilized leader than Christian Richard.* ***Below:*** **Crusader Knights,** *England 13th and 14th c.*

ALAS MOTHER, WHAT IS GOD?

FOURTEEN DAYS AFTER THE DEATH OF GAHMURET HIS SON, Parzival, is born. Herzeloyde leaves the court and settles in the forest wasteland of Soltane. There she brings up the young boy with no knowledge of knights, fearing he will die like his father. Her fears are well grounded, for the child is a natural warrior and is soon making bows, arrows and javelins. But he is also a child of nature and we are told he could often be entranced and overcome just listening to the birds. And such is his nature that when he kills one with his arrow, he weeps when the bird stops singing for he cannot understand the consequences of his acts. His mother mentions God and the boy suddenly asks *"Alas Mother, what is God?"* Her answer: *"He is Light beyond all Light, brighter than summer's day,"* gives an Eastern, almost Zoroastrian flavor to the Deity. She repeats the leitmotif of the dark and the light by making a clear distinction between the loyal, white, brightness of God and the black darkness of Falsehood, and tells her son to turn his thoughts away from the darkness and from from the wavering of doubt. This dualistic theme will be encountered time and again throughout Wolfram's narrative.

One day three knights ride past, followed closely by a fourth, resplendent in shining armor. They are pursuing Meljakanz, who has abducted the fair Imane. The last knight asks if Parzival has seen the abductors, but the youth at first thinks them angels. Even when they manage to explain that they are knights he still has only eyes for the glittering armor and the shining weapons, so merely meets their questions with those of his own. From them he learns of King Arthur and of knighthood.

His mother, realizing that she cannot prevent him from becoming a knight, clothes him in a fool's outfit, gives him a poor steed and tells him of his heritage. He also hears that Duke Orilis is attacking his father's lands and that the Duke's brother has killed Prince Turkentals, who was defending the territory. Parzival swears to avenge his death. But he is impatient to be off and hardly listens to her advice that whenever he can win a lady's ring and greeting, to take the ring and kiss and embrace her.

He then rides off the next morning and the instant he is out of sight Herzeloyde (Herze leide or hearts sorrow) dies of grief. Just as with the bird, the young

Opposite: **The Fool** *from the Tarot, (Visconti deck, 1540).* **Right:** **Knight,** *silver seal, 14th c. England.* **Below:* **The Virgin,** *an ivory triptych showing the annunciation, the death and coronation of the Virgin Mary.*

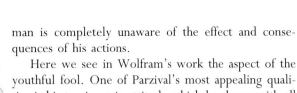

man is completely unaware of the effect and consequences of his actions.

Here we see in Wolfram's work the aspect of the youthful fool. One of Parzival's most appealing qualities is his tragi-comic attitude which he shares with all the great fools. They are essentially lonely, childish and anarchic. They don't mean any ill will, but have no sense of responsibility for the consequences of their acts. They are selfish and determined to get their way. Give them a problem, and the absurd way they tackle it provides the comedy. They are anti-social and, as we shall see, completely inept when it comes to women, being either too shy and gauche or too blunt and offensive.

A Fool in the Tent

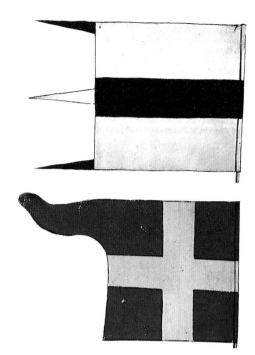

 TRAIGHTAWAY OUR YOUNG FOOL unwittingly changes the fortunes of the innocent Jeshute, wife to Orilis, the very Duke who lays claim to Parzival's lands. Parzival knows nothing of this as he discovers the sleeping Jeshute in a rich tent and, literally following his mother's advice, he wakes her, not only taking a kiss but also her ring and brooch, again thinking he is in accordance with his mother's counsel. Then, ignoring the terrified wife, he hungrily devours the food on the table and leaves Jeshute to vainly protest to her irate husband that her honor has not been despoiled. Orilis forces her to ride behind him as a penitent, clothed in rags and on a worn-out nag.

The simple-minded young man travels onward until he encounters a woman holding the corpse of a knight. She is Sigune, and the knight is Schianatulander, who had ridden out to Baghdad with Parzival's father. She remains a virgin bride to her dead bridegroom. Their love was destined to bring them no happiness in this world. Even though she is distraught over her lost lover, she listens to Parzival and recognizes her aunt's child.

Pennants *of the crusader knights from 14th century Germany.*

She is the first to tell the young hero of his actual name, and explains it means *"to pierce through the middle."* She also tells him that her lover has been killed by Orilis. Orilis is the same knight who had killed Galoes, Parzival's uncle, and he is, unknown to Parzival, even at that moment hot on his tail. Fearing for Parzival's life, Sigune manages to direct the young man the wrong way as he seeks vengeance on her behalf.

We discover later that Orilis had no intention of fighting Schianatulander at all. In his jealous rage he mistook him for Parzival. Schianatulander, as comrade-in-arms of Gahumet, had defended the son's lands and had died in his place. So, unwittingly, Parzival is responsible for the death of his father's friend, and his cousin's lover. We already begin to see how unconscious behavior begets a trail of karma and misadventure. Parzival's path leads him to meet up with a fisherman to whom he trades Jeshute's brooch for food and shelter.

THE RED KNIGHT

The Shrovetide Joust *of Marx Walther. Detail from a 15th century illustrated manual.*

NSTEAD OF MEETING ORILIS as he had planned, Parzival encounters a Red Knight. This account differs little from the one given by Chrétien de Troyes. But we do have a fine description of the armor, if not the man.

"All dazzling was his armor
The eye from its flow glinted red,
Red was his horse swift footed,
And the plumes that should deck its head.
Of samite red its covering;
Redder than flame his shield;
Fair fashioned and red his surcoat;
And the spear that his hand would wield
Was red, yea, the shaft and the iron."

No wonder the young man instantly covets the outfit. The Red Knight has stolen a cup of red gold from the Round Table, but in doing so has accidentally spilled wine upon the queen. The theft of the cup was intended to bring attention to his claim to land that had been withheld from him, and he asks Parzival to carry that message to the king who is holding court in Nantes.

This the youth does, and at court the knights mockingly suggest that the young simpleton meet the Red Knight in combat. Arthur reluctantly agrees to this ploy. The maiden Kunneware, who has taken a solemn oath not to laugh until the best knight would arrive, begins to laugh out loud. This also triggers the voice of the dwarf, Antanor, who has sworn not to speak until Kunneware had laughed. He then prophesies that Kai, who has just struck Kunneware in his jealous wrath, will suffer much sorrow. By then Kai, short tempered at the best of times, is beside himself and strikes the dwarf as well.

Parzival rides out and kills the Red Knight, returns the goblet to the queen, and then rides off in his newly acquired armor in much the same style as in Chrétien's account. From now on it is he who will be known as the Red Knight. What he doesn't know, however, is that he has just killed his own uncle, Ither von Gahevis. This unthinking act creates much sorrow within the court and Parzival will feel it reverberating throughout the entire length of his quest.

So the young hero has now seen death, a loyalty and love that reaches beyond the grave. He has managed to overcome the knight dressed in armor the color of love. His next lesson in life is to learn the rules of social behavior.

Knight *by G. F. Watts, 1875.*

THE EDUCATION OF THE FOOL

ARZIVAL RIDES OFF proud in his new armor, and by the evening he comes to the castle of Gurnemanz de Graharz. It will be noticed that in many of the other versions of the epic the various characters who entered the plot were often unnamed. They were introduced as a function within the narrative. Thus in *Peredur,* or *Perlesvaus,* such a man was an old *vavasour* or an uncle. Wolfram paints these people in the round, and like a novelist develops his characterizations far beyond their mythic roles. Each person is carefully named, and with extraordinary ingenuity is slotted into the interweaving family trees.

Gurnemanz knows the original Red Knight, and so is surprised when the young fool takes off his helm. When he disarms he is still in his bumpkin's clothes beneath the red veneer of knighthood. It is Gurnemanz's role to become his teacher in all things pertaining to chivalry and the conduct of a proper knight. The old warrior immediately recognizes he has an exceptional fighter to teach, even if the first impression was one of a fool. Gurnemanz stops Parzival from always quoting his mother, for now he must enter a man's world, with new manly ideals. By discarding the childish fool's garb Parzival is made to create distance from his mother's influence and become more independent. This is preparing him for the external life and behavior of society. Gurnemanz does not ask the name of his guest, only calling him the Red Knight.

This old *vavasour* teaches the young hero the honor system of the art of knighthood. One particular rule which must be observed is that a knight does not ask unnecessary questions. Around this seemingly innocent and reasonable instruction is woven the whole fabric of Wolfram's message. Because, in trying to live by someone else's rules, howsoever petty or insignificant they may appear, then everyone begins to lead inauthentic lives.

Parzival wants to fit into society but as we shall see, he is ultimately an outsider. At first he stands outside the society on account of his innocent simplemindedness. Later he is to remain outside of the Fellowship of the Round Table because his destiny demands higher values than just those of chivalry. The moment anyone seeks truth then he or she is no longer part of the crowd.

It is significant that Gurnemanz should instruct him in religion and ethics before he is initiated into the art of arms or introduced to courtly love. This is an idyllic and homely period in the narrative as Gurnemanz offers his beautiful daughter, Liaze, in marriage, but Parzival, although he experiences an adolescent crush, nonetheless refuses her hand on the excuse that he is too untried and untested to marry yet. The old host, who has already lost his own three sons, *"now has cast the dice of sorrow one more time."*

As Parzival rides away his thoughts are bittersweet. He thinks of the beautiful Liaze, the daughter who was so rich in blessings and who had offered him honor as companions do. But something had warned him that it was not really love.

In such a mood he allows the horse a free rein. By this Wolfram is showing that the horse represents the natural flow of existence while the rider signifies a ratio-

nal control. This is Nature which knows neither good nor evil. Any Christian rider would attempt to control nature, only permitting what was deemed to be good. But Parzival is in no mood to control and allows the animal to go where it will. This is the Man of Tao who follows the Watercourse Way, trusting in the flow of things. The poet's message is that existence cannot be good or bad because it is one seamless whole and not two separate principles, and that the best outcomes arise when one lets go and allows nature to take its course.

Presentation of Prizes *Treatise of Rene d'Anjou 15th c. French.*

THE GUIDE OF LOVE

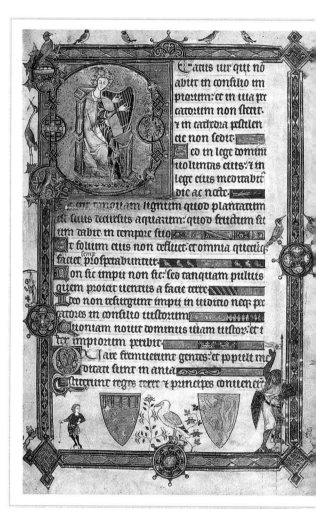

The Alphonso Psalter *c.1284. This elaborate Psalter showing David playing his harp was created for the marriage of an eleven year old son of Edward I of England. Arranged marriages were the norm in Medieval Europe and hardly included love within their contracts. The impact of the Arabian and Sufi love poems upon the courts was a shock and yet the concept of real love remained, except for unusual men like Wolfram, just a poetry.*

BY THE EVENING, after covering an unbelievable distance riding straight across the highest mountains, Parzival comes to the well defended city of Pelrapeire (Belrepaire in Chrétien's account). Like the versions we have already examined he finds the city besieged and the inhabitants starving. But when he meets Condwiramurs, *"a bright light shone forth from the queen as she welcomed him. God had not forgotten a single wish in her, as the rose prompted by the dew shows a new bright radiance from its small bud, a radiance both white and red. That caused her guest great hardship."* Both young man and woman are smitten by what they see in each other. They eat frugally as the town uses up its last foods, and yet Parzival is given a rich bed on which to sleep. In the middle of the night he is woken by the little queen, dressed to kill in a white shift of silk. But even though she has a name of *Conduire Amour*, a channel of love, she is apparently as ingenuous about the courtly rites of love as the young knight himself. He promises not to wrestle with her so she nestles into his bed and tells him her plight.

It transpires that her city is under attack from a suitor she is unwilling to marry. Clamide, the unwelcome suitor, has killed one of Gurnemanz's sons who had once been her betrothed. Condwiramurs swears she is ready to throw herself off her own battlements before she will succumb to Clamide and his desire.

Parzival vows he will fight for her, and the innocent couple go to sleep in one another's arms. The next day he fights Clamide's great champion, the seneschal, Kingrune, and defeats him soundly. He remembers Gurnemanz's advice to be generous to one's enemies

Lover at the Gate of Paradise, *14th century Persia. The passionate, heroic love poetry of the infidel Persia was enthusiastically embraced by Christians who had little to get romantic about under the damning eyes of the Church. The desires of the flesh had no place in such a repressive religion and the suppressed sexuality of the celibate priests and monks hardly made for sympathetic confessors.*

and offers mercy on condition that the seneschal go to the court of Arthur and surrender to Kunneware, the maiden who had been abused so badly by Kai.

Meanwhile two ships land with provisions for the besieged town and the starving inhabitants take heart once more. The tide of battle is turning.

On the second night the two virgin youngsters once again lie in bed together and yet the queen remains a maiden. Wolfram adds, wryly, that the hero lay with such a modesty that would not satisfy many women of his day. However, little Condwiramurs seems satisfied and covers her hair, which signifies to the world that they are married. It is only on the third night that Parzival finally follows his mother's advice of embracing a woman and they *"entwined legs and arms in a way which pleased them both"* and which they then realize they should have been doing all the time. The marriage is truly consummated. But this was not courtly love, nor was it a marriage, which in those times was usually an arranged and loveless affair. This was a marriage of love between two individuals, and in the thirteenth century that was something entirely and radically new. *"And each found their life in the other, and each was the other's love."*

The narrative follows Chrétien's account as the hero defeats the unwanted suitor and sends him off to Arthur and Kunneware. The land is now at peace and the two young lovers rule contentedly. However, one morning Parzival tells his wife that he needs to see how his mother is faring, and Condwiramurs reluctantly gives her permission for him to go. So off he goes in search of his mother and finds the Grail instead.

THE GRAIL CASTLE

NCE AGAIN PARZIVAL lets the horse carry the bridle on its own accord with no restraining control by the rider. We are told that the legend of the Grail Castle is strange, in that anyone actually looking for it will never discover its whereabouts. This brings us to a fundamental principle within this poem and one of the poet's greatest insights. Eastern mystics can never seem to understand Christ's saying, *"Seek and ye shall find."* They insist that this is not the way to enlightenment, to the Ultimate State. And we must make no mistake about it, for Wolfram is moving his hero towards an Ultimate State. Mystics say the gold brick falls when least expected. When there is effort nothing happens. Buddha made every effort for six years in his quest for the Ultimate Goal. But it was only when he finally gave up all effort that he attained that which he had been seeking. The mystical law is subtle, for although enlightenment cannot be forced by effort the seeker still has to make an effort in order to prepare him or herself to be able to receive the gift.

At the time when Wolfram was writing there was a great debate going on over whether one's actions were destined by God, so only required one's abject obedience, or if one had to make some personal effort to gain the inner sanctum. In Christian terms we are talking of Grace. Parzival, in letting go the reins of his horse, is surrendering to the grace of existence. But, as we shall see, he will have to earn the gift.

They reach the land of Brobarz that evening, coming to a sea or a huge lake. Fishermen are anchored near the shore and Parzival calls to one whose hat is adorned with peacock feathers, yet whose face is sad. He asks where he might find lodging for the night. The fisherman tells him there is only one house within a radius

of thirty miles but he is welcome to stay there and the fisherman himself will be his host. He gives Parzival directions but warns against taking a false path. Thanking the man gratefully, Parzival eventually finds the castle. He is welcomed and when he has washed the rust off his body he is lent a purple and gold robe of reverence by the queen of the castle, Respanse de Schoye.

Parzival is taken to a magnificent hall where the fisherman he met earlier awaits him, revealing himself to be lord of the domain. His host sits by the middle fireplace on a couch. But he is a sorry figure, as if "he has been cut off from joy and lives only for dying." We will learn later that this is the Grail King whose realm is now the Wasteland. He is both symbolic of its devastation while at the same time he is the prime cause of it. For while he was born of a line of Grail Guardians he lacked the resolve needed for such a spiritual responsibility. He had fallen in love with the beautiful Orgeluse who was outside the Grail line. He had ridden from the castle with the cry "Amors" on his lips and promptly met a pagan knight from the Holy Lands, significantly from the Holy Sepulcher itself. They fought and the pagan knight was killed but in the battle the king had been wounded between the thighs by the poisonous tip of a lance which had broken off. When it was withdrawn from the wound an inscription could be seen on the blade with the single word, Grail. Although we learn of all this later, what is symbolized is the loss of natural grace. The ideals of the Christian Church of a heavenly 'supernature' had overwhelmed all natural responses. The priests determined what was black and what was white. Nature had been castrated by the laws of a heaven not of this earth. Nature was dead, in consequence Europe was impotent, and the Fisher King,

significantly, was wounded between the thighs. A split had appeared between the body and the spirit. In nature there is no distinction between the soul, the mind or the body; it is one seamless whole. But the religious beliefs of the time had severed any connection between the parts. Europe had entered a schizophrenic state in which the good was believed to arise only from the higher supernature of the spirit, while the bad arose from the material baseness of the body. Strangely this was a distorted extreme of earlier Gnostic beliefs which the Church had seemingly stamped out. Supernature was seen as inherently good but nature, by definition, had to be evil.

Thus we see in the Christian versions of the Grail myth why there is such a fanatical and obsessive insistence upon chastity, virginity and sexual restraint and why there is such criticism of Eve and her kind as being the cause of a man's spiritual downfall. For, of course, sexually potent women drew their power from Nature and were thus deeply threatening to the ecclesiastic body and mind.

Wolfram's great transforming contribution to the legend was to show that the spiritual is inherent in nature. When human laws are used to control or repress nature the consequence of such action is the Wasteland. If one rejects nature, by definition the spirit is rejected as well, for the two cannot be rendered apart any more than one can separate light and darkness. Darkness is the absence of light and light is the absence of darkness. Thus the Wasteland can only be healed by a spontaneous gesture, an intuitive and natural act of compassion. The enchantment of nature is simply the superimposition of the belief in supernatural laws upon the natural order. And that specific enchantment can only be lifted by reestablishing the laws of nature. One compassionate question would be enough, but as we shall discover, Parzival has a long way to go before he can throw off the recently acquired code of social behavior he has learned from Gurnemanz.

Rudolf Steiner, the mystical philosopher so influential in the earlier part of this century, maintained that Gurnemanz was in reality Mephistopheles in disguise, who craftily misguided the emerging natural spirit into entering a prison of what appeared to be reasonable beliefs and ideas of conduct. But in fact what these ideas did was to shackle the human being's ability to be spontaneous.

This point within the narrative is one of the pivotal episodes, although the reader is not actually given all this background until the hero meets Trevrizent, the hermit, when everything begins to fall into place. However, we are privy to the secrets a little earlier.

Above: *Detail from a fresco by Simone Martini, 15th century Italy.*

THE ETERNAL RETURN AND THE INFINITY HORIZON

OISED AS WE ARE, just before the Grail is about to enter the castle hall, it might be helpful to look back at the other two branches of the legend which have been loosely named the Celtic and the Christian. To invoke the Trinity once more, we find that the first, the Celtic branch, corresponds to the Age of Ritual and Magic. It is a cyclic world of renewal and of changes of season. The second is the Christian religious ideal which presupposes a linear and historic line from the Creation to the Last Day of Judgment. In the Grail corpus there is an uneasy mixing of these two essentially incompatible concepts. What Wolfram intuitively does as a poet is to reach beyond them both.

At the time Wolfram was writing, the Middle Ages were dominated by the belief that the history of the world was governed by the influence of cycles, periodicities and the motion of the stars. The forces that produced such effects were thought to be immanent in the cosmos, irrespective of God's will.

The trouble was that in almost the same breath the medieval thinker, especially the scholar-priest, was becoming increasingly eschatological in his conceptions of the line between those two essential moments in existence: the birth and the death of the universe, the supreme moments of Creation and the Last Trump.

The Calabrian abbot, Joachim of Floris, who proved so inspirational to such revolutionary spirits as St. Francis of Assisi and Dante, was the first to divide the history of the world into three great epochs, successively dominated by one aspect of the Holy Trinity – the Age of the Father, the Age of the Son, and the Age of the Holy Spirit. Each Age, then, revealed a new and higher aspect of the Ultimate Divinity.

The Grail epic rocks uneasily between these newly minted ideas and those of the older and more pagan scenarios. So on the one hand we see within the texts the glimmerings of our present-day preoccupation with a continuous sense of historical and linear time, while on the other we find a complete disregard for factual history and a perception of all occurrences as being either cyclic or mythical events.

Within the framework of linear time, the progress of events stretches from a Beginning to an End. On this finite length of historical string, each knot or event is a novelty in itself and no event can be exactly repeated. The belief is that we progress from age to age and gradually evolve from the simple to the complex, from innocence to wisdom. But in this scheme of things the hero is also utterly alone, cut off from any of the deeper cyclic realms of renewal and rebirth. He is surrounded by a universe in which everything is uncharted and unknown, and where the only freedom to make history is by making himself.

In the pagan tradition nature is seen to repeat herself. A hero is not stuck with having to constantly create his own history by swimming upstream through time. The archaic man simply acknowledges no act which has not been previously lived by someone else. For primitive man, reality is a function of the imitation of a previous celestial or divine archetype. Heroes are free to annul their own personal histories and enter a timeless zone in which they actually *become* those great heroic archetypes.

It was through periodically entering a ritual and mythic state, in which time was abolished, that archaic societies were granted freedom to collectively regenerate and begin anew each year. Every time the hero would reembark upon a new life, he would transcend time and live within eternity. Each year he would fail to maintain such a peak of transcendental experience, and would fall back into historical existence. Then, as the next year unfolded, he would wipe out the fall and make another attempt to escape from time.

So, central to the Grail legend in both the pagan and Christian vision is that renewal must be preceded by a ceremonial cleansing, a purging rather than just a purification. It must be a radical departure from what was past. The old world dies in order for the new world to be born. As the new cycle comes into being it is enacted by new characters in new situations. But the underlying principles remain: *"The King is dead, long live the King."*

But Wolfram is offering something quite different. In part he appears to see Parzival as an historical man, a hero in linear time who is alone and often in despair at facing the unknown future. The historical man cannot fall back upon any destiny within the cyclic hero mold, but must learn that only he is responsible for his acts. He has to discover this as he travels on his quest, and he can only walk a path that has never been traveled before. Historical space and time is like the track made by a bird in the sky. Parzival is the first existential European hero, who has to do it his own way. Yet in this powerful legend the linear-hero has to act within a cyclic and mythical arena. So he is both the mythic and the historic man, two profoundly contradictory and incompatible systems trapped together within one heroic body.

When Parzival finally trusts his own inner nature and acts spontaneously, he will be able to burst out of this schizophrenic state and stand on the threshold between the transitory world of time and the eternal world of the timeless. But before he manages to do that he will have to fail completely.

THE GRAIL TEMPLE

S PARZIVAL ENTERS THE GREAT HALL of the Grail Castle he sees a hundred candelabra suspended above the 400 members of the household. There are also candles set within the walls. There are hundred couches seating four to each, and three square fireplaces built of marble and piled with the wood of lignum aloe. The lord of the castle has been laid on a folding bed near the central fireplace. He welcomes the young knight as one of the family (for so he is). The procession of events which follows differs little from the accounts we have already examined, but it is given here in full.

First to appear is *"a squire who rushed in through the door, holding a lance — it was a custom which ever wakened grief. From the point blood flowed, ran down the shaft to the hand, and trickled into the sleeve. Weeping and shrieking arose throughout the wide hall. The people of thirty lands could not shed more tears. The squire bore the lance in his hands around the four walls, and back to the door, and then sprang out."* This appears to calm the gathering. Then, at the end of the hall a steel door is opened and two highborn blonde maidens appear, each carrying a candlestick. Next come a duchess and a companion, bearing ivory trestles. All four bow and set the trestles before the host. All four are dressed in gowns of brown. Eight more ladies enter, four carrying large candles and the other four carrying a wafer-thin slab of transparent red jacinth, known as garnet-hyacinth, which is then laid upon the trestles. These eight are dressed in green samite and join the other four. Two highborn maidens then enter, each carrying a silver knife upon a napkin. They are preceded by four pure maidens who carry the lights. Six more join them also, wearing costly parti-colored robes and bearing six vials of glass with burning balsam. This

makes 24 maidens in all.

After them comes the queen, her face shining as if the sun is rising. She bears an object *"resting on a cloth of green achmardi, the perfection of Earthly Paradise, both roots and branches. It was a Thing men called the Grail which surpassed every earthly ideal. Repanse de Joie was the name of her to whom the Grail granted the office of bearer, for it was of such nature that only she who guarded her chastity and shunned deceit had the right to tend it."* She stands with 12 of the procession on each side, as chamberlains bring water in golden bowls for all the assembled knights to wash their hands, serving them with white towels. A hundred tables are arranged, one to every four. *"And the Grail fed everyone their delight, whether it be fruit or fowl, hot or cold. For the Grail was the fruition of joy, such abundance of earthly sweetness that it nearly equalled what we are told of heaven. Parzival wondered greatly, and would have asked about both the host's infirmity and the Grail but for what Gurnemanz had advised regarding asking too many questions."*

A squire approaches, carrying a sword. The host gives it to Parzival saying that before God had smitten his body he had used it in many lands. When the young knight grasped the weapon it should have prompted him to ask his questions, but he failed for fear of offending.

The procession then returns from whence it had come but as they pass through the door Parzival glimpses the fairest old man he has ever seen, whose hair is "grayer than the mists." Parzival takes leave of his host and retires to bed. Even here he is attended by four maidens who serve him fruit and wine. But he sleeps badly with "sweat streaming from every limb and bone." This corresponds to his dark night of the soul. This is a death experience within the Otherworld but, as yet, the young hero is not ready for it.

Montségur, *French Pyrenees. The remains of what was once the last stronghold of the Cathar heretics in Southern France. Traditionally this has been the Grail Castle of legend, partly through the mystery of an escape from the besieged citadel by four Cathar knights who supposedly carried with them the greatest Cathar treasure — the Holy Grail.*

MONTSALVASCH

HE GRAIL CASTLE WE HAVE JUST SEEN signifies the Mount, the sacred mountain where heaven and earth meet. All temples share that quality of being the Axis Mundi. The center of the world has, at various times, been claimed to be Mount Meru of India, Mount Sumeru of the Urals, upon whose summit is the pole star, Mount Zinnalo of the Buddhists, Mount Tabor in Palestine, and Mount Golgotha, where Adam had been created and buried and where the blood of the crucified Christ falls upon Adam's skull and redeems him. Each of these mountains is the meeting point of Heaven, Earth, and Hell beneath. This center is a *zone of sacred and absolute reality*. The road leading to any Sacred Mount, Fountain of Youth, Tree of Life, or Enchanted Castle, is a difficult one. The difficulties on a peril-ridden, arduous road are those of the seeker on the path to Self, to the sacred center of his or her being. It is understood as a rite of passage from the profane to the sacred, from the ephemeral and illusory to the reality of eternity, from death to life, from humanity to divinity.

This can be especially seen in the Christianized legend of the Grail that does not arise from the Celtic background alone but comes from a sacred yet pagan tradition of the Moors. In this particular version the blood-filled vessel signifies the womb which offers rebirth and reincarnation. *"Repanse de Joie,"* far from being the chaste virgin as in Parzival, was the ancient (and honorable) title of a Holy Whore. The Grail knights were of the Eastern order of the Knights Templar originally formed by her son, John, while the Grail temple was traditionally located at Montsalvasch in the Spanish Pyrenees. The temple was a seen as a microcosm of the universe topped by a huge ruby,

representing the maternal heart of the world and called the Holy Rose. This whole imagery was absorbed, or more likely created, by the Rosicrucians. The temple itself is described as, *"one hundred fathoms in diameter. Around it were seventy-two chapels of an octagonal shape. To every pair of chapels there was a tower six stories high, approachable by a winding stair on the outside."* We are then told of the opulent richness, of a vaulting of blue sapphire, a plate of emerald and *"the altar made also of sapphire."* Upon the inside of the cupola surmounting the temple, the sun and moon were represented in diamonds and topaz shedding a light as if it was day in the darkness of night. *"The windows were of crystal and beryl and the floor was of translucent crystal under which all the fishes of the sea were carved out of onyx as if alive. The towers were of precious stones inlaid with gold; their roofs of gold and blue enamel. Upon every tower was a crystal cross and upon it an eagle with outstretched wings which appeared to be flying. At the summit of the main tower was an immense carbuncle, which served, like a star, to guide the Templars at night. In the center of the building under the great dome, was a miniature representation of the whole and in this the holy vessel was kept."*

In this account, the Knights Templar were named as the Grail guardians who awaited the *Mahdi*, the desired knight, to reestablish paradise on earth, halting the spreading desert wasteland brought about by the loss of the Goddess. So once again we encounter the female aura permeating the deepest strata of the myth, radiant, yet partially hidden within the work. This time its origins lie in the hot and dry deserts of the mystical East rather than the rainswept lands of the Celtic North. This thirst for an essentially female principle within myth and romance became more exaggerated and urgent the more the Church, with its particular male hang-up about

potent women, tried to repress her. The effect of this could be witnessed in the popularity of the cult of the Virgin Mary which was relentlessly repressed by the Church Fathers. It was small wonder that in the Middle Ages people often viewed God as their persecutor and Mary as their defender.

The contact with the East during the crusades was not only limited to a cultural traffic between Christian and Saracen. It was Europe's first real encounter with the Oriental extravagance of the Eastern Christian Church which even actively encouraged the worship of a Trinity composed of Father, Mother and Holy Son

rather than the all-male club of Rome. Such imagery had a revolutionary appeal to a peoples longing for the worship of a Mother Goddess in the wasteland of an all-male hierarchy.

Crusader Castle, *Syria. Wolfram is supposed to have visited the Templars in the Outremer, or Holy lands, and obviously imbibed some of their very unorthodox ideas. For while the huge castles were built to withstand the Saracens, the rich and extravagant ideas of the East did manage to scale these massive walls and many of the Crusader knights returned to Europe with decidedly heretical views. Montsalvasch could well have been modeled on some of the exotic Christian outposts which were hothouses of heresy.*

THE TURNING POINT

HE NEXT MORNING PARZIVAL AWAKENS to find the castle empty. He manages to arm himself and takes the sword he received from his host the night before and leaves. As he crosses the drawbridge it is suddenly raised, making his horse leap the last few feet. He hears a voice calling from the battlements "*You Goose!*" but he cannot see the speaker.

He rides off hoping to find the company hunting but instead comes across his inconsolable cousin, Sigune, who is now clasping the embalmed body of her lover. But Parzival fails to recognize Sigune, as she is so deathly pale.

Sigune then tells Parzival of the Grail King, Amfortas, and his brother, Trevrizent, who has become a hermit in order to balance the deeds of Amfortas. She says, in recognizing the sword of Trebuchet which hangs at his belt, that Parzival, in effect, wields two blades. He is both the Knight of the Sword and a Knight of the Word, which is broken if he does not know how to constantly renew its inspirational powers. He has lost the spontaneous, intuitive and compassionate word which brings spiritual clarity.

From this point we see the whole of Parzival's life going backwards, as he has to make good all his irresponsible or unconscious behavior. He has to see each episode and encounter he has lived through, in the light of his newfound understanding.

So the first person he meets is, by coincidence, the daughter of the King of Lac, the place where the sword he now wears was forged. This is Jeshute, the woman of the pavilion and Parzival's first, unfortunate encounter with the world outside of his home. She is by now a sad spectacle, having been cast off by her husband and riding a miserable nag. He offers her the purple mantle which he had received from the Grail bearer but she refuses

for fear of her husband, who at that moment sees Parzival. And here we come to the relentless interweaving persistence of karmic destiny. For Orilis, the husband, wields the very spear which belonged to Ither, the Red Knight Parzival had slain. And just as Parzival had killed Ither, now that man's spear is turned against him. The very helmet Orilis wears is forged by Trebuchet, whose sword is now held by Parzival. So we see that Parzival has to literally fight against the weapons created from his past errors. Even the dread armor of Orilis is covered with dragons and, as the poet tells us, "*And Parzival won him honor, for here hath he rightly shown. How before a hundred dragons*, one man *might well hold his own.*" Orilis is eventually defeated and Parzival makes good the havoc he has inadvertently caused by reconciling him with Jeshute and sending them to Arthur to bring greetings to Kunneware. Neither had any suspicion that Kunneware is the sister of Orilis, so the outcome is a greater joy than ever foreseen.

In order to swear Jeshute's innocence Parzival enters Trevrizent's cell at a hermitage. A colored spear leans against the hermit's altar. This spear Wolfram compares to the planet Saturn in its multicolored rays, which in terms of the stars will unite Parzival. He absentmindedly takes the spear of forgetfulness with him.

Orilis and Jeshute journey to Arthur's court where Orilis finds his sister, Kunneware, guarding a fountain, which reveals her unexpectedly as a Maiden of the Wells. On the fountain there is the likeness of a serpent with its fangs around an apple. A dragon hovers above it and Orilis, who carries the same device upon his shield, thus recognizes his sister. To round off the sequence we find that the fountain is the selfsame one which will weld the Grail sword that Parzival has been given, and the maiden he has honored is the fountain's keeper.

Knight Errant *by J. Everett Millais, 1870.*

THE FALCON

ALTHOUGH IT IS MAY there has been a freak snowfall. The night before, a falcon has been lost by Arthur's hunters. He and Parzival have spent the night together and suffer the cold of the morning. The falcon pursues a flock of geese and manages to wound one but it escapes. Three drops of blood fall upon the snow. We have already seen the symbolism inherent within both the Celtic and Christian accounts, but Parzival adds a new dimension. Often what happens to Parzival's inner being is reflected in some outer occurrence. If we remember, the squire who raised the drawbridge at the Grail castle called out, *"You Goose"*... Now Parzival sees a goose wounded, just as he is wounded because he has not fulfilled his potential. He searches within himself for the one spontaneous gesture which might reveal his true nature after acting for so long according to someone else's beliefs. With Condwiramurs he had found a natural and spontaneous love, for with her he had been true to his deepest feelings. He is entranced by the sight of the three drops of red on the white snow. *"Then her sweet face arose before him in that night she first sought his side, when on each cheek a tear-drop glistened*

and a third to her chin did glide."

Arthur has camped his retinue nearby but because he believes the Grail Castle to be close by, he forbids any battle in case it might be with one of the Guardians of the Vessel. A squire sees Parzival sitting on his horse with a multicolored spear raised and thinks this is a knight ready for challenge. He rouses Segramours who wakes Arthur and his Queen to ask permission to fight this unknown knight. The king is reluctant but the queen urges him to grant the request. So Segramours rides out, and challenges Parzival. He charges and spins the knight around so the blood on the snow is no longer visible. Parzival unhorses Segramours and returns to the drops of blood and, promptly becomes transfixed again.

Now Kai asks to be able to fight the unknown rider. He rides out and is thrown from his horse, breaking his right arm and his left leg. This tumble has much the same characteristics as Segramours' before him. Parzival's gaze falls upon the blood drops, and once more falls into a deep trance.

Lastly Gawain rides out to meet this superlative knight. But this *"Falcon of May"* is not known as the Lady's Knight for nothing. He recognizes the symptoms of a love trance and he thinks to himself, *"It may be Frau Minne (love) dealeth so with this goodly man, as she dealt with me of old time, so claspeth him in the band of her magic spells fair woven, that his spirit within the snare, she holdeth fast entangled."* He does not challenge or fight but throws a

cloak of Syrian silk over the blood. Instantly the spell is broken. Gawain explains what has happened and that Parzival has jousted and bested both Segramours and Kai, and is now avenged over Kunneware. They both ride back as if brothers or twins.

At this point, as the two champions are feasting with Arthur's court, Parzival is close to being lost in the affairs of an earthly knight of the Round Table. But higher destinies are required of both Parzival and Gawain, and the agency by which they both move on takes a strange and loathy form.

Falcons *Details from illustrations by Audobon, 1838.*

HOLY GRAIL

PARTING OF THE WAYS

ARZIVAL IS BEING FETED AT THE COURT and the feast is well under way when a dog-nosed and be-tusked woman arrives on a mule and interrupts the proceedings. This hideous hag curses Parzival as a traitor much in the same fashion as the other versions we have examined. We already know that she is the goad to the hero to abandon the courtly life and follow his destiny. In this case, before the arrival of Kunrie the sorceress, messenger of the grail, Parzival was dangerously close to being welcomed into the chivalrous life. But the nature and venom of her curses now preclude this. She then offers adventure to the rest of the astounded knights at the Castle of Marvels, where four queens and 400 ladies are held.

As Kunrie leaves, having shamed Parzival, another rider appears who now challenges Gawain, accusing him of the shameful killing of his lord. This is the knight Kingrimursel. It appears that the accusation is without foundation but Gawain agrees to the combat in order to clear his name. They agree that in 40 days both will appear at the city of Schanpfanzun to decide his innocence or guilt.

Now both our twin heroes are cursed, for both represent the two sides of human nature, one striving after the spiritual Grail while the other follows love. One finds the Grail Castle while the other the Castle of Marvels. And yet Parzival has at least expiated some of his earlier mistakes in full. Orilis and Jeshute are reunited and the duke has found his sister. Clamide, who sought the hand of Condwiramurs, now finds Kunneware even more attractive, which releases Parzival from being her protector. Parzival also learns that he has a half-brother called Feirefiz from the heathen, Eckuba.

As Gawain takes his leave of Parzival he says, *"God guide thee on thy way."* Parzival cries out *"Alas. What is God?"* The narrative has now come full circle to his cry of *"Alas, Mother, What is God?"* on killing a bird and recognizing for the first time the consequences of his action. But now the cry is because he has seen the effect of taking responsibility. He has rectified his earlier mistakes and yet there is no reward but instead a curse and the sense that he has failed. *"I served him from the day I first knew of his grace. Henceforth I renounce his service; if he hates me then I'll face that hate."*

Parzival is to go though three stages on his quest. The first was innocence, an unquestioning acceptance of what others tell him and an unconsciousness in his actions. The second stage, which he enters at this point, is doubt. He rebels against all he has been told. This is the adolescent age of his development just as the earlier unawareness was his childhood. The third and mature stage has yet to come.

But he does add something to what he says to Gawain.

> *"And friend in thine hour of peril*
> *As thy shield may a wife's love stand*
> *Wouldst thou know her for pure and holy*
> *The thought of her guide your hand,*
> *And her love from all evil guard thee."*

So here we see Parzival instinctively trusts far more in a woman's love, which is natural and real, than a God who is supernatural and unreal.

Opposite: **The Accolade,** *by E.B. Leighton. 19th C. England.*

QUEEN ON A CHESSBOARD

Treatise on Chess.
*Illustration from a book by
Alfonso the Wise c. 1283.
Chess reached the Middle East
from India shortly before Islam.
The game appears to have been
widespread throughout Europe*

*by the 11th century. The courts
of Northern Spain, where the
ladies played chess and music,
were the main route of
transmission of the Arab culture
to Southern Europe.* **Opposite:**
Phoenix, *12th c. England.*

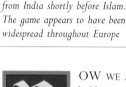OW WE ARE TO FOLLOW Parzival's other
half, Gawain. His adventures are in many
ways parallel to those of his twin, while
at the same time he is to meet Parzival
in a number of guises. This whole
sequence resembles a hall of mirrors where both knights
suddenly come face to face with their own reflections,
or the reflection of the other.

The first encounter in the mirror is when Gawain
fights against the army of Meljakanz, which has besieged
the castle of a king with two daughters. Meljakanz wants
to take the elder daughter by force and Gawain fights
on behalf of the king, wearing the colors of the younger
daughter. In the ensuing battle Gawain and Parzival find
themselves on opposite sides of the mirror, but Gawain
recognizes the Red Knight in time. Through their intercession the affair is resolved.

The next adventure occurs when Gawain arrives
unrecognized at Schanpfanzun where he is to face
Kingrimursel in combat. He is offered lodging by the
king, who tells him to seek out his sister who will look
after him. This Gawain does with some enthusiasm

which is also shared by the lady. However an old knight
passes and sees them together and, recognizing Gawain,
he denounces the knight as the killer of his lord. The
couple have to defend themselves with a chessboard and
its stone pieces against the enraged citizenry until
Kingrimursel himself comes to their rescue, as he had
given his pledge of safe passage for Gawain. The brawl
is resolved and Gawain agrees to seek the Grail, a task
which had been imposed upon the king, and wait a year
before the combat with Kingrimursel.

We rejoin Parzival who, by this time, has been
adventuring for many years. It is Good Friday but he
is unaware of the date. Some penitents are shocked to
see him armed on such a holy day. When he realizes
this he makes his way to the hermitage where
Trevrizent lives. It is at this moment we learn of Kyot
and Flegitanus, and of the fact that the Grail has been
left on earth by the neutral angels. And it is here that
we learn what Wolfram sees as the true nature of the
Grail. The hermit tells Parzival that many Templeisen
abide with the Grail in Montsalvesche. They live by
virtue of a stone called *lapis exilis*. By the power of the

stone the phoenix is burned to ashes, but the ashes restore it to life more beautiful than before. The stone nourishes, restores and promotes youth. On Good Friday a dove descends from heaven bringing a wafer which it places on the stone, and this brings to the stone the power to provide whatever good things grow upon earth, of food or drink. This sustains the knightly brotherhood. The neutral angels were the original custodians of the stone, which then passed into the hands of the knights whose names appear briefly on the stone's rim and then disappear.

Wolfram's fascination with the wonders of the Orient would have certainly extended to the popular legend of Alexander the Great and the Earthly Paradise. In that tale, the stone sent to the leader from the gates of the earthly paradise *"restores youth to the old."* It was brilliant, rare in hue and like a human eye. It would weigh far more than any quantity of gold on a scale and yet, if covered with a little

dust it couldn't outweigh a feather. This symbolized the insatiable human lust for riches. When the eye is closed with dust that lust vanishes. The message within the *lapis exilis* was not lost upon Alexander, and it is said that from that moment he abandoned his ideas of world conquest.

Another explanation is that *"lapis exilis"* derives from *"lapis exilii"* which means The Stone of Death. The poet describes how the phoenix alights on this stone, is burned to ashes and then arises reborn and renewed, suggesting the alchemical transformation and rebirth from what many see as the philosophers' stone. Alexander was reported to have seen a phoenix in the Far East, and much of Wolfram's imagery arises from the contacts with the Orient through the Crusades. Even the Grail Castle itself fits more within the settings of the Near Eastern strongholds of the Knights Templar than any counterpart in Northwestern Europe.

The Grail Guardians

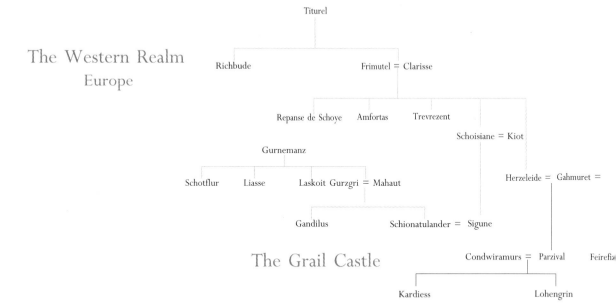

The Western Realm
Europe

Titurel

Richbude — Frimutel = Clarisse

Repanse de Schoye — Amfortas — Trevrezent

Schoisiane = Kiot

Gurnemanz

Schotflur — Liasse — Laskoit Gurzgri = Mahaut

Herzeleide = Gahmuret =

Gandilus — Schionatulander = Sigune

The Grail Castle

Condwiramurs = Parzival — Feirefiz

Kardiess — Lohengrin

THE TWO FAMILIES

ANY COMMENTATORS HAVE ARGUED that Parzival carries a hidden and secret astrological and alchemical description of how an individual is transformed from the gross body to ever lighter and higher forms. Certainly at the core of the poem there is an alchemical spirituality, unique to its times. The hermit Trevrizent appears himself to be more an alchemist than a priest. For one thing he is only a layman and not a priest or monk at all. In fact he is in no way connected to the Church. This hermit is the brother of the Grail King; an individual who was once a royal knight who had immersed himself in the ways of the world, but renounced that way of life and now approaches the divine by himself, with no priestly intervention and with only his own understanding.

Parzival becomes aware as Trevrizent speaks, of the forces of renewal and of the true position of a human

being within nature in the framework of time. The great festival of the year is Easter, which celebrates both a Christian and pagan renewal of the year through the death of the Savior-King. Through this event the realm will be blessed with a new springtime. Parzival must learn how the sun the moon and the stars are involved in the vegetative and unfolding processes on earth. He must also learn that the Grail family carries the Grail, and all it represents, through cycle after cycle, season following season.

We now learn that Amfortas, the King of the Grail, chose a mistress who did not feed him on the Grail. This was Orgeluse, who we will meet shortly when we return to Gawain. One day Amfortas fought the heathen Ethnise, born in Paradise, whose lance penetrated the king's sex. The point was poisoned and the king could not be healed. But the Grail kept him alive, which was an exquisite torture to the poor man. Only one thing

The Sons of Cain

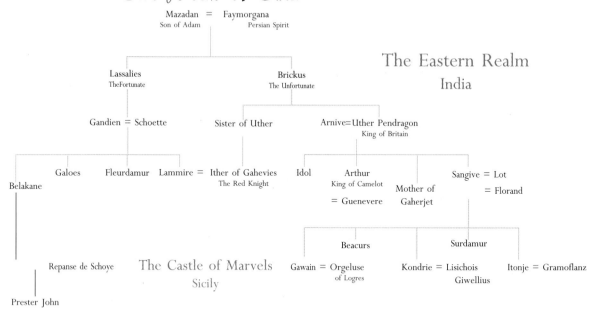

Mazadan = Faymorgana
Son of Adam — Persian Spirit

The Eastern Realm
India

Lassalies — TheFortunate

Brickus — The Unfortunate

Gandien = Schoette

Sister of Uther

Arnive = Uther Pendragon
King of Britain

Belakane

Galoes — Fleurdamur — Lammire = Ither of Gahevies — The Red Knight

Idol — Arthur — King of Camelot = Guenevere — Mother of Gaherjet — Sangive = Lot — = Florand

Beacurs — Surdamur

The Castle of Marvels
Sicily

Repanse de Schoye

Prester John

Gawain = Orgeluse of Logres — Kondrie = Lisichois Giwellius — Itonje = Gramoflanz

can bring about the healing, and that is a knight who will ask the question.

Parzival remains with Trevrizent for two weeks, in which time he learns that he has been wandering four and a half years since swearing Jeshute's innocence at the hermitage and taking the Spear of Troy.

Wolfram then returns to an almost Celtic theme, for the hermit tells him that Adam and Eve came into existence at the moment when Lucifer fell to Hell. So their inner being was intimately bound with Satan's rebellion. The sin of Cain, their son, was to rob Earth of her virginity by spilling his brother's blood. Cain sinned against the Earth and yet remained united with the Earth, and must eventually redeem the Earth. He tells of how the Sybils told of this, and that only through true and divine love could this come about. This is the only reference in Parzival which shows the older legend of the rape of the Goddess poking through. But it is significant.

Parzival admits that two things cause him grief. His greatest sorrow is that of the endless and fruitless search for the Grail Castle and his inability to heal the Fisher King. His other sorrow is his separation and longing for his wife, Condwiramurs.

Wolfram demonstrates a delightful lack of ecclesiastical pomp and ritual throughout the poem. Nowhere is this more in evidence than in the pivotal chapter on Trevrizent. This holy man is a self-imposed hermit attempting to create a balance for his brother's actions. He summarizes Parzival's shortcomings as the irresponsible killing of his kin, Ither (which parallels Cain's killing of Abel), the thoughtless causing of his mother's death, and his failure to ask the compassionate question. Parzival remains in spiritual communion with his uncle for two weeks until Trevrizent, only a layman, absolves him of his sins.

THE CASTLE OF MARVELS

E RETURN TO THE ADVENTURES of Gawain which almost faithfully follow Chrétien's version, so they are given here only in brief. Gawain meets Orgeluse of Logrois (Logres) who slowly teaches him that courtly love must be earned by persevering courtship and daring deeds. Finally, as the hero manages to put up with her provoking scorn and is found partly worthy of her love, she tells him that it was she who was the indirect cause of Amfortas' wound. She admits that Parzival had rejected her love because he was loyal to Condwiramurs and his Grail quest. This showed that she was repeating the pattern of attempting to seduce the future Grail King, but Parzival had avoided the error. She cannot bring disaster upon Gawain because his quest is not the Grail, but love. Gawain gains the Castle of Marvels, which we discover is located in Sicily, survives the marvelous bed, kills the lion that attacks him, and meets the four queens as the enchantments are ended.

Parallel and corresponding to the Grail within the Castle of the Fisher King, Gawain finds in the center of this magical domain a wondrous pillar. The pillar, we are told, sheds its light for six miles around so that everything within that distance can be seen from this point. It had once belonged to Gahmur's wife, Sekundille, until the magician Klingsor had stolen it.

But even when it seems Gawain has completed all his tasks and he is Lord of the Castle of Marvels, there is still some very important business left undone. He has to first defeat the Turkowit who is with Orgeluse. She then sets him a new task of jumping the perilous ford to pluck a bough from the Tree of Virtue which is guarded by the knight Gramoflanz. Gramoflanz had slain Orgeluse's first husband, wishing to marry her in his stead. She had refused, but by now he was in love with

Itonje, Gawain's sister in the castle. And if this plot wasn't convoluted enough for medieval taste, Gramoflanz had sworn vengeance upon Gawain because King Lot, Gawain's father, had killed his father. Gawain makes known his true identity to Gramoflanz, and they agree to combat in sixteen days.

Gawain leaps back with the garland and Orgeluse now completely changes her behavior towards him. She tells him of her first husband Eidegast who died, then of Amfortas who was wounded so he could not avenge her. Gawain tells her to keep his name a secret, and returns to the Castle of Marvels as lord. He secretly sends a squire to invite Arthur to the duel with Gramoflanz, as he is hoping to give both Arthur and his mother Queen Arnive a surprise.

Arthur arrives and is delighted to meet his own mother. Unknown to all, Parzival arrives also, bedecked with a garland from the Tree of Virtue. Gawain, thinking it is Gramoflanz himself, rides full tilt against him. The battle goes against Gawain who is still not fully recovered from his encounter with the lion. As his squires call his name Parzival is horrified by what he has done and dissolves any doubts that the two are twin aspects of a single entity by crying *"Alas! that with gallant Gawain I have fought so fierce a fight, Tis myself whom I have vanquished and my joy shall have taken flight."* And poor bloody Gawain wanly replies *"Thyself hast thou overthrown."*

Parzival fights Gramoflanz on Gawain's behalf and wins easily, and after much complicated arranging all the parties are reconciled under Arthur's guidance. Gramoflanz marries Itonje and Gawain marries Orgeluse.

But Parzival quietly leaves amidst the celebrations and rides out to fight his last battle, that with his brother, Feirefiz.

The Black meets the White

ARZIVAL DOES NOT RECOGNIZE his pagan brother who heads 25 armies. This number reflects the 25 Grail maidens and the 25 lights which stand before the Grail altar. The battle is a reenactment of the ill-fated fight between Amfortas and the pagan knight who wounded him so terribly. But this time the outcome will be completely different.

Feirefiz is magnificent in his armor. Above his head hovers the Ecidemon, Man's angel, who is seen so united with the wearer that the radiant higher being can be seen.

The battle is the most difficult either have ever faced. Many commentators have shown that Feirefiz is protected by armor which draws its power from the sub-earthly will, whereas Parzival draws strength from the super-earthly for he has conquered doubt in God. Thus the threefold nature of man is revealed in Parzival as the head, Gawain the heart, and Feirefiz as the loins and the will of nature. Parzival is loyal and steadfast with the attributes of Saturn; Feirefiz by his own admission calls his gods Juno and Jupiter, while for Gawain it is Mars, transformed into a force of healing.

Both the Christian and the pagan knights are a match for one another. Parzival is beaten to his knees but his battle cry *"Belrapier"* is heard by his lover Condwiramurs four kingdoms away, and she sends him the strength to deal one mighty blow which sends Feirefiz also to his knee. This signals the crisis of the sword which will break, and Parzival finds himself suddenly defenseless. But Feirefiz is magnanimous and throws his own sword away, admitting to Parzival that he would have been conquered if the sword had not broken. As they talk of their father they recognize one another. Feirefiz describes the many facets of one single human nature when he exclaims, like Parzival and Gawain before him, *"To strive with myself have I ridden, and went near myself to slay, Thy valor in good stead has stood us, from myself has thou saved today."*

Feeling entirely at one with one another, as if something essential had been missing before, they are welcomed by Gawain at the Castle of Marvels. The next

Far left: **Knight** *13th c. German. This illustration is traditionally held to be that of Wolfram von Eschenbach setting off to the Outremer to visit the Templars.* **Right:** **Knight**. *Bronze aquamanile, 13th c.* **Center**: **Composite Helmet** *from the 14th century.*

day as they are gathered around Arthur's Round Table the Grail Messenger Kundrie once again appears. This time she does not curse or goad Parzival but falls at his feet begging forgiveness and telling him:

"Now rejoice with humble heart,
Since the crown of all earthly blessings
henceforth shall be thy part.
For read is the mystic writing.
The Grail, it doth hail thee king,
And Condwiramour, thy true wife,
thou shalt to thy kingdom bring.
For the Grail, it hath called her thither.
Yea, and Lohengrin thy son,
For e'en as thou left her kingdom
twin babies thou by her hast won.
And Kardeiss, he shall have in
that kingdom a heritage rich I Trow!"

She now offers to take Parzival and one companion to the Grail Castle that he might heal the king, and he of course chooses Feirefiz.

THE GRAND SCHEME

HROUGHOUT *PARZIVAL* Wolfram intersperses the account with allusions to astrology, alchemy, the Kabbala and the new spiritual ideas of the East. In this Wolfram epitomizes the medieval man in his preoccupations with new frontiers of knowledge. The turn of the thirteenth century was a uniquely inquisitive era. It was the dawn of a new quest of the spirit and Parzival embodies the search of medieval man for some higher knowledge or experience which would give some sense of significance and meaning to life which the Church seemed unable to offer. Astrology is Wolfram's major preoccupation and he intersperses his adventures with precise references to the Zodiac, leading his reader from constellation to constellation as the plot progresses. As he takes us through each of the signs we discover just how well crafted the architecture of his work really is. Each episode corresponds to the forces found within a particular sign. What we experience is the passage of a Sun Hero across the Zodiac and the forces which come into play as he moves from one sign, or from one planetary configuration, to another.

The poem opens under the influence of Gemini, with the double marriage of Gahumet to the eastern and the western queens, and the birth of the two heroes, Parzi-val and Feirefiz. And as if to underscore the theme the opening lines are of the black and white, the forces of good and evil, heaven and hell summed up in the image of a magpie. As Parzival passes through unconscious innocence, doubt and finally an awakening awareness, the author repeatedly returns to this sign of the twins. Parzival comes to the second cycle when he and Gawain, the two essential sides of human nature, set off on their respective quests and of course the poem concludes when Parzival meets his true brother Feirefiz.

But while astrology remains the real, yet almost hidden, force within the text, Wolfram is fascinated by the seasonal and cyclic nature of existence and his poem can be equally seen as branches of the Kabbalic Tree of Life, the 22 stages along the alchemical quest for the philosopher's stone, or the 22 major arcana of the tarot deck, which mysteriously appeared at the same time he was writing. But underlying all these rich new 'sciences,' both Parzival's and the reader's true task is to understand the nature of both macrocosm and microcosm. Wolfram wants us to understand our position within the grand scheme of things and that in order to become the Grail King all the ego's power has to be placed at the service of the whole. In order to allow those natural laws to operate we must personally get out of the way. A man of Tao would be delighted.

2

The Seeker

PARZIVAL

4

The Dualities

CONDWIRAMOUR & PARZIVAL

11

The Test

THE GRAIL MEETING

13

Red White Black

BLOOD ON THE SNOW

22

Philosopher's Stone

PARADISE RESTORED

0

The Fool

THE YOUNG PARZIVAL

6

The Lovers

CONDWIRAMOUR & PARZIVAL

9

The Hermit

TREVRIZENT

12

Hanged Man

THE FISHER KING

21

The World

PARADISE RESTORED

"These are the four amplitudes of the universe
And a fit man is one of them:
Man rounding the way of earth,
Earth rounding the way of heaven,
Heaven rounding the way of life
Till the circle is full."
The Chinese sage of Tao, Lao Tzu

Left:Zodiac. *The twelve figures of the western zodiac circling the sun mark the path of Parzival, the sun-hero. Illustration 9th Century.*
Top: Splendor Solis. *Five of the 22 alchemical stages on the quest for the Philosopher's stone from a manuscript by Salomon Trismosin, 16th Century. There are many intriguing alchemical correspondencies with the 22 Major Arcana cards of the* **Tarot,** *five of which are shown above from the Visconti deck of 1450. The original Tarot suites appeared at the same time as the Grail legends and traditionally are believed to have been created by the Knights Templar.*

Grail Knight *by Alan Lee*

THE MYSTERY UNFOLDS

ARZIVAL AND FEIREFIZ ARRIVE AT THE GRAIL CASTLE and Parzival at last asks the question which will heal the king: *"What ails thee, Uncle?"* By now it is not the question itself which is important but it is the questioning which heals. Underlying the entire poem is the mystery of the Trinity. Man, woman and nature are born out of God the Father, but nature is the principle of life and change, so at some time must age and die. In the Son, nature passes through death but is reborn to live again as the Spirit. Here is evidence of the Trinity in the redemption and rebirth of Amfortas.

Parzival then meets his wife at the very spot where he saw the blood on the snow, but now his unconscious longings have become transformed into love with awareness. He meets Trevrizent again who says something of tremendous importance:

"I mourned for thy fruitless labor
For ne'er did the story stand
That the Grail might by man be conquered,
And I fain had withheld thine hand;
But with thee hath the chance been other,
And thy prize shall the highest be."

What the hermit is saying is that the Grail cannot be won. It is not a goal that one can reach by striving, but only by love, compassion and a let-go. If one is not true to the God within, one will strive in vain. Trevrizent, who had warned Parzival that it was not possible to get back to the Grail Castle by so much striving for it, admitted in the end that it was only through his persistent and unswerving tenacity of purpose that he had managed to change God's laws. But of course those laws are made by the god within us. Parzival's son, Kardeiss, is crowned and becomes the lord of all Parzival's lands and departs with his vassals. Parzival, Condwiramurs, Lohengrin and Feirefiz ride back to the Grail Castle. Inside, both the procession and the castle are as Parzival had experienced them before, but the bloody spear is missing.

As Respanse de Schoye carries in the Grail, Feirefiz instantly falls in love with her. He can only see her but not the Grail she bears. He accepts the condition of baptism in order to wed her. The baptismal font is tilted a little before the Grail, and suddenly it is full of water. Feirefiz is in such a pain of love he accepts the baptism of his love's God. As soon as he is baptized he can see the Grail, whereupon a miraculous writing appears upon the stone which reads, *"If any Templar of this community should, by the grace of God, become the ruler of a foreign peoples, let him ensure that they are given their rights."* This is the first time that such a thought has been expressed. A king then rules, not in his own name, but in the name of his people.

Feirefiz then leaves with Respanse de Schoye. They learn that his previous wife, Secundille, has died so Respanse de Schoye can then feel happy about her voyage.

They sailed to India where they have a son called Prester John. Lohengrin, the son of Parzival, continues in the service of the Grail.

HERE IS A CURIOUS HISTORICAL POST-
SCRIPT to the end of Wolfram's poem.
The son of Feirefiz and the Grail maiden
is said to be Prester John.

An alleged Indian Patriarch called
John arrived in Rome in 1122 with a report of a miraculous relic of St. Thomas who had died in India. From
what we know from the Gospels which bear his name,
Thomas did reluctantly go to India. Patriarch John
described his city in fabulous terms, with a river which
had its source in the earthly paradise flowing through
its walls. A short distance away was the church of St.
Thomas surrounded by a lake. But nobody could enter
it except during the two weeks surrounding his feast day
when the waters receded enough to allow entrance to
the sanctuary. In a silver vessel was the uncorrupted
body of the apostle while in front of it burned a lamp
full of balm that miraculously replenished itself. At the
Eucharist a golden plate with the Host was placed
before the body and the hand, as if alive, would take
the Host and administer the wafer to each person present as if it was alive. We do not hear any more of the
Papal emissaries who were sent to India to verify the
miracle.

Bishop Otto of Freising, one of the greatest historians of the Middle Ages, tells of a Priest-King John, a
Nestorian Christian from the East who fought a terrible battle on the 9th September, 1141, and soundly
defeated a Modammedan army. This battle certainly
happened but the figure turns out to be a Chinese-edu-
cated ruler of a semi-nomadic group of nations who was

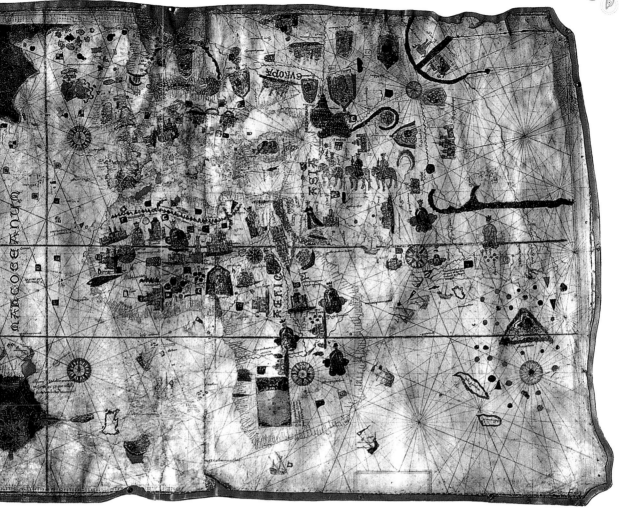

most probably Buddhist. According to the historian this Prester John was descended from the Magi and he was fabulously wealthy. The most famous account of Prester John comes in a letter purporting to be from that ruler and addressed to the Emperor Manuel. It seems to have arrived around about 1170, well before Wolfram ever penned *Parzival*. Pope Alexander III replied to the "King of India" in 1177. That the letter is a hoax is beyond doubt, but the effect upon Europe was far reaching. India was known only through this document for the next two centuries. It describes an exotic and fabulous earthly paradise which would perfectly fit into the end of Wolfram's legend as Feirefiz and his new-found queen ride towards India and an Eastern dawn.

Before we dismiss the document, or the far-fetched tales of Patriarch John, or the descriptions of the tomb of St. Thomas, we might reflect that the vessel in that Indian sanctuary was said to have kept the saint's body ever young. It was the hand of "Doubting Thomas" that probed the wound in Christ's side, and his hand which presents the Host during the Eucharist. This was the atmosphere of Europe when the Grail legend arose, in much the same way that flying saucers, extraterrestrials, channelers, and Higher Selves are so popular today.

PART II

A Myth for our Time

Glastonbury Tor, *rising above the mists of Avalon. The mystery of the Holy Grail is still to be felt in the atmosphere of this most mystical site in Britain.*

CHAPTER I
A LIVING LEGEND

N OW THAT WE HAVE EXAMINED the outlines of the three branches of the Grail legend, we return to the question we raised at the beginning: how does this richest of all Western myths still manage to retain the magical vitality that it obviously possessed in the thirteenth century? What living substance courses through the legend that can still touch our collective unconscious, and can it transform our attitudes in our own epoch? After all the legend was originally forged out of materials found in two very different regions. The original Celtic sources in Northwestern Europe and the Arabic material of the Near East are long since gone and the cultures which gave rise to the Grail Legend have faded into history. And yet this extraordinary phenomenon, which was gestated almost one thousand years ago and then burst upon Europe in a such a flash of wonder and fascination, continues to spread its cult-like ripples even today.

One reason why the myth remains so alive might lie in the fact that real blood flows through its veins – no metaphorical blood, but quite literal and real. Throughout all the various Grail accounts, blood appears as a mysterious and powerful theme. Its image crops up in a variety of surrealistic ways. In the Welsh poem of *Peredur* it is the head of a kinsman that swims in a dish of blood. In all the texts, irrespective of source, a spear, a lance or a sword appears with blood dripping from its tip. When the Grail is described as a vessel it invariably carries the holy blood of Christ. The Grail King suffers from a bleeding wound which cannot heal. The Grail

Guardians are strictly chosen from a sacred bloodline, just as are the descendants of the Maidens of the Wells. There have been so many obviously clear arguments to suggest mythic explanations for the rich imagery found within each account, that we have not paused to consider the possibility that the Grail might actually exist as a real and miraculous artifact.

History and myth seldom make promising bedfellows. History is doggedly linear by nature while myth is cyclic. History appeals to the factual, outer world of singular, novel events which are unrepeatable. Myth resonates with the innermost being, ever renewing its cyclic motifs. These collective dreams have the power to transform a people in much the same way as personal dreams can alter the life of the dreamer. History does not have this unique ability. So when a myth is confused with historical events its whole transforming power is lost.

If we put aside the literary merits of each of the works so far explored and examine the descriptions of the major themes instead, one common factor that might suggest the Grail is a reality, must surely be blood. Three authors, writing in 1982 (Baigent, Leigh and Lincoln), convincingly argue not only why blood is so important, but also, *whose* blood is so important. They argue in their book "*The Holy Blood & the Holy Grail*" that there is no contradiction between the vessel containing Christ's blood, *San Greal*, and a royal blood line, *Sang Real*, stemming from Jesus. The vessel that carried this bloodline was the womb of Mary Magdalene, and the royal blood was that of the Son of God.

Left: **Tassilo's Chalice,** *Anglo-Saxon, 9th C. England.* *Above*: **Mary anointing the feet of Christ** *by a follower of D. Bouts 1450.*

THE HOLY VESSEL

INCE THEIR BOOK WAS PUBLISHED in 1982, more evidence to support the hypothesis of the three authors has been forthcoming which is both impressive and revealing. Even the most orthodox of the Church Fathers have always accepted that Christ was of the royal line from David, even though it appeared he was just a poor carpenter's son. Except when, on closer examination it is discovered that the word for carpenter, Najjar, also meant a holy man in the mystic, Jewish Brotherhood of the Nazarites or Nazorenes.

The Grail romances were set, for the most part, squarely within the great era of the Merovingian Kings of France during the fifth and sixth centuries. As written legends they did not appear until the scion of the Merovingians had been installed on the throne of Jerusalem, even though his bloodline had faded into obscurity for two hundred years. The argument that Mary Magdalene was in fact the wife of Jesus, and was believed to have left the Holy Lands after the crucifixion to settle in Gaul with their child, does have enough real grounds to merit consideration. There were, for instance, many established and flourishing Jewish communities in Southern France where she could have found sanctuary. The Nazarene bloodline she carried could have been allied with the royal lineage of the Franks who, in their turn, were known to have engendered the Merovingian dynasty. This would explain many of the curious traditions which tell of Magdalena landing in Marseille. It might even go a long way in explaining the obscure significance of the mythic birth of Merovee, the founder of the French line, who was said to have had two fathers, one being a marine creature traditionally identified with the mystical fish of Christ. The whole Merovingian blood royal was deemed

to be so sacred and invested with such magical or miraculous powers that a curious pact was made between the bloodline and the Church of Rome at the time of Clovis. This was broken when the Church had Dagobert II assassinated in 679. His son managed to escape to Languedoc, and it is said that his line ended in Godfroi de Bouillon four centuries later. The kings after 680 gradually lost their power to their own administrators, gradually becoming an impotent line of weak monarchs until their dynasty passed into obscurity. This hidden royal blood in Languedoc could explain the source of the fictional origins of the Grail family in the romances. It would certainly fit the atmosphere of mystery and secrecy surrounding an impotent Fisher King, and the young hero who had to be of the royal line in order to gain the castle and win the Guardian's throne. If this interpretation of the scenario is correct then the triumphant entry into Jerusalem by Godfroi was more than just a rescue of the Holy City from the Saracens. It was reclaiming his rightful heritage as a descendant of Christ, King of the Jews, and the royal and magical blood of the Merovigians.

Whatever the historical accuracy of these assumptions, based as they are mostly on circumstantial evidence, the question concerning the role of Mary Magdalene remains one crucial to our own time. It is a powerful message, encapsulated within the Grail.

Mary Magdalene herself has a very strong connection with the early Christian sects known as the Gnostics. Their gospels call her Mary Lucifer the Light-Giver. Mary the Harlot was another of her forms, as well as Mary the Virgin. All three were part of the Triple Goddess Mari-Anna-Ishtar, the Great Whore of Babylon who was worshipped, along with her savior son, in the Temple of Jerusalem. Magdalene signifies

"she of the temple-tower" and it is known that the Temple had three towers symbolizing the triple goddess. A strange and deadly ritual associated with the worship of the Great Whore was the anointing of her male sacrifices. Her priestesses would pour precious oils upon the victims, Christ-ening them so that they would descend into the underworld to be reborn. In the Gospel of Matthew (26:7-12) Jesus says that Magdalene 'anoints him for his burial' and she, like the Virgin, is named the Christening Vase, which held the holy oil of anointing.

Of all the disciples Magdalene was known to be the closest to Christ, something which caused more than enough jealousy from the others, especially Peter. After the crucifixion Magdalene was supposed to have stayed with the Virgin at Ephesus in Greece. She was then said to have been put to sea in a leaky boat without oars or rudder. But she landed safely at Ratis (Les Saintes-Marie-de-la-Mer) and preached near Marseilles (named after one aspect of the triple goddess, Mari). She ended her days in Provence and was buried at St. Maximin. Shortly the mysterious connection of the Magdalene and the Black Virgin will be examined but before this we can briefly follow the fortunes of one man who could claim a descent from Magdalene and Christ, and at the same time was said to be the grandson of either Parzival or his son Lohengrin, and who might be considered the last of the Grail Guardians – Godfroi de Bouillon.

Magdalene, *13th c. Italy. The Church's idea of a penitent whore, clothed only in her hair, holding a scroll which reads,* "Do not despair you who have led sinful lives. Follow my example and right yourselves with God." *From the available evidence it is clear that Magdalene was anything but a whore. She seems to have been a wealthy aristocrat who was both the favorite disciple of Christ and possibly even his wife.*

THE GRAIL WITHDRAWS

I F THE GRAIL HAD NOT BEEN NOT BROUGHT TO BRITAIN by Joseph of Arimathea, as some legends maintain, but had been actually taken to France in the form of Magdalene, then many contradictory and mysterious parts of the jigsaw begin to fall into place. The *Queste del San Graal* explicitly dates the events of the Grail story at 487 A.D. which would have been at the start of the meteoric rise of the Merovingian era just before Clovis, their greatest star, was baptized.

This begs the question whether the legendary Arthur, who was a historical contemporary, had somehow been appropriated by the creators of the romances in order to tell a secret symbolic or allegorical tale of the fortunes of

the vanished Merovingian bloodline. The author of *Parzival*, Wolfram von Eschenbach, situates Arthur's court at Nantes and not in Wales at all. In fact, in all of his long wanderings across the continent he never crosses the sea. Even the appellation of Perceval as "the Waleis" could equally be Perceval from Valais, on the shores of Lake Leman in Switzerland. Chrétien declares Perceval was born in Sinadon, which Welsh scholars have been quick to identify as Snowdon in North Wales, but there are equally cogent reasons to suppose this might be Sidonensis, the capital of Valais.

We know from the legend that Galahad was a scion of the House of David, and his name even derives from Gilead, or Jesus. Parzival's son Lohengrin married the Duchess of Brabant, and according to tradition was secretly the grandfather of Godfroi de Bouillon. While chronologically this would be almost impossible, it is known that there was no clear distinction between the terms 'ancestor' and 'grandfather' in the Middle Ages.

Godfroi, as leader of the First Crusade to the Holy Land, was a supreme and popular hero enjoying a prestige second to none in the Christian world. For he had wrested Jerusalem from infidel hands, saved the Holy Sepulcher and stood for the highest Christian piety and chivalric values. His pedigree within the House of Lorraine included the Plantard family and stretched back to Dagobert II.

As the Merovingian line had become more and more wrapped up in mystical and pious pursuits it lost touch with the peoples it governed until, as we have just learned, the line submerged, becoming invisible like the Fisher King within the Grail Castle, until finally reemerging in triumph with Godfroi.

At this point in history it would appear that the factual Grail of the Holy City, the Temple, and the Sepulcher had at last come to roost and that the objective had been achieved. But, in both romance and reality, things are never quite so simple as they first seem.

The answer to the Grail-Question which the hero

must ask – "Who is served by the Grail?" – was that it "served everyone." Yet, in even the most positive of the accounts, only three seekers ever actually experienced the ultimate bliss and benediction of the vessel. In most cases the Grail is then withdrawn or kept hidden. In fact the real goal of serving everyone is never achieved at all. The quest for the Grail remains only a partial success, just as its underlying Gnostic message was lost once the Church's Crusades turned their attention from looting the Holy Lands to grabbing the treasures of Southern France and slaughtering all the Cathari heretics who were creating an extraordinary new spiritual experiment in Europe. And it was that experiment that was so faithfully detailed within the Grail legends.

Although Godfroi was a hero, the peak of the chivalrous, Christian ideal, he was in reality a merciless butcher prompted by greed and fanaticism. The army commanded by him massacred the entire population of Jerusalem, his knights slaughtering *"a great multitude of people of every age, old men and women, maidens, children and mothers with infants, by way of solemn sacrifice"* to, of all people, Jesus. The Crusaders had proudly ridden into the city *"knee deep in the blood of disbelievers"* and had promptly herded all the Jews of the city into their synagogues and burned them alive. This is a far cry indeed from the inscription on the Grail seen by Parzival, that any Templar who governed a people must respect their beliefs and rights. And yet it is this leader, Godfroi, who was enthroned at Jerusalem just as Galahad, his counterpart of legend was enthroned at the Holy City of Sarras near the border with Egypt. Godfroi's triumphant entrance into Jerusalem happened a millen-

Opposite: **Godfroi de Bouillon**, *the first King of Jerusalem on his way to the Holy Land. 14th c. French manuscript.* *Left:* **Christ Riding into Jerusalem on Palm Sunday**, *Swiss Folk art.*

nium after Christ, his possible forebear, had ridden into the city on a donkey. And from all the evidence available it appears to have been this same Galahad/Godfroi who founded the secret Order of Sion which possibly was the mastermind behind many of the fortunes of Europe – especially that of the mysterious Templars.

THE GUARDIANS OF THE GRAIL

THE ORDER OF THE POOR KNIGHTS of Christ and the Temple of Solomon, believed to have been founded in 1111, twelve years after the capture of Jerusalem, was surrounded by the same atmosphere of mystery as Godfroi's Order of Sion. Originally there were nine founding members and no further candidates were admitted to the Order for nine years. The Cistercian, St. Bernard of Clairvaux, praised them as the epitome and apotheosis of Christian virtue and helped to draw up their covenant. And small wonder he did so – this new order was, in all but one essential, identical to their white robed, Cistercian brothers. But just as these Cistercians were devoted to peace, as can be seen in their compilations of the Grail stories which have little violence within the pages, their mounted brethren lived and breathed for war and daring deeds. The Templars were sworn to poverty, chastity and obedience. Although they cut their hair, they were forbidden to cut their beards, and like the Cistercians wore white surcoats and cloaks, which from 1146 carried the adopted red cross which made them famous. They owed allegiance to no one but the Pope and, like so many orders dedicated to poverty, swiftly became the richest organization in Europe. At the peak of their power and influence they were the most disciplined and formidable fighting force ever seen, respected even by their opposite numbers, the Hashishim, or Assassins of Islam. It was hardly by coincidence that one of the Templars' greatest centers of influence was at Troyes, where Chrétien's *Le Conte del Graal* first appeared. This court of the Count of Champagne contained, among other esoteroic studies, an influential school of the Jewish Cabbala.

Wolfram von Eschenbach was said to have gone to the Outremer (the Holy Lands beyond the sea) to observe the Templars in action, and while in their company absorbed much of their vision. The Templars certainly had many clandestine contacts with both the Islamic and Arabian traditions. But when Jerusalem fell in 1187 they appeared to lose their whole raison d'etre, and while they remained the most dreaded Christian fighting force, their riches were already being eyed by Church and Kings alike.

Center: **Seal of the Templars** *12th c.* **Above**: **Islamic Cavalry**
While the Saracen horsemen were highly manoeverable they were no match for the heavy armor of the Templars. **Right**: *Map of the Holy City. The Templars were housed in stables on the right in the walled enclosure.*

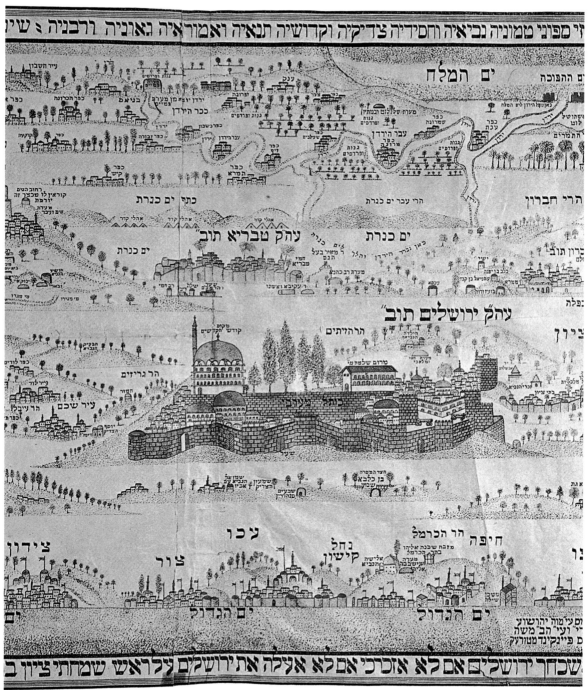

A typical Crusader Castle, **Krak des Chevaliers**, *guarded the northern approaches to the Outremer.*

FALL OF THE GUARDIANS

VENTUALLY THE COVETERS' GREED WON, and the Templars were suddenly arrested throughout France on obscure and trumped-up charges and accused, among other things, of forcing initiates into homosexual acts, of repudiating Christ as a false prophet, of kissing the devil's genitals, of stamping upon the cross, and of worshiping a mysterious three-faced head.

The Inquisition which followed turned up some very mysterious items. Those which appeared to hold considerable fascination for the torturers could be summarized in the list of charges drawn up on August 12th, 1308: *"Being that in each province they had idols, namely heads. That they adored these idols, that they said the head could save them. That it could make riches, make the trees flower, and make the land germinate."* What is most noticeable about these mysterious heads, which were of both men and women, was that they possessed almost precisely those attributes claimed for the Grail itself.

The Order was finally suppressed with great cruelty and their Grand Master, Jaques de Molay, was burned at the stake in 1314, thus ending two centuries of remarkable power and influence.

Having traced the possible, if not too probable, royal bloodline from the Son of God to one of his descendants, Godfroi, we are confronted with an obvious question: "So what?" Even being the son of the son...of the Son of God still doesn't make anyone a Christ. Enlightenment has yet to be proved to be carried in the genes. And even if it had created a Savior he would be unlikely to be recognized any more than was his great, great.... grandfather. But while the history of the Templars, the successive Crusades, or a royal bloodline can suddenly reach a dead end, myth does not. The very stuff out of which myth is created is recyclable and renewable. Myth speaks the language of eternal returns, cycles renewed and heroes reborn. But the Grail myth is somehow incomplete. The legend has not managed to come full circle. So what prevents us from leaping that final gap and closing the cycle? The present barriers don't seem to have changed much during the eight hundred intervening years. We can still identify three unhealing wounds which are as true to us now as they ever were in the thirteenth century – women, the Wasteland and the Wounded Individual.

Above: **Three-Faced Head** *from Salisbury Cathedral, England. The cult of the head was not unique to the Celts, and the dangerous pagan ancestry of the Templar rituals must have especially alarmed the Inquisitors.*

THE THREE
WOUNDS

THE ESSENTIAL FAILURE, or at best the very limited success of the Grail quest, is intricately interwoven with the state of Europe's physical and spiritual health at the time when the legends first appeared. At that time the whole continent was in turmoil. While there appeared to be free access and many pilgrimages around the different regions there was no central authority except for the Church of Rome. The various kingdoms were too busy squabbling and coveting their neighbors' lands to form any secular equivalent. And yet a fresh religious atmosphere and a new uplift of the spirit was trying to assert itself. This new spirituality had its true source in the earlier Christian sects of the Gnostics. At the very heart of Gnosticism lies an essentially female view of the cosmos which was the major ingredient to inspire Cathars and alchemists alike.

As we shall see, the patriarchal priests of Rome overreacted. In response to what they saw as a tangible threat to their power they unleashed the most horrendous and demonic persecution aimed at all those who did not bow to the letter of their dogma. The recipients of their wrath invariably included the most innovative minds of the age and, predictably, the cursed spawn of Eve, St. Peter's pet hatred – women. The Church's principal tool of suppression during the eleventh to the fourteenth centuries was the Crusades. But the violent and looting rabble who usually made up the bulk of the crusading forces ensured there was a complete overkill. It has been estimated that the cost of bringing Europe under the priestly skirts of the Church was about ten million innocent lives. And even after a forced but often only nominal conversion,

appeared out of sight and went underground for the next five hundred years.

The failure of the Grail "to serve everyone" can be seen as a failure to acknowledge the threat of Rome until too late. However the malaise goes deeper, and we might best describe the Wasteland of Europe as a consequence of the Three Dolorous Blows. In retrospect, we can tentatively identify those three great wounds which bled Europe then, as they bleed her still, as being the Repression of Women, the Creation of the Wasteland and the Wounding of the Individual Self. In the following pages we will explore each of these wounds in turn, for they are not just an historical horror which has mercifully passed. These wounds have remained unhealed even after 800 years, although the pain has become so familiar and so much part of our everyday existence that we no longer even notice them. But once all the historical bandaids have been removed, and the wounds are exposed to the fresh air, we are at least able to diagnose what they are and the most effective ways of healing them.

there was still a natural resistance to the New Law which fanned the flames even more beneath the so-called heretics.

The Church reacted to what it saw as heresy with an increasingly fanatical and dictatorial zeal, and was largely unhindered in carrying out its purges. Both the fledgling sciences and the female principle dis-

Galahad Receives the Grail *by Dante Gabrielle Rossetti. The romance of the Grail legend was a favorite theme for the English Pre-Raphaelites surrounded, as they were, with the wasteland of the Industrial Revolution.*

Chapter II
THE LOSS OF THE FEMALE

QUEST FOR THE WOMAN

E HAVE ALREADY OBSERVED that the two basic archetypal elements of the Grail/Chalice and the bleeding Spear/Blade are classic sexual symbols for the masculine and feminine principles. We have also seen that in most of the Grail accounts it is only when these two are united that the waste and barren realm of the Grail Castle is restored to its former state of paradise.

The Grail is not only the nourishing vessel, bestower of food and drink. It can equally signify the uterus or womb of either the earth/mother Goddess, or the sacred vessel of the holy blood of Christ – which can in turn be both the womb of the Virgin Mother or a receptacle carrying the blood of the crucified Christ.

Eve was supposed to have been, at least partially, redeemed by the Virgin Mary. But women were still never allowed to participate, let alone officiate, in Christian worship in any part of Europe except Ireland and Brittany. Within the inner sanctum of the Grail Temple, however, the roles are reversed. In the mysterious ceremony and procession at the Castle of the Fisher King, only women were pure enough to act as bearers of the Grail. So we must be witnessing a tradition which either predates the Church or subscribes to an alternative Christianity in which women reestablish their spiritual equality in direct contradistinction to that of the Holy Roman services.

The quest for the Grail can also be interpreted, in terms of modern psychology, as the return of the son to the mother. In this scenario the hero had originally left the mother's womb when he followed the knights from the wilderness. In this every baby is a hero, passing through psychological as well as physical transformation from a water creature living in a amniotic paradise to an air-breathing mammal who has to face a dangerous unknown without boundaries. All of us have experienced this tremendous change, and if we had con-sciously embarked upon such an adventure we could all claim heroic status.

His mother's death as he left the child-paradise went unnoticed in our hero's egocentric drive and intoxication with a new existence and sense of freedom. But in many versions it was this sin of causing his mother's death that at first prevented him from curing the Fisher King and healing the realm of the Grail. So when he leaves his own queen it is to seek his mother. But he finds the Grail instead. This is no coincidence. For the castle to which he is invited is surrounded by water and invisible to all but the worthy. This can be seen as the womb of the new mother who is now rediscovered by her son/lover, inasmuch as every lover is a son and every mistress is a mother. And if we seek the ultimate image of the mother and son in the Western world then surely we need look no further than the Virgin Mary and the infant Christ. But what of the other, dangerously incestual side of the relationship? The hidden scriptures point towards Christ's lover, Mary Magdalene.

Virgin and Child. *Both images are contemporary with the writing of the Grail legends.* **Left:** *English, 1200.* **Right:** *Anglo-Norwegian, 1220.*

The Queen & The Cup

AT VIRTUALLY EVERY SIG-
NIFICANT POINT of the
hero's quest for the
Grail he finds a female
signpost. Every en-
counter with each facet of the mystic
female is choreographed like the
moves of the pieces in a game of
chess, in which the opposing King can
only be checked with the cooperation
of the Queen, who can assume the shape of all the
other pieces except the Knights. She is the only piece
on the board which can move in any direction, as far
as she likes. This shape-shifting versatility of the Sovereign assumes a number of guises in the Grail quest.
She is both one and many, the epitome of stability while
at the same time continually changing shape. All the
heroes seem to be overly preoccupied with her potent
sexuality, whether it is repressed, as in the prim Christian texts, or randily promiscuous as in the Welsh. But
it hardly matters whether the hero is a chaste, if reluctant, virgin, who has to be reminded at every encounter
to hang on to his purity for at least another chapter, or
whether it is a lewd Celt trying to wrestle a coy but
willing maiden to the floor. Virgin or roue, a Galahad
or a Gawain, this implicit and explicit sexuality does
seem somewhat surprising, in what surely should be a
solemn and sacred quest for a holy object. Such curious lapses are immediately made clear when we know
that the mythic current raging beneath the collective
unconscious is really a quest to reestablish the male's
displaced female aspect.

It will perhaps be remembered
that in the prologue to Chrétien's *Le
Conte del Graal*, which opened our
survey of the legends, the Grail Castle
was at one time visible to one and all.
We were told how the land had been
fair and fertile, the people gentle and
prosperous, and maidens at the
springs and wells around the countryside had served the weary travelers
from their cups. But when a certain King Amangons
raped one of the maidens and stole her ceremonial cup,
and when his retainers followed the king's action with
such dedication, the wells were quickly deserted. The
kingdom lay barren and waste, and the waters dried up. The
only man who could restore the land to its original state was one who could recognize the Fisher King
and the Castle behind the many guises and false reflections. The Grail bearer symbolizes the original maidens
of the wells as dispensers of drink and food. But more
importantly she represents, like them, the Sovereignty
of the land which withdraws and dries up when the king
forces her to his own will and neither serves her nor
gives her anything in return.

A number of themes and motifs can now be seen to
be emerging which are fundamental to the underlying
myth of the hero on a quest. First there is an impotent
or a maimed king who is unfit to rule, or to be in union
with the Sovereign queen of the land. She appears, disguised as the various females the seeker encounters on
his way, finally transforming into the Queen or Empress
who can only dispense the sacred nourishment to a

worthy hero. So the Quest for the Grail is indistinguishable from the Quest for the Woman. Whosoever finds her finds the Grail. The impotent king must have a new, young and vigorous successor, who is able to restore fertility to the woman who holds the cup, and, symbolically, the realm itself.

Perhaps this motif can be traced to some collective memory of those ancient goddesses who were dethroned by the aggressive male gods, most clearly re-enacted by King Amangons' violent rape of the divine water maiden. He stole her sovereignty, symbolized by a chalice, and forced her by blind and brutish male power to become just another possession in his castle.

This predominantly male authority rapes the land until it is destitute. Only when the mother's son comes to either kill or heal the father can there be a restoration of her original Sovereignty. The quest for the Grail can be seen as a celebration of the eternal female who awaits her young son to reinstate her title of Great Mother Queen and restore the harmony of the realm.

THE FEMALE BLOODSTREAM

SO FAR WE HAVE EXAMINED the historical bloodlines. But the blood which courses through the veins of the Grail myth carries with it the hint of something far more dangerous and powerful, like some dark magical ingredient which runs far deeper in ancient tunnels of the collective unconscious. We briefly glimpse the dark spring tides under the moon, and the quickening of life. At the time when the Grail legends first appeared it was generally accepted that the blood women spilled at the moon was responsible for new birth. Blood which was retained in the womb was believed to coagulate into a child. Even Aristotle claimed that human life is a coagulum of menstrual blood, while the Roman Pliny, author of the encyclopedic Natural History, insisted that it formed the material substance of generation. This curious notion was still taught in European medical schools only two hundred years ago. Far earlier, the ancient Mesopotamian Goddess Ninhursag was said to have created humankind out of clay mixed with her "blood of life." The Jews, the Muslims and the Christians borrowed this and similar creation myths to form their own. Even the name Adam can be traced to the feminine "adamah" meaning bloody clay.

So here we find ourselves in the dangerous tabooridden territory of the moon-blood which has magical properties beyond anything man can create. In most cultures men view this life-essence with holy dread, for it is wholly alien to men's experience. But many magical and mystical initiations of the hero, from the Hindus of India to the Norsemen, have the theme of drinking, bathing or worshiping a vessel filled with the magical stuff in order to transform the initiate. In Greece it was called the supernatural red wine. In India the goddess Kali invited the gods to bathe and drink in the flow of her womb in order that they might rise blessed to heaven. The Norse God Thor reached the mytical land of enlightenment by bathing in the moon-blood of the

Primal Matriarchs. And Soma, the archetypal drink which transforms, heals, and allows glimpses of the Otherworlds, was secreted by the moon-cow. In India the Goddess of Sovereignty, Lakshmi, gave her menstrual blood to Indra, who on drinking it became, like the Goddess, the Mount of Paradise with its many hued rivers. We find almost identical images in Egypt or Persia where the vessel of this immortal blood is the moon. In the north any Celtic king could become immortal by drinking the "red sovereignty" and to be stained red with it signified being chosen as Sovereignty's consort.

We have already seen the influence of the mysterious Gnostics upon many of the Grail texts. Consider then the horrified description given by one of their most virulent critics, Epiphanius, of an Ophite "agape" or Gnostic love feast. He is righteously demonstrating the heresies of the Gnostics as he tells in shocked tones how a group celebrates the spiritual event: *"And the wretches mingle with each other and after they have consorted together in passionate debauch the woman and the man take his ejaculation into their hands and offer to the Father, the Primal Being of All Nature, what is on their hands, with the words, 'We bring to Thee this oblation which is the very body of Christ'."* He goes on, *"They then consume it in shame saying, 'This is the Body of Christ, The Paschal Sacrifice through which our bodies suffer and are forced to confess to the sufferings of Christ.' Even when the woman is in her period they offer up her blood in the same fashion."*

The Ophites considered eating both of the living substances of reproduction far more holy than drinking the symbolic but dead blood of the Son of God. So here we find a powerful female motif counter to that of the male theme of Christ's blood and the Eucharistic body, which so often threads through the Grail corpus.

When these twin images of the male and the female blood coalesce in a myth like the Grail, howsoever subterranean the hints might be, then we have a very

potent and transforming power indeed.

In passing it should not be forgotten that Adam-Kadmon, the Gnostic image of the primordial man, was a man of clay and blood who was called the Prince of Fools, and like Perceval/Parzival, a most thoroughly unenlightened man.

Left: **Goddess**, *Mesopotamia. This little figure has a crescent moon above her head signifying both the receptive bowl and the natural life tides which flow through the body of the female.*
Above: **Alchemical Pillar of Life.** *Planets surround the inner core of the body with the male-female caduceus coiled contrawise about the pillar.*

Faith ~ Wisdom ~ Whore

N COMPLETE CONTRAST to Adam-Kadmon, the Great Fool, there is the Gnostic Great Mother, Sophia, the spirit of female wisdom. Just like the Grail Bearer and Mary Magdalene, she is symbolized by a dove. In some traditions Sophia was thought to be the powerful female part of God's soul. She was said to have preceded Jehovah and to have given birth to both Christ and his sister Achamoth. Achamoth, in turn, gave birth to the Son of Darkness and Jehovah, the God of the Church. It was the vain and proud Jehovah who forbade humans to eat of the Tree of Knowledge. But Sophia sent her own spirit to the Paradise Garden in the form of the serpent Ophis in order to teach Adam and Eve to disobey the jealous God. That serpent was also called Christ.

The Eastern Christians held Sophia in great love and devotion, building her greatest shrine in the Hagia Sophia at Constantinople. She also appears in the Jewish Kabbala as the *Shekina* of God. There is a lovely tradition which maintained that the World Soul was born of her smile, which makes a welcome change from the serious business week of the male God's creation.

None of this much appealed to the patriarchs of Rome who dismissed Sophia as a foolish, clamorous woman and knowing nothing. But they had a powerful and charismatic rival in the cult hero, Simon Magus, a disciple of John the Baptist, one time companion of Christ himself, and a brave champion of Sophia.

While Simon agreed that there had been a Creator he insisted on an equal and corresponding Creatrix.

More radically he went on to claim that the Father was actually born out of the Mother. Simon himself traveled with a holy harlot named Helen whom he worshiped as Sophia, the Gnostic Virgin of Light. This was in imitation of the Gnostic Jesus with his sacred harlot Mary Magdalene, who also embodied Sophia and bore the title "Faith-Wisdom-Whore."

The Gnostic gospels insisted that Jesus gave the mystic keys of the kingdom of Heaven to Magdalena which is why Peter, and the Church he founded, were so jealous toward Mary and all women. Simon was succeeded by Menander, "Moon-man," which suggests that the legendary rivalry between Peter and Simon was, in fact, a rivalry between those early Christian sects struggling for power – a struggle between the Essenic sun god and those who worshipped the lunar hero. This might account for Simon's glorification of women. For to Simon, Paradise was the womb, Eden the placenta: "The river that flows forth from Eden symbolizes the navel which nourishes the fetus." This surprisingly female orientation was not unique to early Christianity. Before the patriarchs of Islam arrived in the seventh century, Arabia had been matriarchal for a millennium or so. At Mecca the goddess Sheba had been worshiped in the form of the black aniconic stone which is now enshrined at Kabba, on the site of the old Temple of Women.

Opposite: **Sophia,** *from the Book of Wonders by David Jovis, 16th c.*
Above: **Philosophie,** *14th c. The influence of Sophia was widespread throughout Europe in the Middle Ages. However she had to be hidden from the Inquisition within alchemical treatises or astrological manuscripts.*

THE GNOSTIC FEMALE

IT IS REVEALING TO DISCOVER parallels to Sophia outside of Christianity. Mohammed's "daughter" Fatima has undergone the selfsame transformation as did Sophia and the Virgin Mary. She had once been known as the Mother of the Father, the Tree of Paradise, and the Red Moon Cow which suckles the Earth. The name Fatima even signifies the Creatrix and her symbol, as the crescent moon, appears on Islamic flags.

Both the Shiites and the mystical Sufis maintained that the feminine powers of sexuality held the world together. One of the finest Sufi poets Farid declared that true divinity was female and that Mecca was "the womb of the earth." The Shiites still await the Virgin Pairidaeza who will give birth to the *Mahdi*, the moon-guided messiah and savior known as the Desired Knight. The Shiites had formed the Assassins, the Islamic counterparts of the Templars, and had kept remarkably intimate links with their supposed Christian rivals. It is small wonder that such "heresies" began to spread throughout the Christian ranks to find their greatest expression within the mysterious accounts of the Grail.

While the Christians could easily dismiss any pagan or infidel ideas as the work of the Devil and not have to justify such pronouncements, the orthodox Fathers had great difficulty in pinning down exactly what they sensed was really wrong with the Gnostics. However, on one point they could unanimously agree – that the essentially feminine, and therefore heretical, bias and imagery of the Gnostics clearly branded them as tools of the devil. What particularly incensed the priests was the Gnostic practice of giving women equal status in officiating at all ceremonies and rituals. Tertullian reports with genuine righteous abhorrence that *"All initiates, men and women alike, might be elected as priest, bishop or prophet."* Unthinkable! So we can see the radical nature of the Grail legends in which women were the

The Queen of Sheba. *The child born of Solomon and the Queen was mottled, black and white to signify the merging of Africa with the Jewish state. Parzival's piebald brother symbolizes the union of East and West.*

Grail Bearers in the most holy ceremony. Even worse was the Gnostic claim that the true revelation of esoteric Christianity was transmitted to Mary Magda- lene, "the apostle to the apostles."

However much these sects were repressed or reviled by the Church, their principles of enlightenment were gradually incorporated into the bardic streams through the troubadours and the romances of the early medieval epoch. Tantric-style meditation – which was almost identical to the East-ern Tantric Yoga, in which the feminine power would enfold the original creative

word spoken by God – spread its inner, mystical message by direct experience. In alchemical treaties of the early Middle Ages we find secret symbols and obscure illustrations, which carried that feminine message in a visual language which baffled the orthodox theologians.

Alchemy was said to have been invented by Mary the Jewess who discovered the process of distillating alcohol around the period when the Grail legends first emerged in Europe. One aspect of the alchemical quest was that in which the participant sought the divine female power, Sophia, whose colors were milk white and blood red. The philosopher's stone, the ultimate goal of the alchemist's dream, was often known as the Sophistical stone.

Mercury/Hermes was the alchemical hero destined to fertilize the Holy Vase. This represented the Great

Mother and was referred to as the *Vas Hermeticum* or Womb of Hermes. The vase was seen as a womb-like sphere or egg from which the *filius philosophorum* was to be born. This is much the same imagery as that contained in the Holy Vase being the womb which would carry Christ. The alchemists rejected both Church and Gnos-tic teachings that matter was inherently fallen or evil. They believed that the savior destined to emerge from the womb-like alchemical matrix was, at one and the same moment, both child and the miraculous philoso-pher's stone. Here we discover a mirror reflection of Wolfram von Eschenbach's Grail, the Lapis Exilis.

Mary Prophetissa. *This legendary founder of alchemy spoke of the birth of the Divine Child, created within the miraculous vessel of Hermes. Two cups signify the Union of Opposites; five-petalled roses symbolize the Passion.*

UNIO MYSTICA

THE GREATEST THREAT TO THE POWER of the Church at the time when the Grail legends first appeared were the Cathars. The crusades launched against them in Southern France had the twin objectives of suppressing the influence of a people bitterly opposed to the Roman Church, which they dubbed the Synagogue of Satan, and of acquiring land and plunder in the civilized land of Languedoc. The Cathars had become a real thorn in the Church's side, scoffing at their most treasured symbols of power – the holy idols, the Trinity, the sacraments, the bogus pardons, and the obvious corruption of the priesthood. The Cathars had absorbed the Gnostic belief of the twin principles embodied in the Prince of Light, whose realm was the spirit, and the Prince of Darkness who had created the material existence. This meant that they could accuse Rome of worshipping the wrong God. For they maintained it was Jehovah who was the dark demiurge, who had created matter and who had entrapped souls within its prisons. But what hurt the priests of Rome most was that the Cathari heresy was spreading like wildfire into the urban centers of France, Germany and Flanders, and was rapidly eroding the Church's power base.

It is difficult to reconstruct just what the Cathari beliefs were, as we only have the interrogator's biased records as evidence. But certain clear principles emerge which demonstrate just how near Europe was to becoming a peaceful Paradise on earth – ironically, as it happens, led by a group whose belief was that matter was actually hell. It also shows how deeply the Grail romances were steeped in these heresies and why the Church has refused to have anything to do with the legend.

The Cathari vision was essentially Gnostic in principle. They subscribed to a belief in reincarnation, and an essential and foundational female principle. They denied all clerical hierarchies or official intercessions between human and Deity. Theirs was not a blind faith in someone else's words, but a "knowing" based upon direct, personal and mystical experience of the Divine through meditation. Of course, such a direct individual contact with God made any priesthood completely superfluous and effectively put the Church of Rome out of business. The Cathars were essentially Dualists, seeing existence as being a constant war between the Prince of Darkness and the Prince of Light. Men and women were seen as beings of light, pure spirits trapped within

matter created by the diabolic Rex Mundi, King of the World. And it was this demiurge they claimed was worshiped in Rome. So while both Creator and Church were based on the male principle of power, the Cathar followed the female principle of love.

They also repudiated the crucifixion and all the cross had come to represent. Jesus was regarded as a prophet of love, but was still of the flesh and carnate. Their own teachers, *les parfaits* or *parfaites* could be of either sex. They traveled in pairs across the Languedoc countryside teaching meditation as a direct approach to the Divine. This was further evidence of heresy as far as the Church was concerned, for their own creed was firmly based upon intercessionary prayer and elaborate ritual. So possessive were they of their intercessionary powers between worshiper and God that any lay person caught reading the Bible would be promptly executed.

In 1145 St. Bernard went to Languedoc to preach against the heretics. However, he found that their sermons and morals were far more Christian than his own corrupt organization, and he admitted that he could find no fault in the Cathari *parfaits*. At least they practiced what they preached. Pope Innocent III, on the other hand, found such insights particularly unhelpful and

ordered a crusade to crush the gathering spiritual renaissance. This was in 1208, right in the middle of those years when the Grail legends were being penned. In the following forty years the highest culture in Europe, which embraced Christian, Gnostic, Jewish and Muslim ideas with equal enthusiasm, was reduced to rubble and fell in step with the darkness of the rest of the continent.

But this was not before Bernard's Cistercian brothers, who compiled the Vulgate Cycle, had absorbed many Catharic ideas. In *Parzival*, Wolfram von Eschenbach sited his Grail Castle deep within the Cathar territory. In one of his poems he even names the Lord of the Grail Castle at Montsalvasch, as Perilla. By what can hardly be a coincidence this was also the name of the Lord of Montségur, the greatest Cathar stronghold and the last citadel to fall in the Pyrenees. It is this castle, which resisted the invading inquisition the longest, that is traditionally identified with the greatest of all the Cathari treasures, supposedly whisked away under the noses of the besiegers just before they overran the fortress. Whether that precious treasure was the Grail, as many suppose, remains an unsolved mystery.

THE DARK FACE OF THE VIRGIN

ONE HISTORICAL FIGURE who seems to bob up with disarming frequency, and certainly one who was the most influential of his day, is St. Bernard of Clairvaux. As a child he had received the miraculous grace of the Black Virgin of Chatillon, in which three drops of milk came from her breast. This event was to influence him throughout his lifetime, and have a far-reaching effect upon the Grail legend. He managed to restore the ailing Order of Citeaux and create the most powerful Cistercian multinational organization of its time, exceeding even the Templars in riches and influence. His Order built hundreds of abbeys, in which learning and the arts flourished. And all were dedicated to Our Lady. He even wrote the rule of the Templars, whose founder members included both of his uncles. Bernard was a truly remarkable man who somehow managed to keep the feminine principle alive within the Church by the many hymns and sermons addressed to the Virgin. He also wrote almost 300 sermons devoted to the theme of the Song of Songs, that uniquely female message of love sung within an otherwise sternly patriarchal Old Testament. In the Song the Virgin is shown as the beloved Shulamite, bride of both Solomon and Christ. Her cry that "I am black, but I am beautiful, O ye daughters of Jerusalem" would find echoes in the cult of the Black Virgin which dominated Bernard all his life. He was familiar with the doctrines of the Cathars, although he did not agree with their ideas, and he had much respect for Islamic lore even though he launched the Second Crusade against them. One might imagine that this extraordinary religious figure would have found the mystic Sufis of Islam much to his taste. For the Sufi "the Beloved" is the spiritual bridegroom, and the Sufi mystic must become his receptive bride.

Bernard's essentially balanced approach can be found within the twin orders which bear his influence, the female-oriented Cistercians and the aggressively male Templars. So it is hardly a coincidence that it was these two orders which were so instrumental in keeping the Grail legend alive. The Templars were traditionally the original Guardians of the Grail, while in the Cistercian monasteries clerics labored to compile the huge Vulgate Cycle of which the *Queste del San Graal* is a part. But the mystery surrounding Bernard is really that of Mary Magdalene.

On Easter Sunday in 1146 Bernard chose to preach the Second Crusade at Vezelay. It is significant that among the crowd of 100,000 who had gathered that day was Louis VII and his feisty young Queen Eleanor who, later, as wife to Henry II of England, instigated the famous Courts of Love. Vezelay was the greatest center of the Magdalene cult. Only fifty years before Bernard's

Opposite: **Virgin and Child** *Cistercian ms., Citeaux, France 14th c.*

Left: **The Black Virgin,** *The Madonna of Einsiedeln.*

impassioned sermon, the great basilica of St. Mary Magdalene had been started. It was also the same year that Godfroi had set forth on the First Crusade.

There must have been something very special about Vezelay. In 1217, Francis of Assisi, often called a troubadour of love and one of the very few truly enlightened figures in the Christian tradition, founded the first house of his new Franciscan Order there. It is also highly significant that both the Franciscan Order of the Cordeliers and the later autonomous Order of the Capuchins were traditionally guardians of the Black Virgin.

But who is the Black Virgin and why should she have excited such a devoted cult throughout Europe, especially in Southern France? There is a deafening silence from both scholar and priest about these mysterious black effigies. There were hundreds to be found throughout Europe, but they were heavily clustered in the South of France. They were usually of unknown antiquity, but certainly among the oldest of the statues of the Virgin. Wherever there is a statue of a Black Virgin there is invariably a flourishing cult of Mary Magdalene in the same area. A remarkably high proportion of all the Black Virgin statues which are over 300 years old are credited with miraculous curative powers. It would seem that they represent a continuation of the worship of pagan goddesses, and some may have been idols consecrated to Isis and other early deities which were adopted into the New Law.

MAGDALENE ~ THE MYTH

 HERE IS ALSO AN ODD CONFUSION and merging of Mary of Egypt, Mary Magdalene and Mary the Virgin, as if they retain the three aspects of the Triple Goddess in the one image.

In the Holy Spirit aspect of the Triple God, Christ impregnates his virgin mother Mary. As the Son he both spiritually and physically impregnates Mary Magdalene. In the Gnostic gospel of Phillip we are told that the companion of the Savior is Mary Magdalene. But Christ loved her more than all the other disciples and used to kiss her on the mouth. The rest of the disciples were offended by it and expressed disapproval. They said unto him, *"Why do you love her more than all of us?"*

In the Gospel of Mary, Magdalene is still in communion with Christ long after his crucifixion and his apparent death. Her insightful visions and actual 'knowing' far exceeds that of any of the other disciples. Peter is especially galled by the fact that a mere woman should be in such an honored position. His particular hatred of her was seemingly transmitted down to all the other 'Paters,' who shared both his hatred and his mistrust of what, after all, was yet another one of the daughters of sinful Eve.

We see the polarity within Christianity from the second century onwards between Mary Magdalene and Peter. All the countless manuscripts and hymns which extolled her role as favored disciple and bearer of his inner teachings were carefully excluded from the canon. In *Pistis Sophia* we learn the real cause of the problem when Mary tells Jesus of her fear of Peter. *"Peter maketh me hesitate,"* she says, *"I am afraid of him for he hates the female race."* So here we have the twin, but polar, traditions within Christianity. On the one hand is the Church of Peter, the Rock – orthodox, male, dominant and aggressive. On the other hand there is the rival Church of Mary, of Love – Gnostic, heretical and wor-

shiping a male/female deity. Of course the aggressive Church of Rome, dedicated to Power, triumphed over its gentler rival but it turned out to be a hollow victory. The Church's exclusion of the female principle crushed the heart out of Christianity and drove Mary's church underground where it remained until briefly bursting forth on the wave of a revived and radical spirituality. This new sense of a balanced religiousness was spearheaded by the Catharis' alternative Church of Love and secretly supported by the Templars, the cults of Mary Magdalene, the Black Virgin and the writers of the Grail romances.

The thirteenth century saw the appearance of the "penitent whore," that curious and thoroughly submissive fiction, created by a Church anxious to suppress both women in particular and nature in general. This pathetic creature cringed in stark contrast to the healing Black Virgins and the potent Magdalene, who was anything but penitent. The Magdalene could remind all the "Peters" that it was she who was the Beloved of Jesus and who held the keys of Heaven.

The fanatical zeal of the priests, who denied, subjugated, or tried to transcend nature altogether, was in bleak contrast to the healing and nurturing powers of the Black Virgins. Behind this dark female face was hidden a Catharic leap in consciousness, for they understood the significant relationship between the sexes. A new image of love sung by their troubadours had its real roots in the alternative church of Mary Magdalene and the Black Virgin.

In 633, during the reign of the Merovingian King of France, Dagobert I, an unmanned ship sailed into the harbor of Boulogne-sur-Mer as the King was attending mass. The ship was without oars or sails, and contained nothing but a statue of the Black Virgin and a copy of the Gnostic gospels. This true account strangely echoes the episode in the *Queste del San Graal* when the embalmed body of Perceval's sister is carried in a ship to Sarras. It also demonstrates the veneration accorded to the Cult of the Black Virgin and her mysterious connection with the Gnostics.

The four "heresies" of the thirteenth century, the Cathars, the Templars, the Black Virgin and the Holy Grail, all arose, flourished and declined at almost one and the same moment, as if their flowering depended on some particular season, some special nutrient in the upper atmospheres which appeared between the years 1100 and 1300. All these suddenly sprang to life but within the space of two hundred years had been either crushed or had fallen into obscurity until our own present metaphysical era.

Above: **The Pope-Ass.** *This curious 16th century woodcut purports to be an image of a monstrosity seen in Rome. It is significant that the detractors of Rome still retained the old mind-set in making the monster female. Luther believed this creature to exist and wrote a book about it.* **Right:** *Seal of Peter and Paul, the two women-haters.* **Left:** **Mary of the Miracles**, *Guadalupe, Mexico.*

THE CHURCH OF POWER & THE CHURCH OF LOVE

I IS TEMPTING TO BLACKEN the Fathers of the Church as if they were the only chauvinists on the planet but sadly women have had a hard passage throughout the world for at least five millennia, especially in the realm of religion. Apparently all the religions of the world are dominated by males and somehow see women as, at best, imperfect copies of their rightful masters. This seems a far cry from the matriarchal communities which worshiped a great Goddess.

Even that enlightened being, Gautama the Buddha, when he was finally forced to allow women monks into his company, sadly declared that his real living message, which would have lasted 2500 years without women, would not survive longer than 500 after all.

According to some Islamic theologians women can't enter Paradise and should not receive religious instruction. There are still many orthodox mosques which retain the signs, "Women, dogs and other impure animals are not permitted to enter."

The Jains of India, while they have many women among their monks, do not believe a woman can become enlightened, unless she takes a male body in her last reincarnation. Orthodox Hindus will not allow women in some of their temples and no woman is allowed if she has her period.

But no religion, even today, is so tyrannical and unjust to women as the Christian church, Roman or Reformed. In its entire history there is not a single case in which women are accepted as equals to men. As the nineteenth century American suffragist, Josephine Henry once remarked, "It demands everything from her and gives nothing in return." This is exactly the state of Sovereignty when the king Amangons forces the well

maiden to his own will and neither serves her nor gives anything in return.

The Reformed church has been as chauvinistic as the Catholic. Even the archenemy of Rome, Martin Luther, relegated women to be merely useful childbearing machines for little males. "If women get tired and die of bearing children" he observes, "there is no harm in that; let them die as long as they bear; they were made for that." With such religious leaders it is hardly any wonder that women have found such difficulty in being accepted as worthy of having souls at all. Thomas Aquinas believed that the original sin of Eve was repeated every time anyone made love, married or otherwise. It would appear that Christianity is the only religion in the history of our planet in which it is sinful just to be alive.

While the modern churches do not actively denounce women — "All wickedness is but little to the wickedness of woman" as did their nineteenth century predecessors, nonetheless they doggedly resist the ordination of women into the priesthood. Even in the U.K. which has one of the better records of women's suffrage and equality, a bishop of the Church of England only one hundred years ago insisted that women "are intrinsically inferior in excellence, imbecile by sex and nature, weak in body, inconstant in mind and imperfect and infirm in character."

Against such a background perhaps we begin to see just how revolutionary and radical was the vision of the Grail. And yet even now we can see that it failed.

New Woman Vicar. *The male hierarchy of the Church of England fought a fierce rearguard action against the inclusion of women officiating at religious ceremonies. They cited menstrual impurities as well as women's inherent inferiority as valid reasons to exclude the dreaded Eve.*

Chapter III
The Wasteland

A Blade in Paradise

E HAVE BRIEFLY EXPLORED how a peaceful agricultural civilization, living 6000 years ago, was invaded and overrun by a nomadic and aggressive people who lived by the sword. Suddenly, within the various strata unearthed, archeologists began to find weapons and fortifications as if they had sprung up overnight where there had been absolutely none for the previous six millennia. Obviously, any collective remembrance of these happenings would hardly have cropped up in the Middle Ages. And yet the Wasteland motif was a recurring and threatening theme during this time, kept alive by the myths that were penetrating the soft underbelly of Europe from the Near East and Moorish Spain. We should also not forget the Celtic contribution as outlined in Elucidations.

All the same, the shock suffered by the European pilgrims and the crusaders upon seeing the desolate wastes of the Arabian deserts and the dunes of North Africa must have run deep. Those Easterners who had not fully embraced Islam and who still worshiped the Goddess maintained that the great deserts had been caused by the renunciation of the Great Mother who withdrew her fertility from the land. The deep fear was that the same situation could happen in Europe.

The symbolic Wasteland, on the other hand, was far more pernicious. This was the landscape of spiritual death, in which religious concepts had become so divorced from the feelings and real life experiences. The coming of the *Mahdi*, or the Desired Knight in the twelfth and thirteenth century was identified variously, depending upon tradition and region, as the second coming of Christ or the long-awaited awakening of King Arthur or Merlin, or some other powerful hero who would defy the oppressors.

The Wasteland of Northeast England, with cars dumped on the one hand and advertised on the other, all in the name of progress and novelty.

DOMINATOR

IN VIRTUALLY EVERY ACCOUNT of the Grail legend the final goal of the quest appears to be either the reestablishment or the transformation of the Wasteland into Paradise. This is pretty standard fairy-tale stuff, in which radical transformation is the foundational magic of the story. But in the Grail myth the original paradisal state of both the land and the inner realm of the characters has been somehow lost. Each of the various accounts of the legend give reasons for both its loss and what the hero had to do to restore the earthly Eden. As we have seen, the curative panaceas roughly correspond to the three branches of the Grail. So for the Celts the healing is seen as a renewal of the vital potency of the land and the king. This cyclic and seasonal view is mutated to fit the linear Christian vision of Redemption. In this historical version the original sin of disobedience which happened at the beginning of time can only be redeemed by a new Christ in the form of a pure knight like Galahad towards the end of time. The last, more "alchemical" branch of the legend, appears as a synthesis of the earlier two in which the healing of the wound can only be brought about by the radical transformation of the individual into a whole and complete being, including both male and female natures. All of these resolutions are valid within themselves, but they are also eight hundred years old and much has been discovered since then about social patterns of behavior which was certainly not available to someone like Wolfram. So in trying to determine what any original earthly paradise might have been like, and what possibly could have actually and historically happened, we must examine two models of social interaction, the dominant and the cooperative.

Homeless in Moscow, *1990. The capitalist system is not alone in having poverty as the very base and foundation of the pyramid. This picture surely confirms the Wasteland needed to support the dominators at the top.*

PYRAMID

THE HIERARCHIC/DOMINANT MODEL of social interaction is best imagined as a pyramid or mountain. It implies a number of equally important aspects or characteristics. For instance: a dominant mode is, by definition, a hierarchy, just as any ranking system is, by definition, a dominant mode. Equally, by implication, a hierarchic mode is manipulative, divisive, stratified and class structured. It always requires that some section of the community remains separate from the rest in order to monitor or impose the orders, requests, or desires of the dominator at the top of the pile. This separated group, which can be in the form of a bureaucracy, an army, a priesthood or a police, is also, by definition, an authoritarian hierarchic mode.

Likewise, whenever there is a dominator system there is a heightened division of specialized roles and skills within the dominated community. So whenever a specialized class or group exists within the framework of a community, we can be pretty sure the community operates within a dominator system.

Such a system requires a large production of wealth to keep it operating and fed. This can be in the form of produce made by the large mass at the base of the pyramid or it can acquire wealth and new technologies by simply taking them from others in conquest and pillage. Tragically, this has been the only system we have known for the last fivethousand years.

In terms of social interaction, it matters not which groups dominate or are dominated. But the patterns which are most vulnerable and are most likely to be affected are those of sex and gender, race, religious groups, nation, class, or even all of these at the same time. The particular dominator pattern which is of our most immediate interest is that of gender. But as far as the effects are concerned, it still matters little whether the dominator is matriarchal or patriarchal, just as it wouldn't matter if blacks ruled over whites. One group will simply be the dominator and the other the dominated.

The Fresco above was painted by Andrea da Firenze in 1355 and demonstrates the rigid hierarchy of the Middle Ages. The Church is the backdrop to all the actors. The Pope is at the pinnacle of the pyramid with

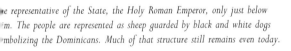
...e representative of the State, the Holy Roman Emperor, only just below ...m. The people are represented as sheep guarded by black and white dogs ...mbolizing the Dominicans. Much of that structure still remains even today.

The ruthless repression of women and their virtual elimination from any position of power or self determination throughout the last five thousand years is a dreadful indictment against the male dominator structure.

But it is a fundamental feature of these social systems that they are so self-regulating that once the desired order is established (in this case, male supremacy) the dominated group is so repressed and conditioned to accept their fate that the system itself is seldom, if ever, questioned.

Less obvious, yet equally insidious signs of this social form are to be found in the inevitable breach that develops between the technological and the social and cultural evolution of a people. It was evident in the Middle Ages in the weapons, castles and fortresses required to support the social status quo. What is more divisive than a fortified stronghold, or what separates men from their fellows more than a suit of armor or a lethal blade?

Just such schizophrenic divisions permeate all aspects of the dominator system, and each split generates new hierarchies of dependence. The State tends to separate from the Spirit, the Sacred from the Secular, the male from the female, individual from individual, the left-hand hemisphere from the right-hand, and the individual from his or her own decision making apparatus.

The very nature of this system is coercive, manipulative, competitive, violent and warlike.

To the mystic the bulwark of the system is seen as the development of a false and separate sense of self, called Ego. Distrust, fear and a death-oriented vision are common features which arise from this condition. And while the clouds were only gathering at the time of writing the Grail legends, Europe was soon to experience the frightful pall which plunged the entire continent into the darkness of the Inquisition, the heretic hunts and the Black Death.

Not, however, before the Grail legends had warned of the coming Wasteland.

PARTNERS IN PARADISE

WHILE WE HAVE FIVE THOU-SAND YEARS' worth of examples of the Dominator model there is almost total silence when we come to the egalitarian model of social interaction. This is hardly surprising as any dominator system will be at pains to remove all evidence of an equal and alternative process. So any evidence we can accumulate will often consist of ill-matched clues from archeologists and anthropologists. However, over the last thirty years a radically new picture has emerged of an ancient, so-called primitive civilization, in which people appeared to have lived life so joyously and in such harmony with their surroundings, that it leaves us wondering if it is we who are the unfortunate and barbaric primitives.

From archeological evidence unearthed over the last thirty years we are now in a position to reconstruct how the neolithic peoples of Old Europe, Mesopotamia and Crete lived. It is clear that the welding force which brought those peoples together was not war but the Goddess. It is, of course, fashionable to extoll the virtues of this vague yet powerful figure in an overreaction to her suppression for so many millennia. But there is no way to avoid the fact that she was to be found everywhere in these early communities. Her image turns up in every aspect of daily life. She appears as much in the shape of the womb-like ovens that baked the pots as the shapes and patterns which appeared on them. Her nurturing and regenerative being permeated and reflected the natural world. That world was seen as Female, and

the Female was seen as the World. And her life-creating and life-affirming spirit was holistic in quality. But while the protective, procreating, and caring view of the world must have been dominant, the male, far from being seen as inferior, must have been regarded as potently essential to the health of the whole.

Equality and shared responsibility for the community is a natural outcome of the cooperative or partnership system. Such a system has to operate on trust and mutual caring, so it is more likely to take on those feminine aspects of the mother – the nurturing quality of receptivity, and a conservationist, cyclical and regenerative view of existence rather than any innovative linear ideas of change. Technologies would tend to grow slowly, out of immediate needs rather than projected futures. Continuity would be through the elders, the wise women and sages. In the dominator system of the thirteenth century few reached old age. The conquered were slaughtered as useless. The changing fortunes of kings and courts, popes and chieftains, and the ensuing feuds, did not favor natural lifespans.

A community based on cooperation is slow to alter its ways. It tends to stay in one place, if it is agricultural, and expands within the confines of the known area. However, given time and equality of opportunity for both sexes, innovations could be explosive. It has been noted with some surprise by historians that the greatest periods of innovation and cultural energy have actually coincided with a period when women were

accorded an unusually high status within their communities. The courts of Eleanor of Aquitaine and Marie de Champagne are perfect examples during the time the Grail was being written, and we only have to consider the Elizabethan era in England or the Italian Renaissance to be assured there is enough evidence to support this.

Left: **Goddess on Leopard Throne**, *Catal Huyuk 5000 B.C.*
Above: **Dancers**, *Tarquinia 520 B.C. When we compare the somber and often cruel medieval images of Christ on the cross, and the unrelenting sufferings of saints and sinners, with this joyous and energetic dance between an Etruscan couple we begin to realize the heavy legacy we have inherited.*

COOPERATIVE

IF A MODERN EXAMPLE needs to be shown so that we can really observe the workings of the cooperative system we can do no better than to turn to the longest lasting and most vital of all the communities which tried to create paradise in the eighteenth and nineteenth century in America – the Shakers.

Not surprisingly the founder was a woman. Ann Lee believed that each of her village communities was, quite literally, a small part of the Garden of Eden. By the middle of the nineteenth century these communities had grown to six-thousand members. The social structure was a classic cooperative and partnership system. Their shared and common ideal was a particular and very unusual theology for the times, which incorporated both a Father God and a Mother Goddess. These deities were equal in the Spirit so there was a similar and complete egalitarianism of the sexes within the community,

although women usually provided the leadership within a central board of elders. Life revolved around the religious meeting with its ecstatic whirling and shaking dances, and the subsequent trance states in which anyone might become a channel for the Father's or the Mother's words. Although the members' material needs and possessions were kept to a minimum, their lives appear to have been fulfilling and rich. Craft skills were particularly welcomed and their traditional houses and exquisitely elegant furniture remain a testimony to their often ecstatic and life-affirming way of being. The communities were beautifully laid out and they managed to be highly innovative in their technologies. And to give added evidence of that innovative power within a strongly feminine community, Sister Tabitha Babbit was the craftswoman who invented the powered circular saw in 1810.

Above: **American Progress,** *by J. Gast 1872.* **Left:** **The Oneida Community***, New York State. This was one of the most successful communities in America. They declared that God was both male and female. This sexual equality was rare in the new and aggressively male nation.*

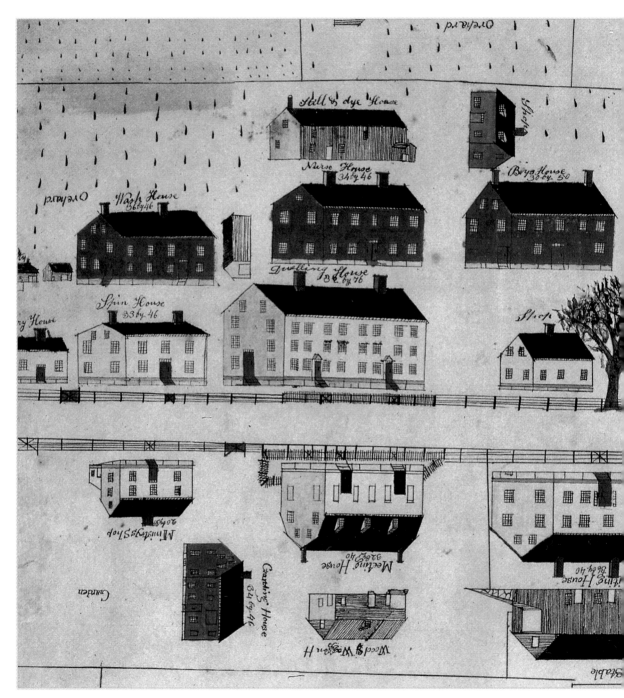

Hall & dye House

Shop

Nurse House
34 by 46

Boys House
36 by 50

Orchard

Wash House
36 by 46

Orchard

Dwelling House
36 by 76

Spin House
33 by 46

Shop

ry House

Ministry Shop
26 by 39

Garden

Coaching House
34 by 46

Meeting House
32 by 40

Wood & Wagon H

ting House
36 by 40

Stable

THE PURSUIT OF HAPPINESS

THE DESCRIPTION of the Shakers' lifestyles could, with little alteration, describe the likely patterns which sustained the communities of neolithic Europe, who were also agriculturalists and consummate craftsmen and craftswomen. Although the neolithic communities appeared to only worship one Goddess, albeit in her many aspects, in the later communities of Crete there seemed to be an acknowledgment of the two interdependent principles of life. On that island paradise the Serpent Goddess was joined by a bull deity; the Pregnant Goddess of the Land was linked to her Son, or the Yearly God. This would seem to reflect the Shakers' dual principle of Father God and Mother Goddess.

It is hardly a coincidence that many of the community experiments which flourished during the eighteenth and nineteenth centuries in America were both religious and often egalitarian. Few, however were to survive the flux of the industrial revolution of the cities. But as far as can be ascertained, their natural predecessors, those peaceful agriculturalists, living over six thousand years ago, also naturally embraced the brave words of the American Declaration of Independence which insists that all are "created equal and that they are endowed by their creator with certain unalienable rights that are – Life, Liberty and the Pursuit of Happiness." We are reminded of the miraculous writing which appeared on the Grail cup which read "*If any Templar of this community should, by the grace of God, become ruler of a foreign peoples, let him ensure that they are given their rights.*" As far as is known both statements are firsts in the annals of Western history.

Left: *Part of a Shaker village map of Alfred, Maine painted in 1845. In that year the total number of the Society's members topped over 4000 living in over two dozen different communities.*

IN MEMORIAM

HE MYTH OF A GOLDEN AND PERFECT AGE of Paradise on Earth, where all beings with their fellows, nature, and the cosmos, appears in nearly all cultures of the world. The compulsion to return to that sacred garden state can be seen as one of the most powerful of human longings, irrespective of culture, creed or geography. As if, somehow, all peoples dimly remember that at one time it did exist.

Certainly the Paradise myths throughout the world are strikingly similar in that they all tell of a time when human beings once celebrated life, the land, laughter, love and the light of the spirit which appeared to permeate all things.

Is one of the reasons that the myth of the Grail remains such a hardy perennial, because it touches a collective and unconscious memory of this Golden Age which might once have actually existed. And does it simply remind us of what went so terribly wrong that we should have lost it all?

The ultimate expression of Paradise in the West must surely be that of the Heavenly Paradise. This is the reward promised by the Judaic, Christian and Islamic religions. The trouble with heavenly kingdoms of perfect happiness and fulfillment is that they only seem to happen post mortem – in the HereAfter, never the HereNow. This is the ultimate Blind Date, offered by the priestly caste of marriage brokers.

Yet on Earth, too, there have been many promises of new worlds of peace and plenty, from those made by the Jewish God to his chosen people, to those given by Columbus to the king of Spain. Both Columbus and Amerigo Vespucci shared the same vision of a virgin but earthly paradise somewhere beyond the western horizon. And Columbus firmly believed he was to be the

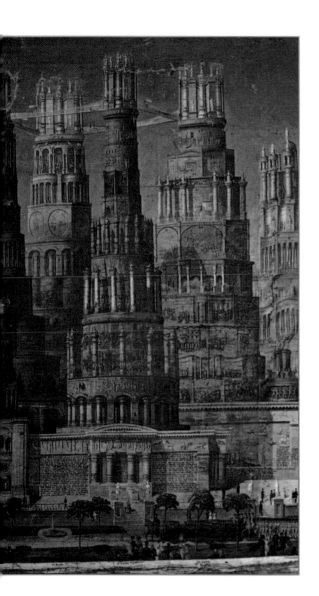

divine messenger and discoverer of the New Kingdom.

Each of the colonizing nations that followed Spain towards paradise carried with them the very virus which would destroy that earthly Eden the moment they put their feet upon its shores. The Old World plague that the colonizers brought to the new world was not the various sexual diseases the settlers carried with them but the far more insidious dis-ease of a society chronically out of balance. Europe invaded the Americas, imposing the same coercive, manipulative, competetive, violent and warlike pyramidal system that had all but destroyed the continent. And that self-regulating system was simply not programmed to ask questions about itself. The worm was already fat within the core of the apple, and Eve once again found that God was the same distrustful, death-oriented, patriarchal chauvinist as the one left behind in the Old World. Once again, only two hundred years after the Grail legends had shown the possibility of a renewal and restoration of the Wasteland, and the spiritual awakening in Languedoc was poised to take a quantum leap into a new realm of consciousness, another extraordinary opportunity to recreate a paradise on earth was lost. It is hardly necessary to belabor the point that we face, as the millennium turns, an almost identical turning point. Whether it is possible to nudge the planet towards the sanity required to bridge the gap, and to properly complete the Wasteland cycle, is another matter entirely.

The Historical Monument of the American Republic by
Erasmus S. Field. However beautiful the monuments they reveal the same hierarchic pattern which has been passed on down 5000 years of history.

CHAPTER IV
THE WOUNDED KING

AN EXISTENTIAL HERO

SO FAR THE NEED TO CALL ATTENTION to the loss of the female principle has somewhat overshadowed any comparable urge to reinstate the hero. But now we can re-examine the role of the hero from a very different perspective and discover how the wounded Monarch can be healed.

If we examine the nature of being a hero, the most recurrent motif in the hero's eternal quest is that of leaving one condition in order to discover a richer or more mature condition. In essence, a hero's journey is towards transformation. And at the very end of that road, the transformation is likely to be a radical change of consciousness. Heroes and heroines are those who give their lives to something bigger than themselves. But this can transpire only when the hero is no longer identified with the ego. Only then can there be a truly heroic transformation of consciousness.

This is not just the path of the hero, but also the path of the mystic. Both the true hero and the mystic have to die to their egos, die to an idea of who they are in order to be reborn as something else and something greater. Only when the identification ceases to be ego-centric can transformation happen at all. It is the fate or destiny of heroes to lose their old way of living in order to allow a new, higher, or more mature life to enter the empty space left by their old selves.

If we examine the lives of the savior-gods, including Christ, we discover this pattern of the hero, who must actually or symbolically die in order to be resur-

rected or reborn. The old gods of the Middle East – Adonis, Osiris, Dionysius, and Tammuz share that essential pattern. And precisely like Christ they all were eaten in the form of bread so their worshipers also might participate in their resurrection.

The Great Fool Parzival, has to die in order that the new Parzival can find the Grail. Only through suffering and the twin agencies of doubt and love can this be transmuted into compassion. And Wolfram is saying that compassion can only arise when one is truly humble. The humbleness of which he speaks is not just some assumed and pious veneer. To be really humble is to be without the obstructing ego getting in the way. By nature a hero is a spiritual being simply by virtue of allowing a greater part of the whole to replace the individual ego. This is nothing less than a death of what one believes to be oneself. It can happen as a voluntary act of self-sacrifice, as in such a savior-hero as Christ. It can happen in an initiatory ceremony, or it can happen in a spontaneous act of love or compassion which suddenly allows the gold brick to fall naturally into the vacuum of the ego-less state. But the master key to any heroic act is letting go of the self, creating an emptiness to allow something greater to enter.

Yet today it is difficult to feel anything but heroically impotent. We appear to live in an intolerable world of wars, violence and catastrophes, in which we can glimpse not the slightest of meanings. Everything appears to be nothing more than the blind play of economic, social or political forces, mostly initiated by those at the top of the pyramid and heading out into a polluted, overpopulated and possibly violent unknown. We have lost the ability to be in touch with our fate because we sense our fates have been lost over the horizon.

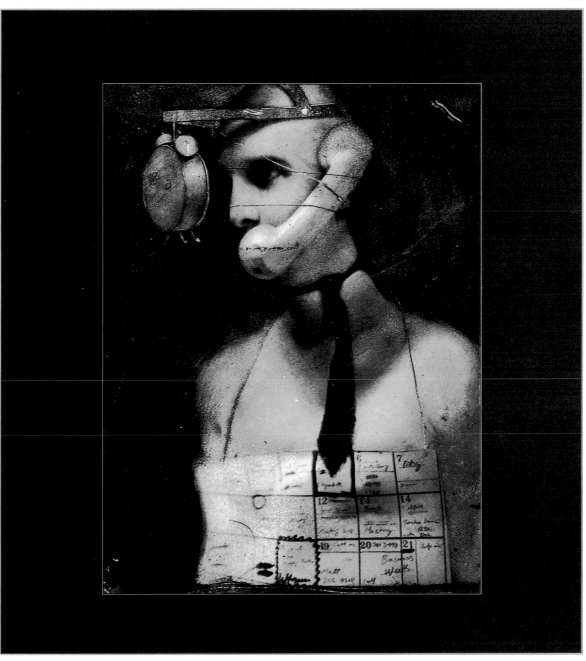

Man *by Matt Mahurin. The present-day hero is dominated by time, money and information.*

Monty Python and the Holy Grail. *This English spoof on the Grail legend demonstrates the continuing fascination with the subject. Two other* *highly successful and popular films, the* Fisher King *and* Indiana Jones and the Last Crusade *continue to keep the myth alive.*

THE HERO'S PATH

HE MEN AND WOMEN of traditional societies accorded the historical event no value in itself. Archaic conceptions of reality were ahistorical, archetypal and cyclic in nature. They defended themselves against what seemed to be pointless suffering in a meaningless drift of historical time, either by periodically abolishing it in sacred rituals, repeating their various cosmogonies, or giving events archetypal meaning. Thus the archaic hero could see himself repeating what the heroes in past sagas had done. In doing so he became that archetypal hero. The modern hero does not have that reassurance, for he has to consciously and voluntarily create history for himself. Yet at the same time he has less and less opportunity to do so, for history is made by those at the top of the pyramid and not those at the bottom. And through an unquestioning and self-alienating social conditioning, the would-be hero fails to act spontaneously out of his or her authentic sense of being.

Perhaps the most cruel legacy of what surely must be the most cruel religion ever imposed upon a people, is to be told that we are born sinners. According to the Christian priesthood, and totally contrary to Christ's original message, the very nature of life is inherently evil because of the original sin. European women have borne the stigma of being sinners for almost two millennia. Under the priestly regime there appears to be no way to change our essentially sinful nature, any more than

we can change the eternal punishments of the Christian hell. So the people of Europe, and the later colonists in the New World, learned that no one is acceptable as they are. And just as human nature had to be changed, by force if necessary, so should Mother Nature. And here the wounded king is revealed: in trying to change themselves into what they were not, an entire people became schizophrenic and guilty. And we all carry the burden of that, even today.

The heroic act of today, as it was in Parzival's age, is to simply trust one's inner nature and act upon it. We are all indebted to Joseph Campbell, that insightful and delightful mythologist, who has pointed out that one of the great heroes of the 1980s was Luke Skywalker in the Star War movies. In the midst of a great battle he is told to switch off all his sophisticated and robotic technologies and to trust in the Force – his own inner nature. And the Force *is* Nature. Like Skywalker, Parzival had to trust that his horse, his inner and intuitive nature, would take him where he needed to go.

That is all the Grail message teaches. It is the most radical, transforming and uniquely Western message that has been delivered down the last eight centuries and urgently needs to be re-read. If the modern hero listens to his or her inner and natural flow, then suddenly the vastness of nature will fill the empty space left by that "false self." We must remind ourselves that, by definition heroes are the ones who give their lives over to something bigger than themselves.

THE QUESTION

LOVVAD·SEIAO·SACTISSIM·SACRAMENTO·

WE HAVE COME FULL CIRCLE in trying to establish the real aims of the quest for the Grail. By now we have seen that the essential theme of the Grail, repeated in all the Celtic accounts, is that of a union of the two principles of the Goddess and the Hero-king. This is the foundational condition of Paradise. But one great dream of man is to create a Paradise to his own specifications which contains all the desirable, and none of the undesirable, elements of the social, economic and spiritual worlds. The trouble has been that the hierarchic paradigm of the last 5000 years remains so firmly in place that our inner conditioning does not allow us to step outside of its conceptual framework. So even those with the best of intentions have fallen prey to the dominator syndrome.

From the Spartans of ancient Greece to the Owenite Communities of nineteenth century America, few attempts at making the earthly paradise have ever lasted long. It is a vindication of the female principle that the Shaker communities of America, which managed to last the longest. Founded by a woman and based on cooperation, equality, and shared living, the Shakers almost created their dream. But they sadly avoided firmly grasping that prickly subject for all spiritual seekers — sexual contact. They solved the problem by pretending it wasn't there. They became celibate, which is not always synonymous with Paradise, nor is it likely to produce communities which last.

Today we are also faced with the same Question which the hero had to ask when he saw the Wounded King and the strange ceremony which symbolically told the story of the king's predicament. All the hero had to do was to ask, "What ails thee Uncle?" and the enchantments of both realm and king would have been ended. If a real and historical hero had asked what really ailed the people of Europe in the twelfth and thirteenth century then, perhaps, the horrors of the Albigensian Crusades, the Inquisition, and the suppression of all female power might have been avoided. As it was, any questions were ruthlessly crushed and the scales crashed toward the side of male dominance, exemplified by the Northern knights and the Church of Peter and Paul. And Europe became a nightmare Wasteland for the next eight hundred years.

But if we look around us today the selfsame nightmare persists in war, fanatical religious and ethnic strife, an empty materialism, a technology which divides us

even further and is out of control, and an undercurrent of violence which can erupt at any moment. There is a sense of hopelessness in the face of a future already predicted to be overpopulated and overpolluted. And the same sense of loss is felt now as it was eighthundred years ago – the loss of a female balance, of sensitivity to cyclic rhythms of the seasons, of growth and nourishment. All the ecological bandaids we can use will not help the deeply engrained attitudes we have, of dominating and controlling nature herself. The Voices of the Wells cannot be heard above the drone of the chain saws cutting the lungs out of the planet, or the chatter of computers printing out the sales figures of the multinational corporations. The voices of cooperation with nature are still far too few.

So what can be done? Is there any message in the legends we have been exploring which might tell us how to go about it?

Left: **The Chalice.** *The Christian flag in the Shimabara rebellion, 17th c. Japan.* **Above**: **Memorial.** *1813, U.S.A. This stylized image painted by an unknown woman, seems to express the loss of the Voices of the Wells.*

THE REALM OF ACTION

N SEEKING SOME INSIGHT into the nature of the healing of the three wounds we might take a look at an unexpected clue – the Tarot, which on close insprection reveals mysterious connections with the Grail.

Most people are at least vaguely acquainted with this deck of 78 divinatory cards. Although the origins of the cards are unknown there have been many theories about where they came from. The most likely route is from the Orient, but when they arrived in the Near East, in what is thought to have been the thirteenth century, they underwent a transformation through contacts with the Jewish Kabbala, the Gnostic Cathars, the gypsies, and Hermetic magic.

The modern pack of playing cards evolved from the Minor Arcana suits of the Tarot deck, minus four cards. Originally there were four knights in the court cards and some scholars are of the opinion that the Tarot was originally invented by the Knights Templar. When the Templars were declared heretics the knights suddenly disappeared from the pack. The Church claimed that the Cathari used cards to teach their Gnostic doctrine but it is possible that the Templars learned their use from their Saracen rivals.

It is yet one more curious coincidence that the Tarot should surface in the years shortly after the Grail legends appeared, when the Cathars and the Templars were being ruthlessly eradicated. The mysterious disappearance of the 22-card trump pack of the Major Arcana and the four knights was in some way connected to the increasing hostility of the church to all forms of playing cards. The priests were especially virulent about those 22 cards, calling them "the rungs of a ladder leading to hell," or the "Devil's breviary." But why, might we ask, was the Church so antagonistic to these seemingly innocuous cards? The answer seems to lie in the fact that religious insights can be taught more easily through a symbol code known only to particular initiates. Thus a teaching can be given right under the noses of the orthodox without arousing any suspicion. But the Church was highly suspicious of anything which might be playful or enjoyable, and rightly so it turns out. Firstly, the Tarot images are very female oriented, suggesting cyclic doctrines of renewal and rebirth such as the Gnostics preached. The whole idea of shuffling the cards was a parallel to moving the major elements across the stage of life. Fate would guide the diviner to choose combinations that captured the moment and could show past or future events around it. The connection of the Major Arcana with Grail legend, and the relationship of the aces of the four suits with the four Grail Hallows, are shown below:

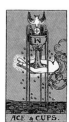

Grail	Tarot	Playing cards	Season	Element
Sword	Swords	Spades	Spring	Air
Spear	Wands	Clubs	Summer	Fire
Grail	Cups	Hearts	Autumn	Water
Dish	Pentacles	Diamonds	Winter	Earth

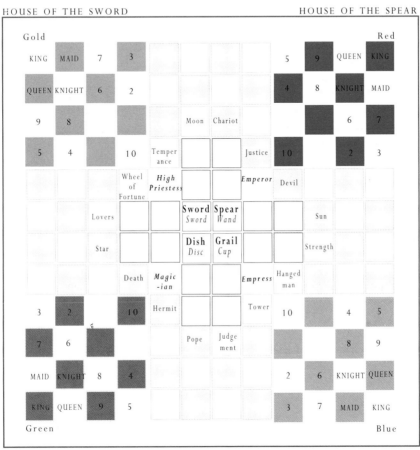

HOUSE OF THE SWORD

HOUSE OF THE SPEAR

Gold

Red

KING	MAID	7	3				5	9	QUEEN	KING
QUEEN	KNIGHT	6	2				4	8	KNIGHT	MAID
9	8			Moon	Chariot				6	7
5	4		10	Temperance		Justice	10		2	3
			Wheel of Fortune	High Priestess		Emperor	Devil			
	Lovers			Sword *Sword*	Spear *Wand*			Sun		
	Star			Dish *Disc*	Grail *Cup*			Strength		
	Death	Magic -ian			Empress	Hanged man				
3	2	10	Hermit			Tower	10		4	5
7	6			Pope	Judgement				8	9
MAID	KNIGHT	8	4				2	6	KNIGHT	QUEEN
KING	QUEEN	9	5				3	7	MAID	KING

Green

Blue

HOUSE OF THE DISH

HOUSE OF THE GRAIL

The Gaming Board of the Grail

RINGS OF ETERNAL RETURN

THE BEAUTY OF THE SYMBOLIC IMAGES within each card is that they bypass the language of the intellect and instead speak the language of the unconscious. Such mythic images can constellate a whole complex vision, opening doors of perception into those subterranean corridors of our collective dreams and our spiritual lives which cannot be accessed through normal language. The story the cards tell is deeply opposed to the tenets of orthodox Christianity, as the illustration opposite shows. The first thing to notice about the mobius-like double Rings of Return is that in contrast to the Christian religion which encourages the idea of a linear historical time, the Tarot points towards a cyclic religion of reincarnation, renewal and transformation. The clue to the importance of the Infinity sign of the figure eight is found in the Magician card, in the card of Strength, and in the Two of Pentacles.

The first circle of cards within the figure eight follow a clockwise, outer, solar path. This the right hand way of the male. The cards themselves are laid facing out, signifying the conscious world of action. The second circle follows a left hand, female, lunar and inner path to the mysteries. Where they overlap lie two mandala cards, the Wheel of Fortune and the World, or Major Fortune. In this arrangement we can observe the Gnostic secrets which were withheld from the Church. Once the authorities discovered the secret it is small wonder that the trump cards were promptly con-

7

8

6

9

5

4

3

1 The Magician ~ The Sun **19**
2 The High Priestess ~ The Moon **18**
3 The Empress ~ The Star **17**
4 The Emperor ~ The Tower **16**
5 The Pope ~ The Devil **15**
6 The Lovers ~ Temperance **14**
7 The Chariot ~ Death **13**
8 Strength ~ The Hanged Man **12**
9 The Hermit ~ Justice **11**
0 The Fool ~ Judgement **20**

21

2

1

0

demned and expunged from the pack.

The secret lies in matching each card in the solar sphere with its opposite number in the lunar cycle. The sum of their two numbers always equals 20, a sacred number in the Eastern decimal system from where they originally came. Listed opposite are the corresponden-

19 18

20 17

16

15

11 14

12 13

The Emperor, in the Gnostic reckoning, stands for the Holy Roman Empire which would eventually be blasted apart by the lightning of Lucifer, while the two figures falling from the uppermost and crowned battlements of the town were the Emperor and the Pope. But of course the real coded message comes with the card which corresponds to the Pope himself, namely the Devil.

When we come to the Lovers the whole underlying message of the Gnostics, the Cathars, and the Grail, finally fits into place. The Lovers is the card of a balanced harmony and wholeness which is reflected in its twin card, Temperance. Here there is the image of the Goddess Isis with one foot on land and one in the water, signifying her sovereignty over both. She pours water into water, from one jar into the other, symbolically merging Isis and Osiris. This ancient image is seen in the Amulet of the Two Jars which would have been known to the Cathars as the merging of God and Goddess. Even the little triangle on the breast of Temperance holds a secret spark of life, the power of the Triple Goddess to bring forth life from her genitals. And the path to the Light in the little landscape at the bottom left of the card lies between the two peaks — *Perce à Val*, the name of the Grail hero.

Now we can fully appreciate the beauty of the figure eight arrangement, for it signifies the union and balance of the sexes. In Celtic marriage rituals, which are still preserved in Scotland, the bride and groom join their right "male" hands and their left "female" hands which then form the double-natured infinity sign so favored by the cards.

cies. From these correspondencies we can see that the Magician is an aspect of the Solar hero related to the masculine power of the Sun, while his female equivalent is a personification of the Moon. The Empress is truly the naked Goddess of Sovereignty who nurtures the Earth with her waters, being the early Astarte or Ishtar.

ARCANA

HAVING EXPLORED THE NATURE of the cards it comes as little surprise that the patriarchal Christians regarded the Tarot as a Bible of Heresy. It is equally understandable that the Cathars and the Templars would have found the original Eastern versions to be as perfect vehicles for their ideas. The Tarot appears to signify the quest of an individual who has to go through a number of initiatory trials and a symbolic death to be worthy to meet the Goddess. This prefigures his actual death and meeting with the Gnostic Great Mother, just as his sexual encounter with his lover signifies his meeting with his own inner female.

How far either the Templars or the Cathari were actually instrumental in creating the cards to describe the secret quest for the Grail is left to the reader to decide but a few possible correspondencies are listed below.

THE MAJOR ARCANA

The correspondences of the Grail Legend with the Tarot Cards

0	The Fool	The Seeker/Parzival
1	Magician	Merlin
2	High Priestess	Lady of the Lake
3	Empress	Guenevere
4	Emperor	Arthur
5	Pope	The Church of Peter
6	The Lovers	Parzival/Condwiramurs
7	The Chariot	The Grail Horse, Natural Will
8	Strength	Gawain
9	The Hermit	The Grail Hermit
10	Wheel of Fortune	The Round Table
11	Justice	Sovereignty
12	Hanged Man	The Fisher King
13	Death	Enchantments of the Land
14	Temperance	The Way of Nature
15	The Devil	Green Man/Nine Witches
16	The Tower	The Wasteland
17	Star	Goddess of Sovereignty
18	Moon	The Grail Bearer
19	Sun	The Solar Way, Male Power
20	Last Judgment	Enlightenment
21	The World	Flowering of Paradise Restored

THE MINOR ARCANA

Four Aces	The Four Hallows
	Sword = Swords, Cup = Grail,
	Wands = Spear, Pentacles = Dish
2-9	The Landscape of the Grail Quest
Card 10	Four Courts of the Hallows
Court Cards	The Page (*originally the Maiden*), the Knight, Queen and King of each of the four Castles being: The Grail Castle, Castle Mortal, Arthur's Castle, Castle Belrepaire

There are many alternative scenarios for the four courts of the Grail and those on the opposite page may clarify some of the complex webs of lineage and bloodline while remaining true to the Tarot cards.

NORTH
Court of the Disc & the House of Benwick
Earth *(Between the Winter and Spring Solstice)*

West side:

WEST
Court of the Grail & House of Pellinor
Water *(Between the autumn and Winter Solstice)*

EAST
Court of the Sword & House of Pendragon
Air *(Between the Spring and Summer Solstice)*

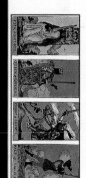

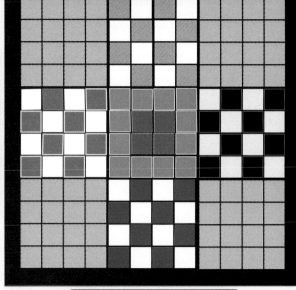

SOUTH
Court of the Spear & House of Lothian and Orkney
Fire *(Between Summer and Autumn Soltice)*

The Vision of St. Eustace, *Pisanello, Italian 15th C. The pagan knight, Eustace, encountered a stag bearing a cross between its antlers. This image corresponds to the encounter of the three knights in the Queste del San Graal. The stag symbolizes the wild and natural state. Its antlers signify the transforming renewal which happens. In this painting there is both a natural and a supernatural message. Our inheritance from the Middle Ages is the apparent loss of the ability to respond to the ways of nature. Religion is too concerned with Heaven so has lost a foothold upon the Earth. This is shown in all of our future-oriented religions which offer a promissory note for the Here-After while completely neglecting the Here-Now.*

Chapter V
The Healing

Transformation

E have witnessed how the Grail can be all things to all people, but if we were able to distill the quintessential juices of this myth then they might be listed somewhat like this:

We are chronically caught within the programs of a self-perpetuating and habitual pattern which prevents us from either seeing our true predicament or doing anything about it. In the legend this is shown in the unreflecting and unquestioning behavior of Parzival as a young man.

This habit-forming is best described as being conditioned to a hierarchic system of social interaction. In the thirteenth century, as well as today, the upper position is firmly held by the male. This is the point where Parzival wants to join the Knights of the Round Table.

In order to maintain this pattern, man has had to separate rather than unite. His blade of separation extends to every activity of life, from splitting the atom to separating the male from the female, or the left-hand hemisphere of the brain from the right. Parzival chooses the severing blade of knighthood and aggressive combat.

The worst split is in man himself, for so enthusiastic was his desire to separate that he has severed his connection with nature, while still being part of it. Thus he has become schizophrenic. And it is the smaller part of himself with which he has identified. The greater part is hidden and is nature, entire and whole. Parzival acts out the teachings of Gurnemanz. He is programmed and conditioned to not ask questions.

While women have suffered cruelly under this system they have largely avoided the worst excesses of the separation simply because their wombs and bodies have closer ties with the natural cycles of life than men's. The Grail Bearers have served the Wounded King and have waited patiently for him to be released from a wound of his own creation.

This separation from nature has not only cut most men from the female principle that exists within themselves, but has prevented access to their inner receptive nature and their spiritual lives. Parzival has denied a God who is only part of someone else's belief system which has been imposed on him. But in throwing out the God he also denies his own natural spirituality.

Of all known centuries the twentieth has witnessed the most extreme manifestation of the Wasteland. And yet each of us carries the deadly self-replicating virus which created it. Each of us carries a microcosm of that Wasteland in the form of conditioning and programming. The Grail legends indicates a way of breaking through that program. The heroic act today, of giving up our lives for something bigger than ourselves, is the only way back to the Spirit. And that heroic act is not for nation, creed, or even for one's brother human, but to simply allow the greater part of what has been severed within us to fill the vacuum left when the false self, or ego, is left behind. Parzival has remained loyal to his love, true to his quest to find something bigger than himself, and has become humble and therefore worthy to receive it. He has trusted in the natural and spontaneous and has avoided other people's ideas of the supernatural. He has managed to stop dividing life into black and white, and accept existence as a seamless whole, as he and his piebald black brother, Feirefiz, become one. Parzival accepts the whole of nature, including himself, as both a spiritual being and at the same time a very normal and happily married family man. His fight with his black brother was the last he needed to make, for he ends in the natural flow of nature and the Grail.

THE SPIRIT OF THE VALLEY

The Spirit of the Valley never dies.
It is called the Mystic Female.

The Door of the Mystic Female
Is the root of Heaven and Earth.

THESE ARE THE WORDS of the Chinese mystic sage Lao Tzu. Tradition speaks of him as the founder of Tao but, like Christ, there is no historical record of the man except his teachings, found in the *Tao te Ching*, or the "Way of Tao," written 2,500 years ago. Lao Tzu insists that the nature of existence is like a female. Not that nature is female but that there is a feminine receptivity in nature. Existence is a womb, and the mystic takes on some of that womblike quality. The Eastern religions of Buddhism, Jainism, or Hinduism are more inclined to the female way, and are noticeably nonviolent compared with the Western male-oriented religions.

The Spirit of the Valley is the spirit of emptiness. Lao Tzu sees it as an empty hollow between two peaks, just as *Perce a Val* is symbolic of the piercing of that valley. The woman is the valley while the man is the peak; one is receptive, the other active. There appears to be a deep imbalance in the male need to act, to prove that he is, while the woman is more balanced and still. Her womb is wholly connected to the life cycles around her. These life tides flow through her in a way that is alien and denied to men. The man is a nomad, constantly needing to move, a ceaseless wanderer and vagabond. The woman, like nature, is more able to allow things to occur in their own time, for she is far more part of the life tides than man. She literally experiences those tides of the moon, the menstrual cycles of her womb and the seasons of carrying life, of birth, nurturing and renewal. This acceptance of life's inner patterns allows a relaxation which is not possible for the male. The two models of society that we have examined likewise can be seen to operate at this natural level of male and female. It is no coincidence that the first societies which settled were matriarchal and matrilocal. It also comes as no surprise that the groups who would overthrow these valley cultures would be the nomadic males, ever looking to prove themselves through danger and death.

Tao is a hollow vessel
And its use is inexhaustible,
Fathomless.

Lao Tzu uses the analogy of hollowness throughout his writing. He insists that a golden pot and an earthen pot are identical in terms of hollowness. The same is true of a sinner or a saint. The actions on the outside are not the inner emptiness. And, says Lao Tzu, that inner emptiness is really existence itself. Existence is not a thing, or a set of things, but a no-thing-ness. And nature appears out of this nothingness, just as the empty space of a room is needed before it can be filled with furniture. The Grail, too, is a vessel of emptiness. It is the principle of receptivity and so, as we have observed, it can be all things to all men. It was the Grail that was said to have nourished everyone "with what they desired."

Snowdonia, *Wales. The legendary birthplace of the original Grail hero, Perceval.*

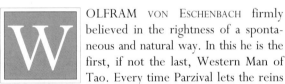

This Very Place the Lotus Paradise
This Very Body the Buddha

Zen Buddhist saying

OLFRAM VON ESCHENBACH firmly believed in the rightness of a spontaneous and natural way. In this he is the first, if not the last, Western Man of Tao. Every time Parzival lets the reins of his horse loose and relaxes into the saddle, accepting that wherever he goes is fine, it turns out for the best. But the moment he tries to take control and impose his superior belief upon the natural order he promptly becomes lost in the Wasteland.

The recent popular interest and fascination with the principles of Tao curiously arise from a scientific base. Many physicists find that the insights of this ancient "religion of nature" closely correspond to what scientists are now discovering in the laboratories and in their mathematical models. In terms of theoretical quantum physics, matter is increasingly looking like emptiness, an endless receptacle out of which forms are created, or at least the illusion of forms. Wolfram's great creative insight was that he had the female bearer of the Grail carry a formless Lapis Exilis which allowed nature to unfold in its season and in its unique form. All Parzival had to do was to let go of all his programming in order to let this enter him.

On the other hand his pagan brother, Feirefiz, being less filled with Christian and chivalrous programming and thus nearer to Nature, immediately understands the beauty of the bearer and her receptive nature. It wasn't, however, baptism that he really needed, for Wolfram is quite clear in the description. He needed the water from the Grail's inexhaustible well to open his eyes to the deeper emptiness.

The new metaphysical age in the West has become a supermarket place for spiritual wares. All seekers are desperately trying to transform themselves. Every guru, therapist and preacher tells us that with only a little more effort we can attain whatever particular goal we desire, be it Moksha, Liberation, Higher Consciousness, Psychic Enhancement or Enlightenment But predictably this new priesthood is just as rooted in the past pyramid hierarchy as the thirteenth century popes.

This twentieth century metaphysical priesthood claims it can change us all into something extraordinary and special, and yet Parzival was constantly being exhorted to be humble. It was only when he ceased to be the greatest knight, on the most sacred quest, seeking the most important object in the world and rejecting the greatest God that... hey presto! It found him.

Dozmary Pool on Bodmin Moor in Cornwall. We now come full circle from Paradise to Waste Land and back to Paradise. The Waste land was the result of the loss of contact with nature, the Otherworld and with Mother Earth. Paradise is the restoration of that essential communion. The mysterious and legendary pool, above, on the lonely moors of the West of England, is said to be bottomless and is the traditional site where the dying King Arthur returned the sword Excalibur to the Lady of the Lake, thus relinquishing his stewardship of the realm to Sovereignty. This water-womb reminds us that we are not separate from nature, and of the simple truth of the Buddhist saying that it is This place which is the real Lotus Paradise.

THE GRAIL FILLS

WOLFRAM WAS DESCRIBING THE ACTION of the ego and its desperate need to be extraordinary. And ego is the mainstay of the dominator system. This system is so engrained and programmed within us that we not only cannot see ourselves reflected in the Wasteland around us but we also cannot see the main perpetrator of both the infertility and the lack of introspection. But it comes from the same source – ego. And there is no strategy of purposefully ridding ourselves of this false sense of self except by being conscious of it and identifying more with the hollowness within than the form created. For the last five millennia we appear to have chosen to be identified with the rich golden vessel embellished overall with rare and precious gems. It is time to take a peek at the emptiness within, for that is the source of healing, the source of wholeness and the Grail.

Lao Tzu seems to offer one of the few sane hints to that crucial question, *"What ails thee, Uncle?"*

What ails us all is that we cannot accept ourselves exactly as we are. We just cannot seem to accept ourselves as being perfectly natural, just as the whole of existence is natural. If only we can act spontaneously, without being programmed into someone else's belief system, we can ask the real question of ourselves. Then, miraculously, for one moment the vessel of the Grail is empty – and in the next it is filled with the wonder and glory of all and everything.

Ideal Government in the Country *by Ambrogio Lorenzetti, 14th c. This is Medieval Paradise on Earth; The legend of the Grail is a myth of Paradise Regained. But the message behind the legend shows that the paradise was never really lost. It was only forgotten.*

The End

Galahad, Perceval and Bors attain the Grail *14th C. Illustration*

ACKNOWLEDGMENTS

Malcolm Godwin, *11, 15, 18, 19, 92, 94, 102, 103, 156/157, 235, 236/237, 239;* British Museum, *10, 12, 36, 38, 39, 66b, 67b, 69c, 86, 143a, 175, 177a;* J. Lathion, Nasjonalgalleriet, Oslo, *21;* Museum of Antiquities, Newcastle-upon Tyne, *23b;* Simon McBride, *25, 35, 43, 106/107, 245;* Trundholm, Denmark, *27;* British Library, *28, 140a, 152;* National Museum of Ireland, Dublin, *29a, 48, 52/53, 67a;* Metropolitan Museum of Art, *30;* Nationalmuseet, Copenhagen, *31, 55b;* Österreichisches Nationalbibliothek, *32;* Musée des Antiquités Nationales, Saint Germain-en-Laye, *33;* Dean & Chapter of Gloucester, *4;* Church of St James the Great, Paulerspury, *5;* Victoria & Albert Museum, London, *51b, 117, 196;* Bibliothèque Nationale, Paris, *16, 17, 23a, 44, 49, 51c, 64, 68, 80, 116, 118, 120, 121, 125, 127, 133, 151, 172;* Guildhall, Carlisle Museum, *54a;* Rijksmuseum Kröller-Müller, Otterlo, *54b;* Bridgeman Art Library, London, { John Rylands University Library, Manchester 7; Schlossmuseum, Weimar, *26;* Private Collection, *45;* Hessisches Landesmuseum, Darmstadt *56;* Birmingham City Museums & Art Gallery, *134/135;* Walker Art Gallery, Liverpool, *149;* Christie's, London, 166; York City Art Gallery, *185;* Private Collection, *199;* Palazzo Publico, Siena, *246* }; Roland Pargeter, *61, 96, 98;* Musée de Cluny, Paris, *63;* Alan Lee, *65, 178;* Bodleian Library, Oxford, *13, 66a, 169a;* Society of Antiquaries of London, *70;* Leiden Universiteits Bibliotheek, Holland, *72;* Kevin Redpath, *73;* Heidelberg University, *75;* Trinity College, Dublin, *76;* Ashmolean Museum, Oxford, *77;* Clonfert Cathedral, Galway, *79;* Scala, *41, 85, 155, 218;* Pinacoteca Nazionale, Ferrara, *87;* Musée Royaux des Beaux -Arts, Brussels, 90; St Mark's, Venice, *93;* S. Apollinare in Classe, Ravenna, *95;* Taunton Museum, *97;* Langport Church, Glastonbury, *99;* Museo Nazionale, Florence, *100;* Courtesy the Trustees, The National Gallery, London, 59, *104, 240;* Tower of London, *101, 108;* St Mary, Chartham, Kent, *109a;* All Saints, Acton, Suffolk, *109b;* Private Collection, *110;* Universitätsbibliothek, Heidelberg, *111,* Chicago Art Institute, *113;* San Giovani, Rome, *114;* Biblioteca Nazionale, Florence, *119a, 130, 132;* Courtesy of Winchester Castle, Hampshire County Council, *122, 123;* St Zeno's Basilica, Verona, *129b;* St. Anastasia, Verona, *131a;* Tate Gallery, London, *138, 163;* Fersfield, Norfolk, *142;* Dorchester Abbey, England, *143b;* Evora Cathedral, Portugal, *145a;* U.S. Games, *144, 177b; 234;* Bayerische Staatsbibliothek, Munich, *148;* Comstock, *159, 161, 207;* Simant Bostock, *182/183;* Galleria Dell Academia, Florence, *187;* Schweizeriches Landesmuseum, Zurich, *189;* Salisbury Cathedral, England, *193;;* Universitets Olsaksamlingen, Oslo, *197;* Public Record Office, London, *190a;* Canterbury Cathedral, England, *204;* Einsiedelnss, Switzerland, *209;* Church of The Virgin of Guadalupe, Mexico, *210;* Lutherhalle, Wittenberg, *211a;* I Berry/Magnum, *213;* Oneida Community, *222;* Gast, Whitney Museum, *223;* Format Partners/Ulrike Preuss, *215;* P. Le Segretain/Sygma, *217;* Library of Congress, *224;* Sandak Inc, New York, *226;* Matt Mahurin, *229;* British Film Institute, *230, 231;* Jean Williamson/Mick Sharp *71, 243;* Kunsthistoriches Museum, Vienna, *255.*

Every effort has been made to trace all present copyright holders of the material used in this book, whether companies or individuals. Any omission is unintentional and we will be pleased to correct any errors in future editions of this book.

BIBLIOGRAPHY

THIS BOOK is not an academic work of scholarship, so the following list of books is, with few exceptions, limited to popular, non- scholastic editions which are mostly still in print or are otherwise easily obtainable and easy to read.

Original texts

This list gives the major source material which forms the basis of all the Grail legends included in our text.

Le Conte del Graal or **Perceval** by *Chrétien de Troyes,* trans. N. Bryant, Brewer, Rowman & Littlefield, Cambridge, N.J., 1982

The Elucidation: a prologue to the Conte del Graal. *A. Thompson* (ed). Publications of the Institute of French Studies, New York, 1931.

Sir Gawain and the Green Knight, Trans. *J.R.R. Tolkein, Allen & Unwin, 1975*

Sir Gawain at the Grail Castle, trans. *J.Weston,* David Nutt, 1903

History of the Kings of Britain by *Geoffrey of Monmouth,* U.K. Penguin,1966

Josef d'Arimathie or the **Roman de l'Estoire dou Graal** by *Robert de Boron,* Francisque Michel(ed.) Bordeaux, France, 1841.

The Mabinogion ed. & trans. *J. Gantz,* London, Penguin, 1988

The Mabinogion, ed. & trans. *Lady. C. Guest,* Ballantyne Press, London ,1910

The Mabinogion, ed. & trans. *G. Jones & T. Jones,* Dent, London, 1976

Le Morte D'Arthur by *Sir Thomas Malory,* ed. Caxton, Penguin, Harmondsworth, U.K.,1969, New York, 1970.

The Legend of Sir Perceval, *Jesse Weston,* David Nutt, London, 1909

Prester John:
The Letter,
trans. *V. Slessarev,*
University of Minnesota Press, 1989

Perlesvaus (The High Book of the Holy Grail),
trans. *N. Bryant,* Brewer, Rowman & Littlefield,
N.J., 1978

Parzival by *Wolfram von Eschenbach,* trans.
A.T.Hatto, Penguin, Harmondsworth and New York,
1980

Parzival, a knightly epic by *Wolfram von Eschenbach*
trans. *Jesse Weston, London, 1894*

Queste del Saint Graal, trans. *P.Matarasso,*
Penguin, Harmondsworth and New York, 1969

Romance of Perceval in Prose (Didot-Perceval),
trans. *D. Skeeles,* University of Washington Press,
Seattle,1966

Titurel by *Wolfram von Eschenbach,* trans. *C.E. Passage,*
Frederick Ungart Pub. Co., New York, 1984

The Vulgate Version of the Arthurian
Romances, Carnegie Institute, Washington, 1909

General Reading

I am indebted to many of the authors whose works
appear in the list below. Much of the material
which has appeared within this book has both its
source and inspiration within these editions. The
dedicated scholarship which the Grail legend
inspires seems to have only one fundamental flaw;
that of an unreachable horizon. The more one
enters into this mythic Otherworld, the more the
chance one will be trapped on fascinating,
unending and diverting paths. At least here are a
few excellent signposts to the major highways.

Achterberg, Jeanne, **Woman as Healer,**
Rider/Shambala, 1990

Adolf, H. **Visio Pacis: Holy City & Grail,**
Pennsylvania State University Press, 1960

Ashe, Geoffrey, **A Guidebook to Arthurian Britain,**
London and New York, Longman,1980

Baigent, M. Leigh,R. and *Lincoln, H.*, **The Holy Blood and the Holy Grail**, London, 1982

Bernard of Clairvaux, **On the Song of Songs**, Cistercian Publications, 1976

Barker,B., **Symbols of Sovereignty**, Newton Abbot, Westbridge Books, 1979

Bogdanow, Fanni, **The Romance of the Grail**, Manchester University Press,1966

Bynner, Witter, **The Way of Life according to Lao Tzu**, New York, Capricorn Books, 1962

Campbell, J. **Myths to Live By**, Souvenir Press, 1973
- **The Power of Myth**
- **The Masks of God: Occidental Mythology**, Penguin, 1976
- **The Hero with a Thousand Faces**, Penguin, 1975
- **The Flight of the Wild Gander**

Cavendish, Richard, **King Arthur and the Grail**, London, Weidenfeld & Nicholson,1978

Currer-Briggs, N.,**The Shroud and the Grail**, London, Weidenfeld & Nicholson, 1987

Eisler, Riane, **The Chalice & the Blade**, HarperSanFransisco, 1989

Eliade, Mircea, **The Myth of the Eternal Return**, London, Arkana, 1989

Ellis, Peter Berresford, **A Dictionary of Irish Mythology**, Constable, 1987

Evan, S., **In Quest of the Holy Grail**, London, Dent, 1898

Gimbutas, Marija, **The Goddesses and Gods of Old Europe**, London, Thames & Hudson, 1989

Goetinck, G., **Perceval: a study of the Welsh tradition in the Grail Legend**, Cardiff, University of Wales Press, 1975.

Hall, Manley P., **Orders of the Quest: The Holy Grail**, Los Angeles, Philosophical Research Society, 1976.

Heline, Corinne, **Mysteries of the Holy Grail**, Los Angeles, New Age Press, 1977.

Jung, Emma and von Franz, Marie-Louise, **The Grail Legend**, London, Hodder & Stoughton, 1971; New York, Putnam, 1970.

Kempe, Dorothy, **The Legend of the Holy Grail**, London, 1905; reprint 1934.

Kinter, William and Keller, Joseph, **The Sibyl: Prophetess of Antiquity & Medieval Fay**, Dorrance and Co. ,Philadelphia, 1967.

Loomis, Roger Sherman, **The Grail: From Celtic Myth to Christian Symbol**, Cardiff, University of Wales Press; New York, Columbia University Press,1963.

-*The Development of Arthurian Romance*, New York, Norton, 1963
-*Celtic Myth and Arthurian Romance*, Columbia University Press, New York, 1927
- *Wales & the Arthurian Legend*, University of Wales Press, 1956
-*Arthurian Tradition & Chretien de Troyes*, Columbia University Press, New York, 1949

Maltwood, K., **The Enchantments of Britain**, London and Cambridge, James Clarke, 1982

Markale, Jean, **King Arthur King of Kings**, Gordon Cremonesi, 1977
- **Women of the Celts**, Gordon Cremonesi, 1975
-*Le Graal*, Retz, Paris, 1982

Matthews, Caitlin, **Mabon and the Mysteries of Britain: An exploration of the 'Mabinogion'**, Arkana, 1987
- **Arthur and the Sovereignty of Britain: King and Goddess in the "Mabinogion"**, Arkana, 1989
Voices of the Goddess: A Chorus of Sibyls, Aquarian Press, Wellingborough, 1990
- and *Matthews, John*, **Ladies of the Lake**, The Aquarian Press, 1992

Matthews, John, (ed.) **At the Table of the Grail**, Arkana, 1987
- (ed.) **An Arthurian Reader,** The Aquarian Press, 1988
- **Gawain: Knight of the Goddess**, Aquarian Press, 1990

Morduch, Anna, **The Sovereign Adventure**, London and Cambridge, James Clarke, 1970

Morizot, P., **The Templars**, Anthroposophical Publishing Company, 1960

Newstead, H., **Bran the Blessed in Arthurian Romance**, New York, Columbia University Press, 1939

Nutt, W.A., **The Legends of the Holy Grail**, London, 1902
- **Studies on the Legend of the Holy Grail**, London, 1888

Oldenbourg, Z., **Massacre at Monségur**, Weidenfeld, 1961

Osho, **Tao, The Three Treasures**, Cologne, Rebel Publishing House, 1992
'- **The Book of Nothing**, Rebel Publishing House, 1992

Rolt-Wheeler, F., **Mystic Gleams from the Holy Grail**, London

Ross, A., **Pagan Celtic Britain**, London, Routledge & Kegan Paul, 1967

Schmidt, K.O., **The Message of the Grail**, Lakemont, Georgia, C.S.A. Press, 1975

Stein, W.J., **The Ninth Century and the Holy Grail**, Temple Lodge Press, 1989

Steiner, R., **Christ and the Spiritual World and The Search for the Holy Grail**, Rudolf Steiner Press, 1963

Stone, Merlin, **When God was a Woman**, London, 1976
- **Ancient Mirrors of Womanhood**, London 1986

Walker, Barbara G., **The Woman's Encyclopaedia of Myths and Secrets**, Harper & Row, 1984

Warner, M., **Alone of all Her Sex**, London 1976

Williams, Charles and Lewis, C.S., **Arthurian Torso**, Oxford University Press, 1948

Weston, Jesse, **From Ritual to Romance**, Doubleday, New York, 1957

Wyatt, Isobel, **From Round Table to Grail Castle**, Sussex, Lanthorn Press, 1979

Poetry and Fantasy

The following short list also includes fictions with an Arthurian theme.

Bradley, Marion Zimmer, **Mists of Avalon**, Sphere, 1984

Chapman, Vera, **The Three Damosels**, London, Methuen, 1978

Elliot, T.S., **The Wasteland**, Faber & Faber, 1991

Hunter, Jim, **Perceval and the Presence of God**, London, Faber, 1978

Jones, David, **The Anathemata**, London, Faber, 1952

Macgregor, R., **Indiana Jones and the Last Crusade**, Sphere, 1989

Mitchison, Naomi, **To the Chapel Perilous**, London, Allen & Unwin, 1955

Monarco, Richard, **Parzival**, New York, Macmillan, 1977: London, Methuen, 1978

Powys, John Cowper, **A Glastonbury Romance**, London, Macdonald, 1955

Stewart, Mary, **The Crystal Cave_ The Hollow Hills _ The Last Enchantment**, Hodder & Stoughton, 1970/73/79

Tennyson, Alfred, Lord, **The Idylls of the King**, Penguin, 1983

White, T.H., **The Once and Future King**, Collins, 1959

Williams, Charles, **Taliessin Through Logres and The Region of the Summer Stars**, Cambridge, N.J., S. Brewer, 1982
- **War in Heaven**, London, Oxford, W. Eerdmans,1978

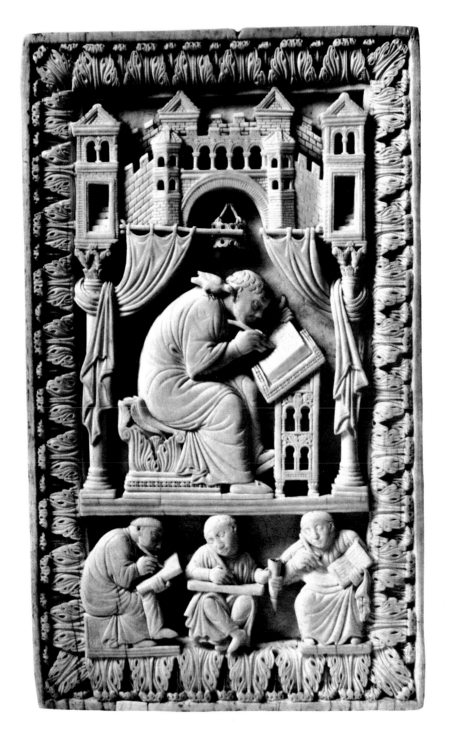